D1480908

OTHER GOOD MYSTERIES BY
GEORGE HARMON COXE

THE GROOM LAY DEAD

The Groom Lay Dead

GEORGE HARMON COXE

TRIANGLE BOOKS

New York

TRIANGLE BOOKS EDITION Published May 1947,
by arrangement with Alfred A. Knopf

5471G

TRIANGLE BOOKS, 14 West 49th Street,
New York 20, N. Y.

THE GROOM LAY DEAD

1

THE clock in the waiting room of the Hoboken station said a quarter of one. Outside, the commuters who had just come over on the tube after an evening in the city dashed for their trains; the others, the travelers with their luggage, came inside and lined up at the ticket windows or sat down on the benches to wait for those who formed the lines. A sailor at the reservation window picked up a lower for Buffalo and after him came a fat, middle-aged businessman who was annoyed because he'd called up two days ago and could only get a lower to Binghamton. When he finally moved away I asked the clerk if he had a reservation for Mr. Wallace on the 1:05.

"Where to?"

"Bath," I said, and watched him thumb some envelopes, extract one, and glance at the tickets inside.

"Alan Wallace? Yes . . . Bedroom C, car 86. They're all paid for, Mr. Wallace."

I'd walked all the way from the tube platform to the station without finding a Redcap but now when I turned I saw one hovering over my bag hopefully. I told him okay and we crossed to the magazine stand.

The headlines on the bulldog editions of the morning papers

said something about Italy. I passed them up. I read my war news once a day and now I wanted something that would divert my mind instead of stimulating it to remember some things I wanted to forget. I picked out one of those quarter mystery novels I hadn't read and slipped it into my pocket.

The two conductors sat at the gate to the train sheds just like they used to when I was in college. "Bedroom C, car 86," one of them said, and handed me my stub. I followed the Redcap through the gate and along the darkened cars.

It was quiet here except for the shuffle of the Redcap's feet as he trudged ahead of me, one arm outflung and his body lopsided with the weight of the bag. Here and there steam curled up from under a car in cottony wisps to disappear in the night, and sometimes I could hear water dripping and, faintly, the hiss of escaping air. When we got to my car the porter met us in the vestibule. I told him what space I had and while he went ahead with my bag I tipped the Redcap and went back to the platform to finish my cigarette and give the porter a chance to get out of my room.

I've never been able to sleep in a Pullman berth unless a train is rolling and I had no intention of trying when I went into my room a few minutes later. I hung up my hat and coat, got the book out of my pocket and stretched out on the berth; then, before I had a chance to do any reading I heard a commotion outside the car and the sound of voices and laughter. I couldn't distinguish any of the voices, but I could tell there were women as well as men in the party and from the sound of it, they were having a good time.

I had an idea it was Johnny Marshall and his gang and I wondered whom he'd brought with him this time. He had phoned me the day before and told me he had a play he wanted me to read. He said he was going up to his place on one of the Finger Lakes for a few days and if I'd come along we could talk over the play and see if it was anything I might want to direct.

I hadn't anything else to do so I took a chance. It did not look as if I was going to get back into the Marine Corps right away and while I didn't expect too much of the play there was a chance it might be something. It might get my mind off other things. I might even have a good time for a few days. I wasn't counting on that either but if Johnny was in good form I knew I'd get some laughs; if he was in one of his mean moods I could take the next train back.

Now I wondered if I should look him up and say hello. I knew he never traveled alone and the chances were that someone in the party would be tight and I was cold sober and didn't want a drink anyway. I thought about it as the train started. Johnny would have Earl Garlin along and Linda Jordan—Garlin as a combination man-friday and bodyguard, and Linda as secretary—but I didn't know who else would be there so I decided I'd pass it up. I didn't feel like a party and I hoped he wouldn't bother me.

We'd gone about as far as Brick Church or possibly Orange when the knock came at the door. I opened it and Earl Garlin was standing in the corridor, his legs braced against the rocking of the car. The instant he saw me his jaw sagged.

"O-oh," he said. "Hello, Alan." He sounded surprised and stared at me strangely for a moment. "Ah—Johnny wants you to come down to stateroom A."

I suppose that look should have warned me. On anyone else it would have gone unnoticed but Garlin was an ex-private detective and his dark, muscular face had been trained to reveal only what he wanted it to reveal. Now, instead of being impassive, he seemed almost embarrassed. I noticed it all right, but I was thinking about Johnny. I didn't want to go, but Johnny was the kind who'd come and beat on the door until the whole car was awake if he felt like it.

"All right," I said, and picked up my coat.

We went down the corridor and Garlin opened the door of stateroom A. I thought there might be a half dozen people crowding that stateroom; instead there were three: Johnny Marshall, Carol Gibson, and Linda Jordan. They seemed to see me at the same time, and as I stopped just inside the doorway, all three of them stayed just as they were, as though the sight of me had turned them into momentary statues.

Even now I can remember how they looked, how they were placed. Johnny stood by the windows. He was just picking up a glass from a small round table and he stayed that way, half bent, looking up, his forehead wrinkled. Linda Jordan was on the settee —the berths had not been made up—with a cigarette in one hand and a glass in the other. Carol was opposite her. She was just putting a glass on the window sill and apparently she had been laughing at something Johnny had said because for that first second part of that laugh stayed on her face and her hand remained outstretched, no longer holding the glass but still touching it.

"Why, Alan," she said and then the sudden whitening of her face erased the smile and she looked at Marshall. "Johnny," she said, her voice shocked and barely audible, "Johnny."

He grinned at her. "Surprise, huh?" he said, and straightened up, a slender dapper man with curly brown hair and pale-blue eyes. His face was flushed when he looked at me and there was something behind his grin that was nasty and unpleasant.

"Hi," he said, and handed me the glass. "Have a drink."

I could feel my face tighten and my skin grow cold. I took the glass and tried not to look at Carol.

"Hello," I said, and drank quickly to give me time to think, to get ahold of myself.

You see, Carol was my girl—or had been until a month ago. It was my fault the engagement was broken and that was the way I wanted it, but I still loved her and trusted her and respected her. In the week that I'd been back from Vermont I'd heard that she had been seeing Johnny Marshall, but it hadn't meant anything. Carol wasn't Johnny's kind of girl. That's what I told myself, what I wanted to believe.

Now, walking in like this and finding her, it was hard to remember that she was free to do as she liked. I had to keep telling myself that if she wanted to come along on one of Johnny's parties it was none of my business. Asking me along, tricking me into coming like this without telling me Carol would be here, was a typical Marshall idea of good clean fun. But I couldn't let him know how much it mattered, how much it hurt to see her with him. I had to be adult and show my sophistication, show that I could go along with a gag. I told myself these things before I spoke.

"Thanks," I said. My voice was thick and I tried to strengthen it. I glanced at Linda Jordan. "Hi, Lin," I said. "Quite a party."

I didn't get the smile I expected. She sat there, a slim smartly-groomed girl with troubled eyes that moved to Carol and Johnny and avoided me.

"Yes," she said. "Quite a party."

Johnny Marshall cleared his throat. "Well," he said, "aren't you going to congratulate us?"

I didn't know what he meant. I looked at him and he was still grinning and I looked at Carol and her face was like chalk. Then I saw her eyes. They were not the smiling hazel I remembered but wide and strangely frightened.

"Show him, honey," Johnny said. He reached for her hand and held it up. It was her left hand and on the third finger was a platinum band paved with small square-cut diamonds. "Come on, drink up, fella! Wish us luck."

I stared at the ring and suddenly something was choking me and a red haze gathered in front of my eyes and I could not see clearly any more.

"When?" I heard myself say.

"Tonight," Johnny said. "At eight-thirty, at the St. Regis. We got the license yesterday and kept it under cover. Didn't I tell you when I phoned you?"

He knew he hadn't told me when he phoned. He'd planned everything, including not telling me. I watched him reach for a newspaper. It was folded and there was a picture of him and Carol taken that evening. It was all there, in that paper I had passed up in the station newsstand.

Then I began to tremble and the rage welled up inside me. I hated them both and what I felt must have shown in my face because I heard Carol catch her breath and saw Johnny back away. Carol sat down suddenly and then Earl Garlin moved quickly from behind me and pushed past. He began to make drinks at the little table, keeping between Johnny and me. And Linda stood up and touched my arm. Her laughter was quick and artificial and she began to chatter about something I could not understand while she pried the glass out of my hand.

"You're 'way behind," she said. "Here, sit down . . . Earl, make Alan another drink."

I was all right then. I couldn't keep the tremor out of my legs but the red haze went away and I began to breathe. Johnny was grinning again, over Garlin's shoulder.

"No congratulations?"

"Congratulations," I said. "It was fast work. How about a little toast—to the fourth Mrs. Marshall. Or is it five . . . ?"

When I got back to my room I sat down on the berth and snapped off the light. I don't know how long I sat there staring out

into the night. Once when the shrill hoarse blast of the train
whistle ripped out of the blackness, my nerves screamed with it
and the old tightness hit me again, leaving me stiff and tense on
the berth. I kept staring out the window, fighting myself, waiting
for the spasm to pass and knowing that I was not yet cured of
this thing I'd brought back from the Solomons, knowing that
what I felt then had nothing to do with Carol Marshall or Johnny
or anything that had happened in stateroom A.

The pounding rhythm of the wheels altered briefly at a cross-
ing and there was a sudden clanging of the safety signal, quickly
lost, and the flash of a waiting car's headlights on the window.
Then the rhythm and the blackness were back and someone was
knocking at my door.

Earl Garlin had a bottle in one hand and two glasses with ice
in them in another. He had his coat off now, but his tie lay neatly
against his silk shirt and there were gold links in his cuffs. He
didn't look tight; he didn't even look tired. He looked like he
usually did—smooth and dark and inscrutable. He nudged the
door shut with a thick shoulder.

"I thought maybe you could use a nightcap," he said. "If you
can't, I'll drink 'em both." He put the glasses on the shelf and
poured Scotch into them.

I thanked him and took the glass and he sat down on the
berth, watching me drink from under thick black brows that
almost met over the broad nose.

"I guess you didn't know about the wedding," he said, and
turned the glass in his hands, watching it.

"Do you think I'd be here if I had?"

"I guess you wouldn't. I figured that's how it was when Johnny
showed you the ring. I could see you start to tremble and your
neck get stiff. I was afraid you'd clip him; that's why I moved in
between you." He swallowed some of his drink. "He told me to

get the guy in bedroom C and bring him to the stateroom. When I saw it was you I almost fell over."

I remembered how Earl had looked when I opened the door. I said I guessed he didn't know I was on the train.

"Not me." He shook his head. "It was a crummy trick. I don't know where Johnny gets ideas like that. I don't know what it is or why, but when he gets mean—"

He didn't finish the thought; he didn't have to. And then I wanted to ask him if Carol knew but I couldn't. The bitterness and resentment had twisted me all up inside and I was afraid it would come out in my voice. So we sat there staring, Garlin at his glass and me out the window, until the door opened again.

This time there was no knock. The door just opened and Johnny Marshall staggered in, half fell, then caught the edge of the panel and pulled himself erect. Twenty million dollars on the hoof. He had his coat and vest off, his shirt open at the throat. His tanned face was slack, his pale-blue eyes glazed, and he had a silly, drunken grin that I wanted more than anything in the world to smash. I could feel the tightness growing in my back again, the sudden trembling, and then Garlin moved in between us.

"Hi," Marshall said. "Need one more drink. Just one, huh?" He reached out and took the glass from Garlin's hand. "Tha'sa boy. Good ol' Garlin."

He took a big swallow and tried to brace his legs against the movement of the train. He peered at me in a half-blind way and chuckled. "Hi, Wallace," he said. "The bride bawled me out—I think."

He reached out to put the glass on the window sill and didn't make it. I caught the glass as he folded in the middle and Garlin caught him, hoisting him, getting an arm around the limp legs. He lifted and dropped Marshall on my berth.

"Cold," he said. "Some bridegroom."

I put the glass down. I was still trembling as I watched Garlin straighten out Marshall's legs and take off his shoes. When he finished, Garlin said:

"He'll have to stay here. I got nothing but a lower up ahead, but you can bunk in Jordan's room and she can move in with Carol. It's only for a few more hours."

I said all right. I said I'd get undressed. I waited for him to go to his berth so I'd have more room, but he stayed right where he was.

"I'll wait," he said.

Maybe he knew what he was doing. After all he was bodyguard for the twenty million dollars that lay snoring in my berth and I suppose he figured there was no point in taking chances. Maybe because he knew I wasn't entirely over my neuro-psychiatric trouble, or possibly because he knew I'd had my share of killing in the Solomons—banty legged, vicious little animals that sniped at you twenty-four hours of the day and screamed taunts at you all night and tortured you if you had the bad luck to be caught.

It's easy to kill when you see what happens to your friends. At first the hate and vindictiveness is hot and driving and then it becomes submerged with other things until you don't realize it's there. A man can only take so much of it at one stretch and some can stand up under it longer than others. The months I'd had without relief were too much for me—and a lot of others. It wasn't the hole in my leg; it was the head that bothered me most.

Shell shock, they called it in the last war; now it was combat fatigue. Some went mad in the field and they'd always be mad; others were in a hospital in San Francisco now. Hundreds of them. I knew because I'd been there for months. The doctors said most of us would be all right in time and I wanted to believe that but I still jumped at sudden noises and fear was always just around the corner and my temper was ragged and uncertain. Because of this I'd lost Carol and thinking of what had happened, what Marshall had done, it would not have been hard to kill.

Garlin watched me narrowly and perhaps he saw some things in my face I didn't know were there; anyway, it was his job to take no chances. So I didn't argue with him. I washed and got into pajamas, slippers and robe, and went down the rocking corridor to stateroom A.

Carol opened the door when I told her who it was, and it was as though a stranger stood there waiting for me to state my business. The light behind her made her hair glistening gold and left her eyes in shadow so I could not tell what they were saying. She wore a heavy silk robe that covered her from neck to ankles and I couldn't see what was underneath.

"Johnny's passed out," I said. "He's in my room. Garlin thinks we ought to leave him there."

She didn't say anything for a moment and she wasn't the girl I loved; she was someone slim and blonde and lovely, with a strange whiteness in her face and a look that was stricken and desperately hurt. I saw the front of her gown rise as she took a breath; then it was still.

"Thank you, Alan."

She started to close the door and I reached out and caught it. I pushed it open a little farther and then I could see most of the room. I guess that's what I wanted to see. The bottles and glasses had been cleaned away and the berths weren't made up. There was a pillow on the settee and I knew she'd been stretched out there, that she hadn't gone to bed.

"Wait," I said. "I'm going to take Linda's room and send her in here. The train is full. There isn't any other place."

I didn't say I was sorry. I didn't say it was tough. I don't think I even felt sorry, nor do I know why it is that sometimes you want to hurt the thing you love. I said, "Good night," and my lips were so stiff they ached.

Linda Jordan had bedroom B. I knocked and she opened the door a crack and said, "Wait a minute, Alan," and moved about in the darkness putting on a negligee. Then she snapped on the light and I went into a room that reeked of perfume.

"Now what?" she said, and her glance was quizzical, anxious.

I told her while she shook out her auburn hair. She had the creamy, flawless skin that goes with such hair and a small, beautifully modeled body. I felt better, just talking to her, because there was no side to Linda. She'd worked as secretary to Johnny Marshall for six or seven years. She'd seen four brides come and go, she knew most of the answers, and she was as easy to get along with as she was to look at.

"Okay," she said. "I was afraid something like that might happen." She began to straighten the berth and gather up some toilet things. "I don't know how a man can be so charming sometimes and so completely a heel at others. I've often wondered why I stayed with him as long as I have." She looked up at me. "Didn't you know they were getting married?"

I shook my head and she said, "I ordered the reservations yesterday and he said to have a bedroom held for you. It didn't make sense—you never seemed like a guy who liked to torture himself— but it was none of my business. It was none of my business either if Johnny wanted to take a gang along on his honeymoon. I only work for him."

I had to get away from the subject somehow before I blew up. I asked her what all the perfume was for. "Do you sponge down with it?"

She laughed and pointed to the small flat bottle on the shelf, partly full. "It fell off and the stopper came loose. I spilled a little."

"A little?"

"With Revel number 4, a little is all you need." She stopped at the door, her eyes concerned, then moved back and put her fingers on my arm. "I'm sorry, Alan, and if it makes any difference, I'm sure Carol didn't know."

"Okay," I said. And to show her I appreciated what she told me I gave her a little slap as she went out. "Sleep tight," I said.

I got into bed and turned out the light. The beat of the wheels was slowing and I knew we were coming into Stroudsburg. We stopped presently and sounds filtered up from the station platform: the rumble of a baggage truck, the accelerating motor of a car, the slam of a vestibule door as the train got under way again. And I was wide awake, the smell of perfume forgotten and bitterness driving thought after thought through my mind.

Lying there in the blackness with the staccato beat of the car wheels for an accompaniment, I kept thinking about Carol. Around and around, like the wheels. Thinking, too, about the man in my bedroom, a man I would like very much to hold by the throat until he was dead. I didn't know then that there were two other people aboard that train in the car ahead that felt the same way. I probably wouldn't have gone to sleep at all if I'd known that deep down in someone's traveling bag was a one-ounce bottle of oil of bitter almonds.

2

WE got off at Bath at ten in the morning and gathered around our baggage on the station platform. Until then, Linda Jordan was the only one I'd seen. She came into her bedroom as we were pulling into Elmira and told me it was okay to go back to my own room. And I stayed right there, having some coffee sent in and battling it out with myself as to whether I should take the next train back to New York or go on with the party.

I suppose it was some sort of angry pride that made me decide to stay. I was here, tricked into coming along on my ex-girl's honeymoon by some sadistic mental aberration of her husband's, and I was damned if I'd give Marshall the satisfaction of knowing how much it hurt. I was going to be tough, to pretend it made no difference what he and his bride did. I'd been engaged to Carol and I'd broken it off and she'd married Marshall. So what? I'd read the play, and when I was ready I'd leave. Deep down there could have been another reason. Carol was not wholly Johnny's wife yet and I guess I was hoping something would happen that day so she'd realize what kind of guy he was and walk out on him before it was too late.

So I stood there as the train pulled out, talking to Linda Jordan and watching Johnny speak to a white-haired man who was taking the baggage to a station wagon. Then I saw the two people coming towards us from the car ahead and knew they were part of the party. The woman was Helen Bradford, Johnny Marshall's sister, and the man who carried the bags was Spencer Haughton.

I took a couple of steps to meet them. I didn't know just where they would fit into Marshall's scheme of things but seeing them did not surprise me much. Helen, however, was surprised to see me.

"Alan," she said. "What're you—I mean—I didn't know you were coming."

"I didn't know you were, either."

"But"—her glance went beyond me and she looked at Carol and her brother—"why should—"

She didn't finish the thought but I knew what she meant. I said I didn't know. "Just one of Johnny's cute ideas, I guess."

She stood there, frowning, looking beyond me, a tall, dark woman, very poised and erect in her tailored homespun suit. Spencer said, "Hello," and put down the bags.

I don't remember what I said as we shook hands because suddenly I was thinking of the things I'd heard about him and Marshall, thinking that here was a man who also had a motive for murder. I was still examining the idea when Marshall came up behind me.

"Hello, Helen . . . Spence. Glad you could make it." He glanced about and continued to Helen. "Where's your lawyer? I thought you were going to bring a lawyer?"

"He couldn't make this train," Helen said. "He's coming to-night."

"Oh, well—" Marshall shrugged. "Then let's go. Bert will take care of your bags . . . Oh, Bert!"

It was a swell day, unusually warm for September and the turning leaves made bright patchworks of orange and yellow and red against the soft green of the valley. Even Johnny was in a pretty good mood, considering how he must have felt. He was sitting up front with Carol and Bert Donelly, the white-haired man who was driving, and he began to tell us how we were going to have to rough it.

"We used to have servants falling all over themselves," he said, "but no more. Right, Bert?"

"That's right, Mr. Marshall," Bert said.

"Only Bert and the Mrs. now. So I hope you guys and gals know enough to make your own beds . . . What about it, Helen?"

"I imagine we'll make out," Helen said. "If you can make your bed I'm sure the rest of us will have no trouble."

Johnny grinned at her. "Oh, Carol will make mine. I mean ours. Won't you, darling?"

Carol didn't say anything. She was staring straight ahead, watching the road, but it didn't seem to bother Johnny any and presently he turned and looked at us again.

"What I want to know," he said, "is who slipped me the Mickey last night."

"Mickey?" Earl Garlin said. "What Mickey? You didn't need a Mickey."

"A little chloral hydrate would have done it." Marshall waited, still smiling. "Sure none of you nice people didn't feed me a little?"

It was his way of kidding about what had happened. He'd been tight and he must have known it, and he didn't want to admit this to Carol. But if he'd thought he was getting away with anything it was a mistake because just then his sister said:

"Maybe it was the bride, Johnny. That's what I'd have done if it had been me."

The grin froze and the pale-blue eyes were cold and bright; then he laughed.

"I know you would, sweet. But Carol's different, Carol's nice. Aren't you, darling?" he said, and squeezed the point of her shoulder.

"I really wouldn't know," Carol said distantly.

"I guess she's sore," Johnny said.

We rode along in silence then and presently I caught a glimpse of the lake through the trees on the right. On the hillsides to the left were the farms and the vineyards. Here and there I could see men and women picking the crop, and sometimes a horse-drawn wagon piled with those wooden trays the pickers used. Once we passed a truck loaded down with grapes on the way to the presses and Haughton asked about it.

"Is this where that good New York State wine comes from?"

Linda Jordan said it was. "And the best of it," Johnny Marshall said, "is made just around the next corner."

He told Bert to stop opposite a low stone building that looked a hundred years old and was. At one end it was two stories, with what looked like an office on the second floor, and the rest of it was long and low and flat-roofed. The flat-roofed part lay right up against the slope of the hill and it was completely covered with row after row of wooden casks.

"Sun-ripened sherry," Marshall said, pointing. "Come on."

On a Marshall party you did what Marshall wanted so we climbed out and followed him through an open double door that led into darkness. You could see then that the walls of the structure were nearly two feet thick, that the floor was packed earth, hard and smooth and damp. Here and there an electric bulb burned dimly, disclosing row upon row of dusty bottles; beyond, built right into the hillside, were other rows of casks that extended farther than one could see.

A man in khaki shirt and trousers came down from some inner stairs that led to the office. He said Hello to Marshall and was introduced as Jim Ingalls, the manager. Marshall asked him to get an empty case. He said he wanted to take some stuff to the house, and as Ingalls went away, he began to select bottles from the racks.

"Green Valley Wines," he said. "The best in the world."

I watched him a moment and then I looked round for Carol. She was standing off to one side, near one of the electric bulbs, and against the black background her face seemed white and distressed. She'd left her hat in the car and her hair was like honey and she looked very slim and young and alone in her tailored green flannel dress with the buttons down the front and the red-leather belt. Seeing her now the old resentment hit me again and I told myself I didn't care how unhappy she was, and yet, somehow, I wanted to go to her and speak and make her smile. As

though my thoughts had reached her, she turned and looked
at me.

Then something exploded close by, a quick, sharp report that
echoed through the cavern of the cellar and turned my blood
to ice.

Someone screamed but all I could think of in that blind moment was my own safety. A sudden, torturing tension knifed
through me and I wheeled, looking wildly for a fox hole, for some
shelter, as the old panic struck me. I took a step before I could
think, before I could yank myself to a stop; then I waited, shaking
all over while I fought for control of my ragged nerves.

Someone laughed and I saw then it was Marshall. He had
noticed my hysteria and so had Carol. She stood very still and
there was pity in her gaze now and I could feel the blood rush
to my face as I glanced away.

"What's the matter, Alan?" Marshall said.

I felt the others looking at me. I swallowed fast and tried to
think of something to say. Marshall didn't give me a chance.

"Nobody's shooting at you . . . Come here." He gestured to
us to follow him and led the way round an intersecting aisle to
another bottle-lined passageway, parallel with the first. "That was
champagne," he said. "I'll show you."

A bulky, grotesque figure looking like something from another world moved out to meet us. Then I could see he wore a
mask like a fencer, and pads had been fastened to the front of
him. Marshall asked him where the bottle exploded and the
fellow showed us.

I didn't go any closer but I could see the jagged fragments of
the battle on the floor and in the rack. Wine still glistened from
the adjoining bottles and as we stood there we got a lecture from
Marshall on the manufacture of champagne.

"First," he said, "you've got to have the right kind of juices and then you've got to know how to blend them. Just what you use is a matter of personal taste and that's why each champagne is a little different from any other. We have our own formula and we think it's the best . . . After that you age the stuff in oaken casks."

"For how long?" Earl Garlin asked.

Marshall grinned at him and said that was a trade secret. "After that," he said, "you bottle, adding yeast and a temporary cork. You age further in a horizontal position and then shake with a French-made device to loosen the sediment. At the proper time you then leave the bottles upside down so the sediment will settle on the cork."

There was a lot more, and though I didn't follow his explanation closely, I did get the main idea. The bottles had to be turned twice daily by hand at a certain stage and the indented bottoms were no guarantee against a hundred and twenty-five pounds of yeast pressure. They exploded frequently, dangerously, and without warning, which was the reason the attendant wore a mask and pads.

I went out before the lecture was over. The doctors tell you certain things to do when you're suffering from combat fatigue. Even when they turn you loose they tell you to keep practicing. One of these things is called "demobilizing yourself." They tell you about the cat whose back and hair stiffen when confronted by a dog or some danger and how, when the danger is passed, the cat then demobilizes herself by going to sleep so that she will be ready for instant mobilization when some new attack threatens.

Well, that's how it was with me, and that was what I had to do. I'd got through this experience without cracking completely and now, before I had any trouble with Marshall or let my temper get out of hand, I had to demobilize myself and get my mind entirely away from what had happened. I edged back to the aisle we had entered and went out to the station wagon. Bert Donelly was sitting behind the wheel and I talked to him about fishing for lake trout.

3

JOHNNY MARSHALL's place was right on the edge of the water, a sprawling, white-framed structure complete with tennis court, boat house and swimming pool—an addition which was more essential than first appeared, since the lake seldom warmed up enough for pleasant swimming until late July.

There were three or four acres in all, I suppose, with the house about halfway between the highway and the lake, and a high hedge fence around two sides, with the lake and a small stream which came from a gorge in the hills, making up the other two boundaries. I couldn't figure why he wanted the place, since he had even more pretentious estates in Palm Beach and Southampton, but it was very nice, with plenty of privacy and no neighbors. The sort of place most anyone could enjoy, though I doubt if anyone had a good time that day, not even Johnny.

Lunch was dull and rather awkward. With the exception of Johnny and Earl Garlin, everyone seemed to be watching everyone else and figuring out privately why each of us was there. I know I wondered about Helen Bradford and Spence Haughton and practically every time I glanced up someone was watching me and I could imagine what they were thinking. As for Carol, she looked cool, reserved, lovely. She didn't act much like a bride. She was pleasant enough in her conversation but I'd never seen her so matter of fact. Not once, as far as I knew, did she look at me.

Afterwards Johnny wanted to play some tennis and finally he got some doubles going with Linda and himself against Garlin and Spence Haughton. Even if I hadn't still had the hole in my leg where the shell fragment had been I wouldn't have played, and neither would his sister. Haughton played because—and I found this out later—he had a plea to make and a favor to ask. He wanted to be agreeable. As for Carol, I don't know what excuse she made but I do know she stayed upstairs until dinner, which was all right with me since I had nothing to say to her anyway.

I told Marshall I could be reading the play if he'd give me a copy, but he said there was no hurry so I sat around listening to the tennis from the terrace and wondering how I could find out what this was all about.

I knew why I was here. In spite of all the money in the world and a lot of surface charm when he wanted to use it, there was a mean, sadistic streak in Johnny Marshall and it seemed to manifest itself mostly where women were concerned. He had married my girl, but she had loved me once and Johnny wanted to be sure that anything that might have been left between us was killed. That seemed obvious enough now. He was top man now and he wanted to rub it in and he was doing it. But the others—I didn't learn anything more until just before dinner when I found Earl Garlin alone on the dock.

"Look," I said. "What kind of a party is this, anyway? What does Johnny expect to prove?"

"I don't know."

"You could guess maybe."

He took out cigarettes. When he offered me one he gave me a slanting, one-eyed glance that seemed veiled and half-smiling.

"I do best on this job when I don't do much guessing," he said. "Maybe he's combining a little business with pleasure."

I asked him which was business and which was pleasure. He didn't bother to answer but looked out across the lake towards the checkerboard hills on the other side and as I studied him I realized I didn't know much about Earl Garlin except that he was Marshall's bodyguard, and that before that he had been a private detective. Wherever you saw Marshall, you saw Garlin— at the race track, first nights, supper clubs. He was always in the background but he was always there.

Now he wore an expensive yellow sport shirt and gabardine slacks. He had a star ruby on his little finger. His hair was dark and sleek, his teeth good, his mustache well kept; I suppose you could call him handsome if you liked them smooth and hard. That hardness was reflected in his mouth and eyes, but if you didn't happen to notice it, he looked more like a playboy than Marshall. I found myself wondering what kept him out of the Army.

"I know why I was invited," I said.

"It was a crummy trick."

"And maybe I know why Haughton's here," I added, "but what about Helen Bradford? Why does he want his sister on his honeymoon?"

Garlin looked at me and let his glance slide past. "I don't know," he said.

"Did you know she was coming?"

"No."

"And you didn't know I was coming—or Haughton?"

"I don't know anything about Haughton except that he writes plays."

"He wrote a good play once." And then I was remembering the things I'd heard. Marshall once backed a Haughton play and it had been a pretty good play. There hadn't been another one in two or three years and some people said there would never be any more produced because of some personal agreement or contract Haughton and Marshall had signed. I didn't know the details, but the way I'd heard it this contract had nothing to do with the usual author's minimum basic agreement, and I also remembered that Haughton had married a girl, now dead, who had once gone around with Johnny Marshall. I filed this away for future reference and kept at Garlin.

"But why bother to come up here? He's got a bigger place than this on Long Island."

"That I can answer," Garlin said. "There's one other guy Johnny's got some business with. Fellow named Dr. Samson Penzance." He grinned crookedly when he saw me stare at him. "You think I'm kiddin'? I'm telling you—that's his name. Samson Penzance."

"All right. What about him?"

"He runs some kind of cult. Calls it the Brotherhood of Horus. Sun worshippers or something."

"Nudists?"

"Semi-nudists," Garlin said, and grinned again. "At least that's what Linda says. I never sat in on the act but she says the men wear trunks and the women shorts and a halter or scarf or something up top. Ought to be something to see, huh? And not only that, the Doc is supposed to be something of a hypnotist. That's so he can cure the body and the mind."

I still didn't know how Johnny Marshall was concerned and when I said so Garlin told me that back in the days of prohibition, when repeal began to look hopeful, Marshall had bought the winery down the road and the property that went with it—a matter of fifty acres or so up the hill and some abandoned buildings.

"There was this house too," Garlin said, "that the other owner had. Of course it was just a modest little shack of ten or twelve rooms so Johnny had to fix it up and add another dozen and put in the court and pool."

He flipped his cigarette away and watched it hit the lake.

"Johnny never bothered much with the acreage. There was a run-down vineyard up the hill but he wasn't interested in growing grapes; he only wanted the wine end. Then about three years ago this Penzance comes along and offers to lease the land, says he wants it for a small health camp. Well, in some ways, Johnny is a fast man with a buck so he has a lease drawn up for twenty years with the stipulation that he can break it should there be any infraction of the law in connection with the running of this camp."

"How?" I said. "What sort of an infraction?"

Garlin said he didn't know. "I don't know how it was worded but the idea was maybe the guy was a phony and if he was, or if he got out of line with the law, Johnny could toss him out."

He rose and brushed off his slacks. I tried to read his mind, to see what else was behind the words, but if there was anything showing on that broad face I couldn't see it. "And now Johnny's sore at the Doc," I said.

"He's been checking up. He's found some things. Also"—and Garlin wasn't grinning now—"his sister, Helen Bradford, is a customer of the Doc's."

I saw Doctor Penzance that evening but before that I had a chance to talk to Spencer Haughton. It was after dinner and I went outside for a smoke and found him on one of the benches beside the tennis court.

He was a tall, lanky man with thinning sandy hair, shell-rimmed glasses and a lean angular face that, in the light streaming from the house windows, seemed drained of all vitality, all energy. He looked old, though he was not much more than thirty, and his mouth and shoulders had the slackness of a beaten man. He shoved over on the bench without speaking and I sat down.

"I've been trying to figure it out, Spence," I said. "And I'm not doing so well."

"Figure what?"

"Why we're here. Specifically, why you're here."

He looked at me and his voice was tired. "Yeah," he said. "I was going to ask you the same thing."

I told him. I said I'd been tricked. "I guess Johnny thought it would be a cute idea, in a sadistic sort of way, to bring me along on Carol's honeymoon."

"I wondered," Haughton said. "I didn't know what to think when I saw you this morning. But it sounds like Johnny, all right . . . I came because I wanted to make a deal," he said.

"About that contract?"

I saw him nod. He wasn't looking at me now but towards the lake. And what he saw was a lot farther away than that darkened shoreline.

"He's got me tied up. He optioned two of my plays a couple of years ago and he keeps them optioned so they can never be produced."

"It must be a funny contract," I said.

"It is. Very funny, according to Johnny. He never forgave Alice for marrying me, but I never realized how much he hated me until after she was killed in that automobile crash. She was playing in Hayride when he met her . . ."

I remembered then. Alice Murray. She'd been in the chorus of Hayride four years ago, one of those flamboyant musicals that are so successful once they catch on. And Johnny had seen her there and there was a month or so when you could find him two or three nights a week at the Stork or El Morroco with Alice Murray. Then, the week the show closed, she married Spencer Haughton and became one of the few women who had successfully turned Johnny Marshall down.

"I'd known her long before she went into Hayride," he said now. "I'd been engaged to her right along and she told Johnny that. I was in California at the time and I guess he thought it wouldn't be hard for a guy like him to cut me out." He hesitated and I didn't say anything, and presently he said:

"He never forgot it. The trouble was, I didn't know how he felt. I was hard up and went to him with this play. He said he thought it was great. He had an agreement drawn up. He was going to subsidize me while I did some rewriting. He made it sound wonderful but what I really did without knowing it was give him the right to control everything I wrote for ten years. I should have gone to the Guild before signing with him, but he had some reason why he wanted to keep it under cover and I believed him."

I knew there was more and presently it came out. "This last year," he said, "I kept the money he paid me and I've been working in a defense plant. I've got enough now to pay him back for everything. I'm going to get my release before I leave here."

That was all he said, but the last sentence was different from the others. There was something cold and hard in the cadence of the words that startled me and made me remember them later on. . . .

Doctor Samson Penzance arrived about ten thirty accompanied by a pounding on the door that rattled nearby windows. "What the devil is that?" Garlin said. "An earthquake?"

"Penzance," Johnny Marshall said. "At least I think it might be." He pushed back from his heart game and called to Bert Donelly, who came down the hall to open the door. "If that's Doctor Penzance, ask him to come in."

You could understand the windows rattling when you saw Penzance, for he was a very big man. Not so tall, though he must have stood six feet, but massive, with huge shoulders, a hard, muscular neck and a leonine head topped by thick black hair. He might have been forty, or fifty; you couldn't tell by his face, which was deep bronze and unlined except at the forehead, but as he stood there in the living room doorway you could tell his eyes were as black as his hair, and at the moment, extremely un-friendly.

Johnny rose and put on the act. The charm was all there, in his grin and in his voice. Handsome, debonair, the perfect host, he ignored the formidable stare of his visitor and introduced us.

"Well, well," he said. "It's good to see you, Doctor."

Penzance ignored this and let his gaze travel from face to face until it touched Helen Bradford; there it stopped. He did not say a word but I saw that she was on her feet. Johnny saw that look too and his smile got wise and speculative.

"Perhaps we'd better go into the study."

He crossed the hall, opened a door and stood aside to let Penzance enter. The door closed and almost at once we could hear the muted rumble of the Doctor's voice.

Earl Garlin blew out his breath. "A character," he said. "Any time you want a house haunted, there's your boy."

Helen Bradford was watching the library door. She stood very straight and tall, a stately, high-breasted woman of twenty-seven, with chestnut hair and a classic beauty marred only by the rigidity of her face and the pallor around her cheekbones.

Linda Jordan rose and went to her. "What is it, darling? You're not ill, are you?"

Helen blinked and then, as though the spell had been broken, became aware of us.

"What?" she said. "Oh, no. Just tired." She glanced at her wrist-watch. "I didn't sleep at all well on the train last night. This will be a good time to catch up."

She smiled at us and left the room, and as I watched her go I felt sorry for her. I don't know why. She had all the money she'd ever need, she was beautiful, and yet she looked like a girl who'd never had much fun. I wondered why as I listened to the rumble of voices in the study.

Earl Garlin poured some champagne for Linda and himself and for me; Spence Haughton refused and so did Carol. She still had some in her glass and she was sitting in the corner with a book. She'd been sitting there all evening while Johnny and Spence and Linda and Earl played hearts, but I never saw her turn a page.

Presently Spence got up and said he guessed he'd go to bed. I tried to read the play Marshall had given me. I'd had it two hours now and I was still on scene two, act one. I kept looking at Carol. She wore a sheer black dress with a touch of white at the throat; her hair was flaxen in the lamplight. She was lovely and she wasn't mine any more, and for that I had myself to blame.

The study door banged open while I was thinking about Carol, and this time all we saw of Doctor Penzance was a glimpse of his back. The floor shook a little as his weight stamped down the hall and then the door slammed and the windows rattled again.

Marshall came into the room, his face red and warped into a tight, mirthless grin. "A very violent man," he said. "How about a drink?"

Ever since dinner he'd had two silver ice buckets working and now the bottle in one was empty, the other half full. When he had poured some into his glass he rang for Bert and asked for another bottle.

"That's all there is, sir," Bert said.

"What?"

"Yes, sir. That's the last of the champagne. There's some port and sauterne and sherry and maybe some—"

"Never mind," Johnny said.

"I could drive down and get some."

Johnny waved him away. "Never mind, I said. Mrs. Marshall
and I'll get it ourselves."

Carol looked up from her book. "Really, Johnny—"

"What's the matter?" Johnny said. "I'm not drunk, am I? It's
only a quarter of a mile. We can take the station wagon. The
air'll do you good . . . Soon as we finish this hand."

I sat there reading the same speech over and over while they
finished the heart hand and totaled the score. Johnny got up.
"Now," he said, "for more wine."

"Not for me."

Johnny looked round to see who'd said that. It was Linda.
"What do you mean?" he said. "The evening's young."

"I know," Linda said. "But not for me. I'm going to bed . . .
Good-night, kids."

Johnny looked at me. I told him I was going to bed too. Garlin
yawned and said he guessed he'd get a bit of air and turn in too.
Johnny muttered something about a fine damn bunch of wet
blankets but Garlin kept on going and when he strolled through
the French doors to the terrace, Johnny went to Carol. He took
her hands and pulled her from the chair. He put his arms around
her. He was a little drunk and I didn't like the way he eyed her
but I couldn't look away.

"Get a scarf or something, baby," he said. "We'll get the wine
ourselves."

I thought she was going to say no. I think she would have if she
hadn't glanced round and found me watching her. I don't know
how I looked but however it was her chin came up and her lip
tightened and spots of color daubed her cheekbones.

"All right," she said and, releasing herself, went into the hall.

Johnny came over to me. He was grinning but his eyes said he
was gloating.

"How's the play?"

I said I hadn't read it yet and he asked me if I was having fun. Until then I'd been polite. I'd avoided him when I could but I hadn't been out of line because I didn't want to give him that much satisfaction. Now the wall of good intentions I'd constructed cracked a little and some of the hostility I felt leaked out.

"Yeah," I said nastily. "It's wonderful. It was swell of you to ask me. How does Carol like it?"

That wiped the grin off but he didn't have a chance to answer because just then Carol came back. She'd slipped into a camel's hair coat and wore a red-and-white scarf over her hair. She didn't look at me as I walked past on my way upstairs.

4

WHEN I got to my room I didn't bother to turn on the light, but felt my way over to the windows and stood looking out. The house was quiet now and there was a faint glow in the sky, as though somewhere up there a moon was trying to break through the clouds. Presently I heard a car door slam. The sound came from the rear, round by the parking court, and I thought I heard Carol's voice before the motor started; it sounded as if she were arguing.

I waited there until the station wagon came down the drive and rolled into the highway, turning left; then I undressed in the darkness and put on pajamas and a robe. I got cigarettes and pulled a chair over by the window and sat down.

It wasn't very long before I heard the station wagon coming. I saw the lights sweep the road and turn into the drive, brushing the hedge with brightness. The motor died suddenly somewhere behind me. A car door slammed again and there were steps on the gravel and I knew they were coming back, Carol and Johnny and the champagne, and this time there hadn't been any argument. I don't know how long I sat there, but I know what I was thinking. And it was torture, a type of mental torture that was new to me, a powerful corrosive that ate away my reason. When I could not stand it any longer I jumped up; then I knew I was going to Johnny's room, and knock, and ask for some champagne.

I didn't want champagne, I wanted brandy. I guess it was a crazy thing to do and it is hard to justify even now. But I could not forget that Johnny had passed out the night before and I suppose I thought I could put on an act and get him drinking and maybe he'd pass out again. It wouldn't prove anything and if Carol really loved him it would be a lousy trick. But I didn't want to think she loved him and I was grabbing at straws. Tomorrow I could leave and then what happened would be all right, but tonight, being in the same house with them, I had to do something.

I crossed to the door in the darkness and opened it silently. There was a night light at the head of the stairs and I turned here and went along the ell. I stopped at Johnny's door. I listened a moment, wondering if I heard someone moving in the room, and then, because I knew I'd quit cold and be sensible if I faltered, I knocked and grabbed the knob. When it turned in my hand I stepped into the blackness of the room and right then I knew something was wrong.

It wasn't anything I heard or saw; it was the way I felt. Not scared, nor panicky like I used to get in the hospital, just tight all over and holding my breath and trying to see through the thick blackness about me.

"Johnny," I said, "Johnny."

And then I saw it. Some movement, a shadow of some movement by the windows. For an instant this shadow blocked off the light from the night sky and was silhouetted shapelessly against the glass. Then the French window was open and someone was going through to the balcony beyond.

I guess I called out. I know I started for the window and it seemed to me that some reflected light danced briefly from the man's eyes before he disappeared. I was about halfway there when I tripped over a chair and went down on my hands and knees.

I scrambled up and kept going, through the window and out on the little balcony. I could see it was not much of a drop to the ground but I could not see nor hear anything else, and as I hesitated there was some new sound behind me. When I turned a door had opened, spilling light across the rug. A switch clicked and the room was bright, and Carol was standing in the connecting doorway.

"Alan!" Her eyes were wide open, her face white. "I heard someone," she said. "I thought it was Johnny."

I glanced about the room. There was a heavy maple chest near the bed and the drawers were partway open. I started towards it before I realized that an inspection of these drawers could tell me nothing. I swerved and went to Carol.

I told her why I'd come. I said someone had been in the room and had gone through the window. I saw, finally, that she still wore the black dress with the white at the throat and then I thought of something else.

"It wasn't Johnny," I said. "Didn't he come back with you?"

She shook her head and her mouth trembled.

"Why not?"

"Because"—she caught her lip and tried to stop the trembling—"because— Oh, what difference does it make?"

That was the time I should have taken her in my arms. If I had I think it would have saved a lot of trouble later on. Her defenses were down and she looked shaken and miserable. I don't know what was the matter with me, what stopped me. Pride, stubbornness, sheer stupidity, whatever it was I stood stiffly, holding back, waiting. Then she was looking at me and something happened to her eyes and her chin came up. She gathered her defenses quickly and was secure behind them.

"I wanted to come back." Her voice was low, controlled. "He didn't. That's all, Alan. I expect he wanted to stay down there and get drunk."

I felt the tension come around my mouth. It was hard to swallow but some damnable thing inside me made me key my mood to hers. I told myself this was Mrs. Johnny Marshall, and by her own choice. It was silly, it was awful.

"I'll get him," I said.

"No." She shook her head and now her eyes were afraid. "He—he'll be ugly."

"I don't care if he's blind drunk." I went over to the door and opened it. "If he can walk I'm bringing him back."

I went down the hall to my room and put on trousers and jacket over my pajamas. I put on some shoes and without bothering to lace them, I went down the main stairs. I didn't tiptoe. I didn't care who heard me.

Outside it was darker than I thought. There was a moon, but it had been blacked out temporarily by a low-hanging overcast and I had to feel my way to the road. After that it was all right and I moved along with quick hard strides until I saw the rectangle of light from an open door of the wine cellar.

I stopped short of the door, watching the dim yellow glow beyond. I was breathing hard and my heart was pounding and a thin breath of fear blew along my spine. There was no reason for it; it was simply a hangover from the nervous condition which had kept me in the hospital and warped my thoughts and made me break off with Carol.

I wasn't afraid of Marshall. I wasn't afraid of anything tangible

I told myself this. I told myself it was imagination and the reluctance to explore the unknown and I tried to remember what the doctors had told me. I waited a half-minute and then I marched through the door, still scared and every muscle tense.

I crossed the damp, hard-packed earthen floor and the murky gleam from the scattered electric bulbs made all the shadows black and impenetrable. I started down the aisle we'd used that afternoon. Then I called out.

"Johnny," I said, and listened to the echo and marched on, telling myself the shadows were friendly. I turned a corner, remembering the inner stairs to the office above and wondering if he could be there.

I stopped and stared ahead, at the rows of casks that reached endlessly into the pitch black of the hillside beyond. *You won't have to go in there*, I thought. *Johnny wouldn't be 'way back there.*

I started to walk and my neck was on a swivel, rigid but turning from side to side as I marched to the corner and started back along the next aisle. I was halfway to the first light when I saw him there on the floor ahead of me.

He was on his back, his ankles crossed, and all about him the earthen floor was red. I stood staring down, seeing now the dark stain on his neck and the wound just under the chin. And though I'd seen much worse things, I felt all sick inside; not shocked or scared, just sick.

I forced my gaze from the still, white face with the closed eyes and half-open mouth. I forced myself to look at something else. That's when I saw the shattered champagne bottle.

I did not stop to think then why Johnny Marshall was in this aisle, I remembered only the sound of the exploding bottle that afternoon, the explanation of the pressure which caused such explosions and the frequence with which such accidents happened.

I stepped carefully around the stain and the fragments of glass and squatted beside the body. Then I saw the base of the triangular splinter protruding from the throat and knew for sure how Johnny had died.

It sounds cold-blooded now, but my immediate reaction as I straightened was an overwhelming sense of relief. It was not that I had ever felt Carol could be involved, it was simply that now no one could be involved. Johnny Marshall was dead and it was an accident, brought about by his own hand.

I backed away, thinking of the office upstairs, knowing I must find a telephone at once. I turned at the intersecting aisle and as my gaze slid across the rows of bottles I saw something white tucked far back, yet visible enough from where I stood. I kept on going, heading for the stairs which mounted along the far wall. I took two or three steps before I stopped.

Why I went back I'll never know. There is no explaining such things and I only know what I did. Something stronger than any conscious thought made me stop, and having stopped, made me retrace my steps. I went back to the white thing I'd seen, slowly, pushing one foot ahead of the other. I reached in between those rows of bottles and pulled out a wadded ball of silk.

For a second or two I just stared at it and the cold from that hard damp floor seeped through the soles of my shoes and slid quickly up my calves. When I moved, everything seemed in slow motion.

I shook out that ball of silk and it was a square scarf with a red-and-white pattern. It was a scarf with a three-inch rip near the center and an irregular stain about ten inches across. It was red, that stain, but it didn't match the red in the scarf; it was dark and faintly sticky.

For a while I could only stand there, numb and frozen and unable to think. It took me a long time to fold that scarf—with the dark stain inside—and figure out what I had to do. Then it was all very clear and when I moved, I moved fast. Too fast, I guess.

I looked over at the shadow of those stairs. I knew I still had to telephone and I knew I'd have time then to get rid of this scarf. I wouldn't have to carry it any farther than the office. I could burn it and put it down the drain. So I started to run, blocking off the rest of my mind, refusing even to admit that this scarf had been around Carol's blond head when she left with Johnny.

I barged down the aisle, tried a short cut between a row of casks and found it was no short cut. I dodged left and made another quick turn and as I did so some shadow bulkier than the rest moved at my elbow.

I was going too fast. I couldn't stop nor turn in time and my reflexes never had a chance. A bomb exploded in my head and when the lights went out I was falling through some vast and limitless blackout.

Something cold was pressing against my cheek. My head was hot and filled with pain and my stomach was quivering. I opened my eyes slowly and realized the thing that felt so good on my cheek was the damp, earthen floor. I wanted to stay right there until the fit of nausea passed, and then I began to think.

That fixed everything up. I put my hands against the floor and pushed, fighting my giddiness until I sat erect; then I turned my head and found myself staring at a pair of brown-and-white shoes two feet away.

I thought of a lot of things then but none of them were any good. I kept my eyes where they were until I got hold of myself and then I looked up, past gabardine trousers and a tweed jacket to the swart blocky face of Earl Garlin. He was leaning against a row of casks watching me through lids that seemed practically shut.

"You were out quite a while," he said.

I remembered the scarf and instantly I was afraid. I glanced round. I couldn't see it and I wondered if I could be sitting on it. I said:

"How do you know?"

"I've been here four or five minutes and you were here when I came."

I asked him if he knew about Marshall. He said he did.

"I found him first," he said. "I found you when I started looking for the stairs. What happened?"

"Somebody slugged me."

"I mean before that?"

"I was looking for Johnny. When I found him I started for the stairs the same as you did. I made a wrong turn and ran into somebody who'd been hiding here."

"I guess you didn't see who it was."

This was a different Garlin; a damned unpleasant Garlin. There was no grin, no trace of friendliness in him now. His voice was clipped, incisive, and his mouth beneath the mustache was hard and mean. I felt my temper flare and the ache in my head was nagging me.

"No," I said. "It could've been you."

He skipped that one. He looked me over with those hard fathomless eyes. After a moment he said, "How come you were looking for Johnny at all?"

I told him I went to Johnny's room to get some champagne, that Carol told me he hadn't come back. "I came down here to see what had happened to him."

The mustache flattened out. "You were pretty concerned about him, weren't you?"

In the next half-minute I realized I was very nearly a well man again. An irrational, ungovernable temper is one of the after effects of this mental condition which had brought me from the Solomons, and a month ago I would have been raging at him. Now I deliberately turned my mind away from him. I thought about the scarf. I started to get up, carefully, so I could feel beneath me and hide the scarf if it were there. There was nothing but that damp floor.

I wanted to ask Garlin about that scarf; I nearly did. Then I saw how it was. Either Garlin knew about the scarf or he didn't. If he didn't, I saw I could not mention it at all. I said:

"As a matter of fact, I've been wondering how you happened to be here."

"I was reading in my room," he said. "I hadn't gone to bed. I heard someone clumping down the stairs and when I looked out the window I saw you come out of the house and head this way."

"So you got suspicious."

"A little."

"Enough to follow me—so you say." I hesitated. "Funny you didn't run into the guy that slugged me."

"That's what I've been thinking."

I brushed myself off and felt the lump on my head. I said I couldn't figure it out either but one thing was obvious: Johnny was fooling with that champagne bottle and it exploded, drove a glass splinter into his throat far enough to sever an artery or vein, and killed him.

"We ought to call the police or the coroner or something," I said.

"Yeah," Garlin said. "Come on. Upstairs."

"Go ahead," I said carelessly, thinking about the scarf. "I'll wait here."

Garlin shook his head and pushed away from the cask. "You'll stay with me," he said, "until the law comes."

5

THE coroner was a round-faced little man named Ryder. He rattled up in a five-year-old coupe a couple minutes behind the State Police car and he was not particularly interested in what Garlin and I had to say to the troopers. His one thought was the victim and we all went down in the cellar and stood around while he made his preliminary examination.

One of the troopers was a husky, heavy-nosed fellow named Tait; the other, a slender blond man with glasses, was Whelan. Tait had a sergeant's chevrons on his sleeve and he was the one who was putting things down in a notebook. He also suggested that everyone else stay away from the body while Ryder was working.

"We may want those pieces of bottle," he said. "The lieutenant may want to have us reconstruct it."

Ryder was one of those bustling little guys with a lot of energy. His unpressed gray suit showed signs of hurried dressing, and the hair over his ears—he was bald on top—was tousled, but he worked with quick, sure hands and made clucking noises and a running fire comment.

"A most unfortunate affair," he said. "Treacherous things, these champagne bottles, yes, sir."

Garlin mentioned the one that exploded that afternoon and the coroner said yes, he knew all about such accidents.

"We had a couple of similar cases a few years ago," Ryder said. "Not fatal, of course, but could have been. Yes, sir. Just a matter of luck, you know . . . Now this fragment here, for instance. Looks like it struck right to catch the carotid artery."

I listened vaguely to him and to Sergeant Tait's questions but mostly I was thinking about Carol's scarf. I didn't want to wander too far but I moved about a little, smoking, pretending I wasn't interested in the examination. When I got the chance I'd take a couple of steps and look into a new row of bottles. Two or three times I saw Garlin watching me and now and then Tait would glance around. I hoped I looked pre-occupied and I guess I did because no one said anything. Neither did I find the scarf.

"There's one other thing," Ryder said when I moved back to the group. I saw he had Johnny's head in his hands and had twisted it so he could see the back. "There's a contusion here of some sort. Don't know how important it is."

"Could he have got it when he fell, Doc?" Tait asked.

"Could have—if he hit the right sort of thing."

"Would that splinter going into his neck like that knock him down?"

"Doubt it. But he had to fall some time, didn't he?"

"How long would it take," Whelan asked, "for a man to die?"

"Hard to say. A few minutes . . . Well." Ryder straightened and brushed his hands. "Guess that's all for now. I'll get on the phone. Probably be a half hour before I can get the ambulance up here, maybe longer. Can you stay with him, Sergeant?"

"Whelan can," Tait said. He put his notebook away and studied Garlin and me absently. "You say you notified those at the house? His wife and sister?"

Garlin said he had. He had telephoned just after he had talked to the police and spoke to Linda Jordan, telling her that she had better tell Carol and Helen what had happened.

"Then I think I'll go along with you," Tait said. "There's one or two things—"

I cut in on him. I asked him if that was necessary. "Can't you wait until morning?"

"I'd rather not."

I didn't like the way Tait said that, nor the steady, unblinking way he looked at me. I told myself that he could not possibly suspect that this was anything but an accident; I assured myself that it was the strain I had been under that made my imagination play tricks like that.

But my growing uneasiness made me feel all empty inside. All I had to do was remember the scarf and the red stain on it and the ragged hole in the center. I didn't believe Johnny's death was any accident. I hadn't believed it for some time. But without the scarf it could still be an accident and that was what Tait must believe. I tried to get the right amount of annoyance into my voice without overdoing it.

"But look," I said, "what good can it do to get the whole house upset? It was an accident and he's dead and there isn't anything anyone can do about it."

"There are still some things *I* have to do," Tait said. "This is my job. I like to do a good job. To do a good job I've got to get all the information I can. The lieutenant's going to want all the details I can give him. Take that crack on the head you say you got."

I bent my head, pointing to a spot on the side near the top that was swollen and sore. "What the hell does that look like?" I asked him.

"Like what you said it was. That's what I mean. This is an accident, yet something bops you one. Why?"

"How do I know? Maybe someone came in and found Johnny like I did and didn't realize it was an accident. Maybe when I came in he got scared or was afraid he'd get mixed up as a witness. When I ran past he might have thought I was trying to grab him or something."

I was making it up as I went along and wondering how it sounded. I glanced at Garlin and he was watching me and that did not help much. "There could be a dozen explanations," I finished lamely.

"Maybe," Tait said. "But I still want to see Mrs. Marshall for a few minutes. She was here with her husband. Maybe she could—"

"If you think she knew anything about it, you're crazy," I said. "Mrs. Marshall was here, yes. But he must have been all right when she left. She wouldn't run out on him if he was hurt, would she?"

"The guy that socked you did," Tait said.

They were waiting up for us when we got back to the house. They did not seem particularly surprised to see Tait, and Garlin introduced him and said the sergeant merely wanted to clear up a couple of points so he could complete his report.

"Just a matter of routine," Tait said.

There was coffee and sandwiches on the big refectory table, also a decanter, ice and glasses. I noticed that Spence Haughton, in a blue flannel robe, had settled for whisky, but Helen, Linda and Carol all had coffee cups nearby. Helen wore a straight-hanging house coat with a fitted top and Linda had a quilted robe with some sort of flower design. Carol still wore the black dress with the white at the throat. I think Tait noticed this right off but he did not refer to it until later.

Linda acted as hostess. She asked Tait if he would like some coffee, or would he prefer a drink.

"Coffee would do nicely," Tait said.

Not for me, though. I needed a drink and so, apparently, did Garlin. We poured out a couple of good hookers and after I'd had a couple of swallows I had a chance to see how things were. Tait was explaining his version of what had happened and when he got to the part where I was slugged Helen spoke up.

"But, Alan," she said, "don't you know who it was?"

She was sitting on the divan with Carol. Her face was pale but composed and she had a ribbon around her chestnut hair. I told her I hadn't the faintest idea who hit me, but what I was thinking was that if Helen felt any sorrow or any sense of bereavement, it certainly did not show.

Linda was different. Linda was nervous. She lit one cigarette from another and her eyes looked red-rimmed and bloodshot, as though she might have cried a little. And Carol—Carol sat very still, her hands in her lap, her eyes fixed straight ahead. Her face was drawn and colorless and she looked as if she were getting by on sheer nerve. Haughton just slumped in his chair, the glass in his hand, staring down at his slippered feet. He didn't say anything; he did not appear even to be listening to Tait's account. Then I saw that Tait was looking at Carol's dress. He cleared his throat.

"You went to get champagne, Mrs. Marshall," he said. "You didn't bring any back?"

Carol looked at him as if he didn't exist. "No."

"You didn't wait for your husband?"

"I thought we were going to ride down and get a few bottles and come right back. He wanted to stay and—I didn't."

"So you took the station wagon."

"I"—Carol hesitated, glanced down at her hands and then back at Tait—"he told me if I didn't want to wait I could take the car. He said he'd walk back."

"And that's the way you left him . . . Do you remember where he was standing—that is, in relation to the door from the road?"

Again Carol hesitated but her glance did not waver. "I don't really know. You see, I'd only been there once before and I'm not very familiar with the place."

"Do you remember the bottle that exploded this afternoon?"

"Yes."

"Was your husband in that aisle when you left him?"

"He—he might have been. I'm afraid I didn't really notice. I'm sorry."

Tait nodded and closed his notebook. Then he came back to the dress he had first noticed. "Did you go to bed when you came back?"

Carol saw where he was looking and glanced down and sudden color tinted her cheeks briefly and went away.

"No," she said. "I intended to wait up for him."

Tait rose and put aside his coffee cup. "Thank you," he said. "Thank you very much. There isn't anything else any of you could add?"

I thought about the intruder I'd discovered in Johnny's room but not for long. This death had to be an accident and I wasn't going to have some prowler louse up things for me.

"Then I'll run along," Tait said. "I'm sorry I had to bother you now but Mr. Marshall was an important man and we want to have as much information as we can ready for the inquest."

He went to the doorway and hesitated. "Perhaps Lieutenant Dunbar will stop in in the morning."

No one moved, no one spoke until we heard the door close. Then Carol stood up. For the first time since I'd come in she looked at me and not until then, until I could see what was really in her eyes, did I realize what made her look so white and strained. She was scared, badly scared. She glanced at the others and seemed about to speak and then she turned without a word and started for the stairs.

Helen jumped up and followed her. "Wait, Carol," she said. "I'll go with you, darling."

Haughton followed them up and Garlin waited until we could

no longer hear them on the stairs; then he went over and poured another drink. When he turned his face was black and his eyes glittered.

"A fine Goddam thing," he said viciously.

"What do you mean, Earl?" Linda said.

"Yeah," I said. "What's your trouble? You may be out of a job, but so what? There're worse things than that. Johnny got fooling around with those champagne bottles and he—"

"Yah—" Garlin snorted derisively. "Who the hell do you think you're kidding? Not me, brother. And you won't kid that lieutenant when he comes in the morning. Not for long, you won't."

"Earl!"

Linda's voice had a snap to it and he looked at her.

"Just what are you trying to tell us?"

"I'm saying it was no accident," Garlin said.

Something hit me in the pit of the stomach and began to spread coldly, emptily, inside me. I couldn't think of anything but that scarf.

"You're mad," Linda said.

"You can say that again," Garlin said.

"But wasn't a piece of the champagne bottle in Johnny's neck? That's what you said."

"Sure that's what we said." Garlin took a big swallow and put down his glass. He hooked a thigh over the corner of the table and leaned on it. "Look. Johnny's lyin' right where the bottle is. There's pieces all around him."

"Certainly," I said.

"Nuts," Garlin said. "You heard what the coroner said. And even if he hadn't I could spot that as a phony. I've been around and I've talked to too many medical examiners to fall for that setup. It would take minutes for a guy to bleed to death, to lose consciousness even. If it happened to you would you lay down and die? Like hell. You'd run for help or a telephone or something."

I was cold all over. It was hard for me to talk. "But if he fell down and hit his head—"

"That piece of glass wouldn't knock him down. Ten'll get you twenty he was out cold when that glass hit his neck." He made angry noises in his throat, tossed off the rest of his drink and stood up. "Don't quote me. Just wait and see." And like that he went out and left Linda and me sitting there.

We sat quite awhile without speaking and finally she said, "Do you think he's right, Alan?"

I told her I didn't know what to think. I said it was an accident until the police proved differently. There wasn't any more talk. I didn't offer anything and I guess Linda realized I wasn't going to. After about five minutes she got up and started for the hall. At the doorway she stopped.

"You can turn off the lights when you come," she said.

I waited until she was upstairs and then I fixed another drink. I kept thinking about that damned scarf and wondering if the guy who slugged me had taken it. I couldn't seem to make any sense out of anything and I wasn't doing myself any good trying.

I finished the drink and a half dozen cigarettes and got up to make another and while I was up I snapped off the room lights. I sat there in the darkness for a long time with all those things going through my head. I even thought about Carol and wondered, reluctantly, if she could have done this thing. Then I knew she couldn't have. She could not have done a thing like that, with a jagged glass fragment from a broken bottle. Even if she had, and I could not admit this, she would not have been so foolish as to leave a scarf behind. Yet she had been scared when she stood up and left the room. And if she was innocent, why should she be scared?

When, finally, I saw a reason, it gave me a nasty shock. If she was innocent, and Johnny was alive when she left, then how could she know that I had not killed him. Suppose she thought *I had* killed him?

The thought left me sick inside and I got up and put down my glass, and then I knew I had to go back to the wine cellar. I had to be sure that there was no scarf hidden somewhere for the police to find, once they took the line of reasoning that Garlin had given Linda and me.

I moved quietly along the hall to the study and closed the door before I turned on the light. I knew I had to have some kind of flashlight if I was to search the wine cellars and I hoped I might find one here. I turned to the desk and what I saw then told me that someone else had been going through that desk. I don't know why I was so sure. I had no standard of comparison, since I'd never seen the desk before, but it did not seem to me that there should be such disordered confusion among the papers and things I found in the drawers I opened. Somehow the disorder did not seem to be an accumulated one that had grown that way through the slackness of the owner; rather it seemed to be a disorder of haste, as though someone had gone through these things swiftly and with no thought of covering his intentions.

But I did find a flashlight and my success promptly erased further speculation from my mind. I turned off the light and went out, taking care not to make any noise with the front door.

The moon was still under the overcast and the night was still. Far across the lake I saw a flash of light as some car sped along the highway, and somewhere off to the left I could hear bullfrogs croaking at each other. Then the shadow of the winery loomed up in front of me and I crossed the road to the grassy strip on the side and moved cautiously along the front of the stone wall to the door.

I slid my hand along the wooden panels to where the doors met and then my fingers found the hasp and the lock. I don't know why I hadn't considered this possibility before; I just hadn't. The doors had been open when I had seen them before and it never entered my head that they would be locked. I was standing there trying to swallow my disappointment when I heard the faint sound on the road behind me.

It startled me, that sound. It wasn't loud but it was distinct and I wheeled instantly and got my back to the doors. Something, blacker than the night, was moving swiftly across the road and making very little noise. I could hear the rasp of shoes on the macadam and saw, vaguely, a hand move up with something dark in it. A low deep voice said:

"Hold it, Mac!"

I slid one foot forward and waited, the muscles tensing in my back. Then light exploded in my face and I was staring blankly into the lens of a flashlight.

"Oh, hello, Mr. Wallace," the voice said.

The light swept down and clicked out. I blew out my breath and sagged back against the door and wondered what I was going to say to Sergeant Tait.

"Were you looking for something?"

"Yes," I said. "I—don't seem to be able to find my cigarette lighter, Sergeant. I thought I might have lost it down here when I was knocked out."

"Oh, yes . . . Hmm . . . How'd you expect to get in, any-way?"

I said I didn't know. "I guess I didn't think much about it."

"I guess you didn't," Tait said. "Well, if we find it tomorrow, we'll let you know."

"Thanks."

"Or maybe you'll find it somewhere else. Anyway, I think you'd better get to bed, Mr. Wallace. It's pretty near three o'clock."

6

THE telephone began to ring the next morning about eight o'clock. It kept ringing every few minutes all the time I was dressing and it was still at it when I was eating breakfast.

First it was one New York paper and then another. Then it was a Rochester paper. And in between it was the district correspondents for the New York papers. Somebody had got the dope from Doc Ryder, the coroner, the night before and put it on the wire and if it had been known then that Johnny Marshall had been murdered I think the house would have been overrun before noon.

When he could, Garlin was doing some long distance phoning on his own and right after breakfast I discovered there was a state trooper stationed at the main gate, so that when the reporters from the Rochester paper and the one from Penn Yan and from the Elmira *Star-Gazette* got there they couldn't get in.

But Lieutenant Dunbar of the State Police got in, and with him was a red-face husky by the name of Corrigan. Sergeant Corrigan, I found out later, from the District Attorney's office. I didn't see Carol all morning, nor Spencer Haughton, and Dunbar and Corrigan didn't bother me then either. They went into a huddle with Garlin and I took the opportunity to stroll out on the terrace. When no one said anything I went on down to the dock.

The boathouse doors were open and someone was working in there. It was Bert Donelly. He had on paint-stained coveralls and was working on the deck of a small sloop and I went over and sat down nearby and said Good Morning.

" 'Mornin'," said Bert.

He kept working and I watched him for awhile without saying anything. I thought about saying something about Marshall and then I thought, "The hell with it. He'll get plenty of that before the day is over." I said:

"How long is she?"

"Twenty-six feet."

"Marconi rigged?"

"Yep. Fast too. Take anything on this lake 'cept maybe them One-designs, and they ain't hardly what you'd call a boat with them six inch drafts."

It was a nice job, all right, with lines like the old Ranger and a fin keel that looked as though it would take a lot of weather. There was a small cabin, with maybe five foot headroom, a couple of berths and a boxed-in one-cylinder marine engine for getting in and out of tight spots.

I glanced about the interior of the house. There was one wide platform in the center and two slips with narrow·catwalks on either side, next to the walls. The sloop rested on a cradle over one of the slips and in the other was a mahogany speedboat which looked a couple feet longer than the sloop. Two dingys had been swung up at the far end of the platform and over everything, and stretching from wall to wall but planked only part of the length of the house, was a sail loft.

I watched Donelly working with his brushes. He was a small, wrinkled man, deeply tanned. He had a battered briar clamped between his teeth and though there was no tobacco in it, he'd take it out once in a while and spit and then put it back in his mouth. If he was at all affected by last night's tragedy, he certainly gave no sign of it and I suppose I sat there watching him for a half hour or more before footsteps came along the dock and Helen Bradford appeared in the doorway.

"Bert," she said, and then she saw me. "Oh, good morning,

Alan . . . Bert, I think you'd better let that go for today."

Bert said, "All right, Miss Helen," and kept working.

"Mae needs you in the house," Helen said, "and there are men from the police. They may want to talk to you."

Bert began to clean his brushes. Helen watched him a moment and then she said:

"And Bert. This won't make any difference, last night, I mean, to you and Mae. You'll stay right on, you know."

"That's all right, Miss Helen. Mae and me'll make out. I been thinking maybe I'd get me a job in the boat works up to Penn Yan."

"But we need you here. I don't know what will be done about this place. Nothing probably. I want you to stay."

"I'll speak to Mae," Bert said.

Helen went out and I went with her. "Let's sit down a minute," I said, and steered her to a bench at the front of the dock.

It was a swell morning. The sun was warm and the air was so clear you could almost see the farm fences on the other side of the lake. A hundred yards away a man in a rowboat was moving slowly our way, a pole and line propped over the stern. He seemed to be trolling and yet he wasn't rowing fast enough for that. I watched him a moment and then Helen was talking.

"Was it really an accident, Alan?"

I sat up and looked at her, jarred back to realities not only by the question but by her tone of voice. She was wearing a simple dark blue dress with a fly front and a belt and her hair looked soft and warm in the sunlight. She was looking out across the lake, and with her regular features and her clear delicate skin her profile was strikingly beautiful.

"Why sure," I said. "Of course."

"Then why do the police ask so many questions?"

"You mean this new guy, Dunbar? Why, what's he been doing?"

"Oh—he wanted to know how we all happened to be here and—"

"What did you tell him?"

"I told him Johnny always traveled with a crowd . . . And he wanted to know if Johnny had any enemies and what would happen to his money."

"What does happen?"

Bert Donelly came out of the boat house and Helen waited while he walked towards the house. The fellow in the rowboat was about thirty feet from the end of the dock, drifting now, and fooling with one of those straight bamboo poles you used to be able to buy in any country store.

"I'm not sure," Helen said. "Earl Garlin telephoned to New York. I imagine one of Johnny's lawyers will come up."

That made me think of a question Johnny had asked on the station platform yesterday morning when he had first spoken to Helen. I said:

"What about that lawyer of yours?"

She glanced at her wristwatch. "He should be here almost any time now."

There were other things I wanted to ask about that lawyer. I wanted to know why he should come at all, and that made me think of what Garlin had told me about Helen being a customer of Doctor Penzance. Now, as I thought of these things, Helen stood up and I rose with her.

"Pardon me."

The voice came from the lake and close by. I turned. The fellow in the rowboat was standing up. He was a red-headed youth, hatless and grinning, and his boat was only about fifteen feet away from us and he had a camera—a small Speed-Graphic—propped in front of one eye. The shutter clicked before I could move.

"Thanks," he said, and reversed his film-holder. "Now if you'll give me your names."

I looked round for something to heave at him and there was a square concrete block with an eye-bolt embedded in it under the bench. I guess somebody'd used it for a small boat anchor and it weighed about twenty pounds. I don't know why I was so sore; probably it was just a case of nerves. Anyway I picked it up and stepped to the stringpiece.

"Wait a minute, Mister," the red head said in quick alarm.

"Alan!" Helen said and put her hand on my arm.

The red-head grinned. "I only rented this boat. I got to take it back. I couldn't get past that state cop and the hedge was too tough for me. I had to get a picture of somebody."

The grin helped. It was the infectious kind that once you think about you're lost. I put the block down and I felt pretty sheepish.

"You had me scared," the red-head said. "I'm from the Elmira *Star-Gazette* . . . Now if you'll just give me your names I'll take this scow back where it belongs."

I looked at Helen and she looked at me.

"It'll probably get printed anyway," the red-head said. "Might as well have the names right."

Helen shrugged and a smile came faintly to her eyes. "This is Alan Wallace."

"A friend of Mr. Marshall's?" the red-head asked.

"Yes," she said. "And I'm Helen Bradford. I'm Mr. Marshall's sister."

"Ahh, thanks." The red-head let out a sigh I could hear from where I stood. "You're swell . . . Now if you could tell me who else is staying—"

"Beat it," I said.

"Okay, chief." He sat down and picked up the oars and that grin was still there.

Helen and I walked back to the house and we were just entering the living room from the terrace when a plump, balding man with pink cheeks and metal-rimmed glasses, came in from the hall. When he spotted us he rushed forward.

"Helen," he said. "You poor girl. What a frightful thing to have happen."

"Hello, Douglas," Helen said. She let the man take her hand and cover it with his own. "Alan, this is Douglas Eddington— Alan Wallace."

Eddington was the lawyer that should have come the day before. He was very glad to meet me and he had a soft hand though he pumped mine vigorously. I said what I had to say and left them in the living room and then went down the hall and out the front door. The state cop was still there but I couldn't see any newspaper men so I strolled out to the road and turned towards the wine cellars.

I still had that bug in my head about the scarf. I remembered with some chagrin my encounter with Sergeant Tait the night before and now I wanted to have another look, just so I'd be satisfied in my own mind that I had done what I could. I'd gone about a hundred yards when I heard someone hurrying up behind me.

It was the red-head. He had a platecase slung over his shoulder and I saw now that he walked with a slight limp. "Hi," he said. "I'll walk along with you. I'm going down to the winery. Might as well get a shot of that, there's nothing more at the house so long as that lieutenant's in charge."

I kept walking and he moved along beside me. "My name's Kiley," he said after a few seconds. "I sure wished I could get a shot of that Mrs. Marshall. I'll bet she's a looker if she's like those other dames he married. What a guy. Known him long?"

I was exasperated but in spite of myself I had to grin at such exuberance and ingenuity. "What are you," I said "a photographer or a reporter?"

"Both nowadays. Mostly a camera, though. Only on an assignment like this where they can't send but one guy I have to get all the details I can." He grunted softly. "If that damned lieutenant hadn't clammed up on us . . . What the hell is so hush-hush about a guy getting killed accidentally? Even if he is a rich guy that's been married five times. Hell, I can't hang around all day; we're running an afternoon sheet."

The door of the wine cellar was open again and when I walked in Kiley stayed right beside me. I knew I wasn't going to do any looking for a scarf with him here but I couldn't figure any way of getting rid of him so while I thought about ways and means I kept walking.

I turned into the aisle where I'd found Marshall the night before and then I saw a man with pads and a mask. At first I thought it was an employee of the place because the light wasn't very good, and then I saw the gray uniform, and the bottles piled on the floor instead of in the racks, and the long handled pushbroom the fellow was using.

He put the broom down when he saw us and came forward. Then I recognizeed him. It was Whelan, the slender blond trooper who had been with Tait the night before.

"Better not come down here." He smiled. "You know what happened to Marshall."

Kiley came to life instantly. "Hey," he said, "was this where he died? Right here?" He didn't wait for an answer, but unslung his platecase and opened it hurriedly. "Boy, this is more like it. It's okay, ain't it, for a picture?"

"Well"—Whelan bunched his lips and glanced at me—"I guess so. Who you with?"

Kiley told him as he screwed a flashbulb into the synchronized gun. "Why don't you stand over there by the spot," he said to Whelan. "There . . . that's it . . . now hold it."

The flashbulb went off with a burst of light. "Boy, this is the nuts," Kiley said. "Atmosphere, huh? Spooky as hell. Look, how would you like one without the mask, chief? What're you doin' with the broom anyway? What're you looking-for?"

He was working all the time he talked. He was ready with a fresh bulb when Whelan took off the mask and posed and after the picture had been taken Whelan said:

"We're reconstructing the bottle—incidentally, the name is Whelan. W-h-e-l-a-n. Thomas J."

"Okay," Kiley said, writing this down.

"Yeah," Whelan said, expansively now that he had time to think about the publicity he was going to get, "reconstructing the bottle."

"What for?" I said.

"Just routine. We'll have it for the inquest. You know, show the bottle and where the fatal splinter came from."

"You mean you sweep up all of the pieces," Kiley said, "and paste 'em together? Can you do that?"

"Why not?" Whelan said. "We already swept up the pieces. Last night. A laboratory guy has been working on it since early morning. The bottle's practically perfect."

"Then what're you lookin' for?" Kiley said.

"Well—there's one piece we haven't got. There's the one in his throat of course—that was about three and a half inches long and an inch and a half wide at the base; then there's another which should be maybe three-quarters of an inch long and half as wide. That's what I'm looking for now."

"Think you'll find it?" Kiley asked, and when Whelan said, "Sure," Kiley said, "And all that trouble just to get a perfect bottle."

"That's the way we like to do things," Whelan said. "Course it'll have cracks in it and some may be sort of wide on account of the glass sometimes powders some but it'll be pretty good."

"Okay," Kiley said. "Now if I could only get a shot of the splinter they dug out of Marshall's throat—"

"Well, see the coroner."

"Damned if I won't," Kiley said. He started away, then stopped and thanked Whelan and me. "I'll send you a print of that one on the dock," he said to me. "And if you get to Elmira look me up. It's quite a town."

Whelan sighed and put on his mask. "These damn newspaper guys," he said. "Well, I got to get back to work."

I told him I was going to look around. I said I wanted to take another look at the spot where the guy had slugged me last night. Whelan said it was okay with him so I moved on. I started where Garlin had found me and began to search systematically from that point, widening my range as I went. I stayed there until it was time for lunch but I didn't find any scarf.

7

Lieutenant Dunbar of the State Police brought us all together in the living room after lunch. With him was Sergeant Corrigan and a fellow named Quinn, who proved to be the assistant district attorney. When I found that out I watched the preliminaries with a sinking sensation in the pit of my stomach because I knew what was coming, knew they didn't need any lieutenant or assistant D.A. to tell that Johnny Marshall had died accidentally.

I sat down over in a corner where I could watch everybody, and tried to look dumb. It was the first time I'd seen Carol. She was sitting on the divan between Helen Bradford and Linda Jordan, wearing a plain dark dress that made her face seem paler, her hair more golden. She looked at me just once and her eyes made some plea I could not understand; then she sat there, her hands folded, her face somberly composed. I suppose it helped that she was an actress, but she could take it too; she was pretty wonderful.

Helen Bradford was just the same, stately, remote, her face untroubled. Linda Jordan had changed. Linda's charm depended greatly on her easy camaraderie, her quick wit, her resiliency and vitality. With these gone she was just a pretty, auburn-haired girl, paler than usual and strangely subdued.

Garlin sat off by himself, watching Dunbar, his dark face sultry and his eyes morose. Spence Haughton slumped in his chair and folded his hands across his stomach as he stretched his feet. The lawyer, Douglas Eddington, sat on the edge of his chair and waited impatiently for Dunbar to speak.

This Dunbar looked more like a bookkeeper than a lieutenant of the State Police and I think he cultivated the impression to kid people along and soften them up for the kill. He was quiet-voiced —at the beginning—partly bald, and with a patient easy manner that belied his alert gray eyes. He began by saying that we were probably wondering why he had asked all of us to listen to him.

"And now that you're here," he said, "I don't see any reason for beating around the bush. You might as well know now that Mr. Marshall did not die accidentally. He was murdered."

For once I was ready. I was all set for that announcement and I didn't look at Dunbar; instead I tried to see the reaction of the others, with the idea, I suppose, that if anyone here was guilty he might do something that would give himself away. Maybe the idea was sound in its premise but for all I found out it was a sheer waste of time.

I couldn't see everybody at once because the room was too big. I did hear a sort of concerted gasp that seemed to come from all over and then a jumble of shocked, protesting words that did not make much sense. One of those words came from Carol. She sat up straight, her eyes wide open, her face incredulous. Haughton said something too, and Eddington bounced off his chair and spat out something that sounded like, "Ridiculous."

Helen Bradford's shoulder sagged. She put her hands together and looked at them and then lifted her face and if there was anything there but utter resignation I couldn't see it. The other two— Linda and Garlin—didn't bat an eye. Garlin had warned Linda last night and she apparently accepted his verdict as I had. She glanced at me, tightened her lips and gave me a combination nod and shrug, as though to say, "Now we are in for it."

"I don't believe it," Carol said finally.

"What about the bottle?" Haughton said. "There was a bottle, wasn't there? And it did explode?"

"Yes," Dunbar said. "It exploded—but only after someone had dropped it." And then he began to explain his theory.

I'd heard it before. Last night. From Garlin. And as I listened I felt a mounting respect for this man who had been Johnny Marshall's bodyguard. He had given us a theory last night that matched almost exactly the things Dunbar now told us and I mentally ticked off the points as Dunbar brought them up.

There was the coroner's opinion that it would take a man minutes to bleed to death from such a wound, the statement that the glass splinter would never have knocked Marshall down nor caused him to lose consciousness. Even Dunbar's reasoning was the same.

"A man with such a wound," he said, "would look for help,

unless he contemplated suicide. He'd run back to the house or go to the office and telephone for help. Certainly he would make some movement." He hesitated, as though to accent his words.

"But in this case, the blood was all in one place. Marshall did not move around after that glass entered his neck. This fact, considered with the contusion on the back of his head, leads us to believe that he was unconscious when the glass splinter was driven into his neck."

"If someone was going to kill him," Spence Haughton said slowly, "why bother with all that bottle business in the first place?"

"Because in the beginning the murderer must have thought he could frame a recurrence of the explosion you all witnessed yesterday morning. Either something went wrong or else he did not give the plan sufficient thought; perhaps he thought the police would jump at conclusions and accept the obvious without further investigation. We don't know, naturally, but the coroner says, and we say, that Mr. Marshall was murdered."

He waited. When no one argued the point he glanced at Quinn and got a nod of confirmation. "We'll have to question all of you," he said. "And there's just one other thing I'd like to say now. It may be a bit difficult for you to understand, especially if you are all friends, but the fact remains that there is a very good chance that one of you here in this room is a murderer."

That got him about ten seconds of absolute silence in which people looked at each other and then quickly away; then Haughton said:

"What about this guy Penzance?"

"He is the one outsider we shall also consider . . . The point I'm making is simply this: Whoever killed Mr. Marshall must have done so with the hope of getting away with it. He knows, now that we know it is murder, that if he is caught he will pay for the crime with his life. I doubt if he would hesitate to kill again if he thought his safety was jeopardized. Just remember that when we ask our questions. It's a pretty silly and futile business trying to protect a killer, you know, even if you are under the impression that he is a friend of yours."

He pushed away from the mantlepiece and glanced at a slip of paper he took from his pocket. "We'd like to talk to Mrs. Marshall and Mr. Wallace first. In the study, please."

I looked at Carol and she looked at me and I felt that everyone else was looking at us too. I got up and so did she, and then she started for the study and I followed without having a chance to say a word to her.

Corrigan shut the door. Dunbar pulled a straight-backed chair around for Carol and when she sat down he moved another chair to the edge of the desk and sat down and Quinn sat down opposite Carol. The big leather chair was empty so I took that. And then I found out why this investigation—insofar as I was concerned—had been delayed.

Dunbar and Quinn had not only gathered all the physical facts of the murder, but they had been burning up the wires for hours getting our dossiers. He had mine cold.

"Captain Alan Wallace, U.S.M.C." Dunbar looked at me with those gray eyes and his voice was mild. "Five eleven, a hundred and seventy, age twenty-nine, medical discharge—"

"With the privilege of standing a physical for re-instatement," I said coldly.

He nodded. "You were at Guadalcanal, decorated with the Silver Star and Purple Heart. You were wounded in the left leg and you spent four months in the Bay City Hospital as a mental patient." He leaned across the desk. "Are you cured?"

"They released me, didn't they?"

He was very patient. "But are you cured?"

"I am now."

He glanced at a sheet of paper that he had placed on the desk. "You were engaged to Mrs. Marshall until about a month ago. Mind telling why that engagement was broken?"

I thought it over. I knew he couldn't force me to tell the truth and I hated like hell to have to explain all of it in front of Carol. But I had to consider something else. Carol might be in a spot— I didn't know how much Dunbar knew at the time—and I realized that I must make it clear that the break-up between Carol and me had been my doing and mine alone.

"All right," I said, and I told him. Once started I was glad to get it off my chest, and yet, even as I spoke I became aware that what I said was not too convincing. It was the truth, and a month ago, when I made the decision, it seemed like the only sensible, honorable choice I had. Now, coldly examined, I realized I had been a complete and utter fool.

"I was afraid I'd be a permanent crock," I said.

"You mean on account of your leg?"

"Not the leg. I knew the leg would heal eventually. It was my head that bothered me."

"Oh," Dunbar said.

Quinn cleared his throat. "You suffered some injury there too, Mr. Wallace?"

I didn't know if he was trying to trick me or not but I didn't like it. "If you know about Bay City hospital you ought to know the other," I said.

"It wasn't what they call traumatic war-neurosis?"

"No," I said. "That's an entirely different thing. That hits a man suddenly, like a shock. He sees some friend of his get his head blown off and he goes berserk, or maybe he pulls a fit. What I had is combat fatigue. I don't know what the technical name for it is, but plenty of men suffered from it. It comes from just what the name says—combat and fatigue. Too much of both without rest or change."

"Go on, Mr. Wallace," Dunbar said. "About your engagement."

"Well, that's what I had, and I had plenty of time to think about it. I watched men go into tantrums over nothing. I watched them dive under hospital beds when a plane went over; I've done it myself. I've fought four orderlies one minute and sat quietly crying the next. Even when they let me walk around I couldn't always control my temper—"

"Alan!"

Carol's voice was strained and ragged. I saw Dunbar wave her to silence and stare back at me. Not until then did I realize what a build-up I was giving myself as a suspect. I could almost see Quinn constructing a case around this made-to-order killer I was picturing for him.

"That's how it was," I said, knowing it was too late now to stop. "I thought about Carol and I made up my mind to break off the engagement. I made it up long before I came East. I knew it was no good telling her the real reason. I knew if I told her I was afraid I'd never be a normal guy she'd stick with me no matter how long it took. I guess I made up my mind too early. If I had waited a little longer—"

I hesitated; then stumbled on, anxious to get it out. "Anyway, I'd made up my mind and I stuck to it. When I came back we went out a couple of times. She saw something was wrong and asked me and I told her I'd changed my mind. I said war changed a man and what he thought he wanted before he went away was not necessarily what he wanted after he had been on the battlefield. She didn't believe me at first but she did before I finished. She asked me if there was anyone else and I told her there was—a nurse in San Francisco. There wasn't but I convinced Carol there was and—"

I stopped suddenly, out of breath and all used up inside. I couldn't look at Carol but Dunbar was studying me and finally Corrigan said, "You musta been some actor."

I glared at him. He was a ruddy-faced man with a square rugged jaw and small deep-set eyes, and he chewed gum incessantly. I looked back at Dunbar.

"Does it say on that paper that I used to be a director?"

He glanced down. "Yes," he said. "Before the war you directed two Broadway plays, one a flop, and you worked for American Broadcasting as a producer-director on some programs.

I said, "And I can act if I have to."

"Okay, okay," Dunbar said. "Now let's get back to this trouble you had with your head. Ever suffer any from amnesia?"

The implication behind that one brought me up with a start. I couldn't tell whether it was just another question or whether he was trying to get at something else. I hoped he wasn't.

"No," I said.

"It's true though, isn't it," he said, "that amnesia is sometimes the result of the condition you describe?"

I said I didn't know, which was a lie, because I'd heard of several men in the same hospital with me having amnesia. Sometimes it was a temporary matter, sometimes it seemed almost permanent. I was sure then what he was driving at and I thought about it a moment and then scoffed mentally at the idea. I never had amnesia. I didn't have it last night. I said:

"If you've got the idea that I might have gone down to that wine cellar last night without knowing what I was doing, you're nuts."

Dunbar let his brows come up. He did a good job of looking surprised. "Why, no," he said. "I just wondered if you could corroborate some of the information that came to me this morning from the Bay City hospital.

He glanced at Quinn, who was making some notes, and then turned to Carol. "Now, Mrs. Marshall, this isn't the sort of question that you have to answer if you don't want to—at least not now." He paused and smiled and his voice was oozing persuasiveness. "But it might help us get at the bottom of this business if you would tell us how you happened to marry Mr. Marshall."

"Why—I don't understand," Carol said. "I liked him and—"

"What I mean," Dunbar said, "is it didn't take much time. You broke off with Mr. Wallace"—he glanced at me—"and then a month later you marry a man you hadn't even known before."

"But I—" Carol got that far and then stopped.

She was sitting up, her back stiff as a board. She looked at all of us this time and if I expected any expression of affection or understanding after my confession I certainly didn't get it. Her eyes snapped and there were spots of sudden color on her cheekbones. When she spoke her voice was frosty.

"I'm sorry," she said, "but that is something I do not care to talk about, Lieutenant."

I guess I was more disappointed than Dunbar; I know I was just as interested because this was the thing that had bothered me and made me bitter. I just couldn't understand a girl like Carol marrying a heel like Marshall so quickly. If it had been some guy who worked for a living or some young officer I might have rationalized things. I would still have been hurt, I guess, but I could see how a thing like that would happen with a girl who had been on an emotional rebound. But Marshall, with twenty millions and four ex-wives. . . .

Suddenly I wanted to get out. I growled at Dunbar. "And anyway," I said, "what's that got to do with what happened last night? We've told you all we know about that." I started to get up.

Corrigan said, "Sit down. He isn't finished."

I sat back, held by Dunbar's steady gaze. "Have you?" he said.

Quinn leaned forward and took it from there. "I'll tell you what it has to do with what happened, Mr. Wallace. You two are engaged." He hesitated long enough to look from Carol to me. "And for a reason that any smart lawyer would certainly question, you suddenly break it off. A month later the girl marries twenty million dollars."

"So what?" I yelled. "She liked him and she married him."

"Yes," Quinn said without raising his voice. "The point is that unless Marshall made some express provision for her in his will she is entitled to dower rights—one third of twenty million dollars."

He was all right, this Quinn. I'll bet he's a good district attorney, and I know he made me feel as though I was already sitting in the prisoner's box. I heard Carol catch her breath but she didn't say anything.

"You were married the night before last," Quinn told her, "and your husband passed out. I believe he suggested that he may have been doped."

"He was drunk," I said.

"At any rate, the marriage was not consummated that night. Last night your husband was murdered, and about that same time"—his eyes came back to me and his voice got hard and curt —"you were in Marshall's bedroom, in your pajamas, talking to his wife."

I felt like I'd been slugged. I said, weakly, "Who says so?"

Dunbar said, "The caretaker's wife—Mrs. Donelly. She saw you from her window."

Quinn sat back and spread his hands. I was still in the prisoner's box and it was all over. At least that's the way he acted. It was all over and he had won and now he was giving the jury the crusher.

"And that," he said, "is a lot of motive. It is also a lot of money for a man and a woman to split up."

How could you argue with a guy like that? It was silly. "Plenty of people had a motive," I said.

"Possibly." Quinn gestured idly, magnanimously. "I'm merely giving you an idea of the sort of spot you're in. Whether you killed Marshall or not—either of you, or working together as part of a plot—it's the sort of case I could do something with, given a few more additional facts."

He studied Carol a moment. "By the way, Mrs. Marshall, why did you run away and leave your husband in the wine cellar?"

"He—he wanted to stay and I didn't," Carol said. "He had been drinking and—"

"He got ugly?"

She regarded him coolly. "I didn't feel like arguing with him, that's all. So I left."

"There's just one more thing," Dunbar said. "Recognize this?"

That was when the room fell in on me. I don't know where it came from or how it got into Dunbar's hand—I know I didn't see him bring it out—but there it was: that blood-stained scarf with the gash near the center.

Carol's "Oh—" was a sucking sound and when I looked at her, her lashes were pinned back and her cheeks were like tallow.

"Recognize it?" Dunbar said again.

I wanted to signal her, to make her deny it. I wanted to tell her that with Marshall dead I was the only one who had seen her wear it last night. I think she would have told the truth anyway, and for the same reason she would never be a top-flight actress. She was too genuine.

"It's mine," she said. "I—I must have lost it when I left Johnny."

"Hmm," Dunbar said; then, matter-of-factly, "We've had a laboratory man make some tests. The blood on this scarf is human blood. It is also the same blood type as Mr. Marshall's. This gash here—well, it's pretty obvious how that got there."

"From—holding the glass splinter?" Carol asked faintly.

Dunbar nodded. "Whoever plunged that splinter into Mr. Marshall's throat, held it in this."

"Listen!" I said. "If you're suggesting she did it you're out of your mind. She wouldn't be fool enough to leave that scarf behind if she did, would she?"

"You forget that if the plan had worked the murder might have been accepted as an accident. It would be simpler to go back later, much simpler than to risk carrying a scarf which at the time was wet with blood."

This Dunbar had answers for everything, and there was one more I wanted. "Where did you find it?"

He glanced at Quinn. "Not far from where you were attacked, Mr. Wallace. At least not far from where Garlin says he found you. It was tucked between some casks in the row behind you—between where you were and the stairs to the office."

It didn't help to realize I had passed this spot twice—with Garlin. When we went upstairs to telephone, and when we came back. And he had been right beside me both times and I had no chance to look.

"I suppose she slugged me too," I said. "Or maybe I slugged myself."

"There could be several explanations for that." Dunbar put his hands on the desk and stood up. "When I think I have the right one, I'll tell you."

And like that, the interview was over. Corrigan had the door open and Carol and I were in the hall and Corrigan was saying, "Miss Linda Jordan, please."

Carol headed for the stairs. I couldn't catch up with her without running and I didn't want to do that with the others in the living room watching. I called to her twice. I knew she heard me

but she didn't stop. Her back looked stiff and uncompromising
and if anything she seemed to hurry even more. She started up
the stairs. I watched her a moment and then turned away.

8

LINDA JORDAN came out of the house about twenty minutes later.
She walked very slowly across the terrace, her head down, her
gaze fixed on the grass. She did not see me at first and when she
did she started to turn away. I called to her and she stopped and
then we walked along towards the dock. She'd been crying and
I asked if Dunbar and Quinn had bullied her.

She shook her head. "It isn't that," she said and then, unexpectedly, "Did you know I was leaving Johnny?"

I didn't know what she meant but I thought it would do her
good to talk. "No," I said. "But I often wondered why you stayed
as long as you did. It must have been six or seven years, wasn't
it?"

"Seven. Nearly eight."

We were at the end of the dock then and she sat down on the
bench and made a place for me. She took a cigarette and a light
and pushed the auburn hair back from her forehead.

"So did I often wonder why I stayed so long," she said. "Maybe
I was in love with him at first. I was twenty. I was a model with
ideas and I'd never had anything except what I could make for
myself and I suppose the thought of having a glamorous person
like Johnny Marshall interested in me gave me a lot of romantic
hopes. I guess I thought I might be the first Mrs. Marshall. He
already had two secretaries but he said he needed another and it
seemed like a good chance so I took it."

She made a funny deprecating sound that was half laugh, half sigh. "I got over the marriage idea when he married Mary Tracey six months later and I also began to see the other side of Johnny Marshall. He wasn't all charm and fun and graciousness. There was a mean streak in him too. Sometimes he was hateful—to me and everyone else who happened to be around at the time—and you only have to look at Spencer Haughton to know it."

"I don't have to look that far," I said.

"Spence made the mistake of marrying one of Johnny's girls. She was killed later in an automobile accident but Spence is still paying for it—or was. Look how Johnny married Carol and then tricked you into coming along on the honeymoon."

"I know."

"I guess I stayed because it was the sort of job a girl dreams about. There was money and big estates and travel and nightclubs and being with the kind of people you read about in gossip columns. It was fascinating. And there was always a fur coat or a bit of jewelry for Christmas or your birthday and if he was mean one day he might make up for it the next—if you could take it.

"Apparently I could. First one of the secretaries left and then the other and after Mary divorced him I thought it would be my chance. For awhile I was almost sure of it—until he met Beryl Jennings. That one lasted three months and then there was Nora DeWolfe, and after that Jean Nolan. I suppose I quit a dozen times but Johnny could always talk me into staying. He'd have some man with him, like Earl Garlin, to take care of people who wanted to get tough and he said he needed me for another sort of protection. I was his protection against girls who were angling for him and that's why I was with him wherever he went—except when he was actually living with one of his wives."

She looked at me, a faraway gleam in her eyes. "I guess it was Carol that made me realize how it was. For one thing she seemed different from the others. She'd been hurt by you and she wanted so much to make a go of things and I thought she was a little afraid of me because I'd been there so long. And Johnny always liked pretty things around him and I guess I realized that one day I wouldn't be pretty and then it would be too late to find any happiness for myself. So I told him. I told him if I was going to have a man of my own I'd better get started; I said it might be better for him and Carol if I left now. Well, he was sweet about it. He said all right, that he'd have a present for me and that I must promise to take this last trip."

She looked down at her hands and I saw something glisten wetly on her eyelids. What she said then told me what had brought the tears.

"They found a check in his pocket, Alan. A check for me—for twenty-five thousand dollars. It—it was my present." Her voice was thick as she finished and she rose hurriedly and turned so I could not see her face. "They've got to find out who did it," she said. "They just got to."

"Yeah," I said, and had to swallow fast to speak at all. "They've got to," I said, and then I wasn't thinking about Linda, I was thinking about Carol and me.

It was after four when Lieutenant Dunbar came out to his car with Sergeant Corrigan and Earl Garlin. I was waiting, and when Quinn didn't come out of the house I spoke to Dunbar.

"Look," I said, "you've been giving all of us the third degree. What about this Doctor Penzance? Did anyone ever tell you he might have a motive for murder?"

Dunbar looked at me, his eyes half-shut, and something about that stare made me wish I'd kept my mouth shut. "Why, yes," he said. "I was just going to question him. Suppose you come along."

I climbed into the car. That mild voice of his hadn't fooled me any. It made me sore—at myself. I was maybe his number one suspect and here I was popping off and reminding him of that fact all over again. The car had hardly started before he confirmed my reasoning.

"Find your cigarette lighter?" he asked casually.

"What cigarette lighter?" I said, before I realized what he meant.

"Sergeant Tait told me you went back to the wine cellar around three in the morning. He said you—"

"Oh," I said. "Yes . . . I—I found it. It was in another suit. I forgot to change it."

"We found this in your room." He turned and there was a flashlight in his hand, the one I'd taken from the study desk the night before. "Is this the one you got from the study?"

For a moment I just stared at him. I wanted to ask him how he knew and then I saw that it didn't matter. Bert or someone had probably identified the flashlight and in any case it was no good denying it. And then I had a funny thought. I thought it would be a lot of fun to watch Dunbar work if you could do it objectively, without being under suspicion yourself.

"Yes," I said. "And before you get any other ideas I might add that the desk looked as if someone else had searched it before I started hunting for the flashlight."

"Oh?" He chewed on that awhile. "You didn't see a briefcase?"

"Is one missing?"

"We think so. Not a briefcase exactly, one of those flat leather things with a zipper—for carrying papers."

"I didn't see it."

"Also, there was a gun. A .32 Smith & Wesson revolver."

I sat back and looked at the scenery. "I didn't see that either."

We rolled up a gently winding road through a patch of woods to a semi-clearing of a dozen or more acres and now I could see the buildings. On one side there was an impressive, new-looking structure with sloping walls, like the Egyptians used to build them, and small high windows. On the other side was a white, two-story house and scattered here and there were a dozen modernistic little houses, each with a high-walled enclosure at one corner that made me think of sun bathing. Three women in play suits were walking lazily in the sunshine as we rolled up in front of the white house and got out.

Doctor Samson Penzance met us on the porch and I was more impressed this time than I had been the night before, for he was really a formidable guy with those tremendous shoulders and that massive head. It was not difficult to imagine those intense black eyes as having hypnotic powers, but I think the most impressive thing of all was his voice. It was deep, sonorous, with an almost gentle sing-song quality that was strangely soothing as he explained about the Brotherhood of Horus.

"Your idea," Dunbar said, "is to cure people by the sun and a dash of hypnotism."

"The use of the sun and air in modern therapy is too familiar to mention." Penzance ran his fingers through his hair and smiled. "Directly or indirectly, the energy derived from the sun accomplishes most of the work done on this earth, and this was known by the Egyptians as far back as 4000 B.C."

"Um," Dunbar said. "I thought the sun God was called Re or Ra."

"In upper Egypt he was called Horus. The symbol was the hawk."

"Oh, yes," Dunbar said dryly. "You're an upper Egypt guy, huh? And this hypnotism—"

"I prefer to call it mental suggestion."

"Nothing supernatural?"

"There is no supernaturalism in my school of thought, nor do

I believe that everything occurs by Cosmic, natural law. However, I am sure that many of the mysteries of life can be understood through the proper exploration of one's nature, by one's self. My purpose is to help the honest, courageous lovers of truth to achieve a greater understanding, to help them find the power of useful knowledge that has been passed down through the ages."

"By whom?"

"By those who have learned the mastery of life."

"And you have learned this mastery?" Dunbar sounded annoyed and the Doctor's unruffled manner didn't help any.

"I try."

"And what can you do that a sun lamp and a psychiatrist can't?"

"I can pass along certain truths, certain esoteric knowledge that has been handed down by word of mouth through countless centuries."

He went on easily and at length. He said it was ridiculous to assume that all the secrets of the ancient Egyptians were put down on stone tablets and papyri rolls; he began to quote people I'd never heard of and spoke intimately of cults which existed in various dynasties. There was Merkure in 2800 B.C., the king of the IVth Dynasty and Khafre, his uncle, and something about the Pyramid of Gizeh. There were others that he quoted in that sonorous, sing-song voice and the first thing I knew I was drowsing.

I sat up with a start, remembering something I'd read somewhere. It had to do with some man who demonstrated that he could hypnotize certain people by his voice alone, and I knew right then that Doctor Penzance might do all right at that sort of thing if you gave him a chance and happened to be in the mood for it. I was glad when Dunbar broke it up.

"Very interesting," he said. "And just how did you happen to pick out this spot for your camp? You've been here about three years, I understand."

The Doctor said that was right. He said he learned of the place through a friend. "And upon further investigation," he said, "I discovered that this property was first settled by a colony, a cult if you like, of Swiss immigrants. I have reason to believe they also were seekers of the truth; may even have practiced some of the same esoteric principles that I now try to inculcate in my followers. Later there was a man named Scheiner who—"

"Nuts."

Penzance straightened in his chair and his lids came down. "I beg your pardon."

"Scheiner was nothing but a nudist and you know it. The Swiss settled here originally because they had an idea it was good grape country. General Sullivan came through here in 1779 chasing Iroquois. His soldiers saw what kind of country it was and some of them asked to settle here as a reward for military service. A few of those soldiers were of Swiss descent."

He waited to see if Penzance was going to give him an argument and when the Doctor remained silent, Dunbar continued.

"By 1820 there was a Swiss colony here. They built part of the present winery and kept to themselves and were pretty nearly self sufficient. For awhile. Those sort of things generally fold eventually and when this colony began to break up as some of the families moved to land of their own, some religious screwballs—called themselves the Cradelers, I think—set up a chapel and started raising hell with the good people of the district. The original founders got in trouble with some of the young girls who wanted to be converted and the farmers finally burned the place down and chased the ringleaders out of the country."

He said, "By 1880 a man named Johnson had bought up the wine cellars and fifty acres of vineyard, and the Johnson family owned the place until prohibition killed the wine business. That's when your friend Scheiner—"

"He was not my friend."

"—came along. Around 1930 that was, when nudism was a fad. He leased most of the acreage and put up some buildings. His addicts that used to come here didn't bother anybody and there wasn't any trouble, but it was nothing but a fad anyway and after about three years that business folded too. Right after that Mr. Marshall came along and bought out Johnson and—"

Dunbar broke off suddenly, as though realizing that he had been doing a lot of talking, and not about murder. "We'll skip the rest of it," he said. "What I'm here for is to find out what you know about the murder of Mr. Marshall."

Penzance let his brows come up. "I know nothing."

"You called at his house last night and you had an argument."

"That is true. But I came directly here. Mr. and Mrs. Talmain—the couple who look after things now that the regular season has ended—will tell you that I remained here throughout the night."

"I don't doubt it," Dunbar said. "What were you quarreling about—with Marshall?"

"A personal matter, Lieutenant."

Dunbar didn't like it. There were ridges along his jaw and his lids drooped dangerously. "You quarreled about a lease. A twenty-year lease that Marshall was going to break."

Penzance shook his head. "You are mistaken."

"Am I?" Dunbar leaned back and nodded to Earl Garlin and Garlin took it from there. He studied the Doctor a moment and his dark face was morose.

"There was a clause in that lease," he said, "that Marshall put in to protect himself. It said that if it turned out you were a phony or guilty of any illegal practices he could throw you out. And when he came up here from New York yesterday, he had what he wanted. He had a detailed report that—"

"Where is that report?"

Garlin stopped. He looked at Dunbar.

"We will produce it at the proper time," Dunbar said, and suddenly I was thinking about the briefcase that was missing and wondering if it could have contained the report they were now discussing.

"May I ask who collected this so-called evidence against me?" Penzance asked.

"Several people," Garlin said. "Marshall had been working on it for months."

Penzance stretched out his arms, bent them and passed both palms over his wavy black hair. "I shall be glad to see it," he said. "Was there anything else, Lieutenant?"

Dunbar colored faintly but his voice was still controlled. "Yes. Marshall's sister was a client of yours, wasn't she?"

I just looked at Dunbar and then at Penzance. It was going a little fast for me now and I felt my respect for Dunbar mounting.

"At one time, yes. You mean Helen Bradford? Yes, I was able to help her, I think. She'd had an unfortunate love affair many years ago. I believe her brother broke it up in some way, and then in 1941 she married Mr. Bradford. He held a commission in the Naval Reserve, and was killed aboard a destroyer somewhere in the North Atlantic early in the war. She came to me in a highly nervous condition and I'm glad to say that—"

"All right, all right." Dunbar's neck was red, his gaze frosty. "Did she give you thirty thousand dollars to build that funny-looking chapel out there or not?"

"Yes."

Dunbar nodded and digressed abruptly. "Did you see Mr. Wallace after you left the Marshall house last night?"

He nodded at me and right then I knew why he'd brought me along, why that look he gave me back at the house had made me wish I'd kept my mouth shut. Dunbar was going to play me

THE GROOM LAY DEAD

against the Doc and see what happened. He'd known that when he told me to climb into the car.

He spent about ten minutes on us, always going back to the wine cellar and my story of how I had been slugged, trying to get either the Doc or me to make a slip or contradict our previous stories. I was sweating when Dunbar finally gave up, and I was awfully glad I wasn't the guilty one; it was tough enough for a guy in my condition to stick to the approximate truth. As for Penzance he simply continued to insist that he had come straight home.

"Okay," Dunbar said. "I'll talk to your Mr. and Mrs. Talmain."

The doctor rose and left the room. As soon as the door closed Corrigan said, "He could've done it, all right. Without battin' an eye."

"Certainly he could have done it," Dunbar said.

Garlin was inspecting his fingernails. "He gave you the run-around on that report."

"If Marshall gave him a copy," Dunbar said. "We don't know that he did."

"All I know is, he said he was going to," Garlin said, "and Johnny usually did what he said he'd do. I don't know what was in the report and I never saw it—I haven't been doing any private operating since I went to work for him—but Johnny brought two copies up here with him and he said he was going to give one to Penzance, just to show him where he stood."

"Was the other copy in that briefcase you said was missing?" I asked.

They looked at me and at each other. Dunbar rubbed his chin and stared out the window. You'd have thought I had been eavesdropping the way they ignored me, and I sat there unanswered and grousing inwardly until Penzance came back.

They were a strange looking pair, this Mr. and Mrs. Talmain.

He was a squat, swart fellow with a round head, nearly bald, and heavy jowls that were blue-black with beard. She was an inch or two taller than her husband, with a clear olive skin and straight black hair. Her cheekbones were prominent, her mouth full and ripe and red. She wore a cotton peasant dress with a round neckline and a full skirt, and while it was difficult to speculate accurately on her figure I had an idea it was full and ripe, like her mouth.

Dunbar asked them when Penzance had come in the night before. They stood side by side before the desk and though the man hesitated, the woman did not.

"It was about eleven-thirty."

"Did he go out again?"

"No."

"How do you know?"

I liked her voice. It was throaty, vibrant, low-pitched. I thought there was a trace of a smile in her eyes, and she had nice hands.

"I should have said he did not go out between then and two o'clock. I was reading until then. I would have heard him."

"Oh, yes," Dunbar said. He exhaled noisily and gave Corrigan a disgusted glance. "I see . . . and are you the only help the Doctor has?"

Mrs. Talmain said no. She said there was a woman in the kitchen to cook. A woman who lived down the road. Her husband and brother helped take care of the grounds and the vegetable garden. "The guests are required to take care of their own little houses. They take their meals here."

She talked perhaps five minutes, easily and with complete confidence, and not once in that time did Talmain open his mouth. He stood with his hands at his side and a truculent, sullen expression on his face until Dunbar questioned him directly.

This time it was vital statistics—where the man came from,

how long he had worked for Penzance, what he did in the winter. He had, it seemed, come from Seattle; he had worked for Penzance for five years and in the winter he and his wife continued to work for Penzance—in his home in Westchester.

Dunbar wrote some things in his notebook and stood up. He said he would probably be back. He suggested that they stay on the grounds so that they would be handy in case he needed them again.

9

WHEN we got back to the house and Dunbar and Corrigan had shoved off for wherever it was they were going, Garlin went upstairs and I made a beeline for the dining room cellaret. There was plenty of ice and I fixed a long one and strolled into the living room.

There wasn't anyone about so I went to the windows overlooking the terrace and found Spence Haughton sitting down on the lawn with Helen Bradford, or rather she was sitting and he was standing talking to her.

I don't know why I watched them so long but I was glad I did, for presently I got the feeling that something about Haughton had changed. The way he gestured as he spoke suggested some new vigor and it seemed to me that his shoulders were straighter, more erect. He no longer had that beaten, hopeless look, and wondering about it I thought of something else and a quick excitement boiled inside me.

I took a couple of fast swallows from the drink, put down the glass and started for the stairs. I didn't meet anyone there or in the upper hall so I went quickly to Haughton's room and opened the door. I didn't know what I expected to find but I remembered vividly now the darkness of Johnny Marshall's room the night before and the shadowy figure that fled through the window when I entered. For an instant there had been an odd gleam of light around that figure's eyes, and now that I had a chance to think about it there was an explanation: the man had worn glasses. The only ones with glasses were Haughton and Helen's lawyer fellow, Eddington. But Eddington hadn't been here last night. That left Haughton, and my idea was that if he had found what he wanted, it might be here now.

I closed the door and glanced about. There was a closet door, slightly open, a Gladstone bag on a luggage rack, a maple chest with the top drawer partly out. When I started for the bag I glanced at the mirror atop the chest; that's how I happened to see the closet door move.

The reflection stopped me cold. I turned, took a step towards the door and got my feet where I wanted them, feeling the tension in my back and liking the effect it gave me.

"Okay," I said. "Come out."

For a second or two nothing happened; then the door moved an inch or more. Finally it opened wide and Earl Garlin stepped out. It was the only time I ever saw him look sheepish. He grinned crookedly and wiped the moisture from his forehead and brushed his mustache back with his handkerchief.

"That's once I got caught," he said.

"Did you get what you wanted?"

"I didn't get a chance. I just got here."

"I guess this wasn't the first stop," I said. "How was my room. Find anything?"

"Nothing that interested me. And anyway the police have already cased your things."

"But not Haughton's?"

"I don't think so," he said, and for a moment the sheepish grin remained. Then it slid away and he was the Garlin I knew again. He didn't waste any time or bother to ask me why I was there. "Let's get going," he said, "before we both get caught."

He was already at the chest. He went swiftly through the drawers, closed them, opened the Gladstone. Looking over his shoulder I saw there was a soiled shirt here, some handkerchiefs, matchfolders, miniature pieces of soap that Haughton had picked up in various hotels. Garlin pawed over these until he came to a pair of used sox that had been rolled together. When he lifted them a small, cylindrical bottle fell out.

He picked it up, frowning as he turned it in his fingers. I figured the bottle held about an ounce and I watched as Garlin gingerly removed the cork and sniffed. Then something happened to his blocky face and he looked at me, his eyes hard bright slits.

"Smell," he said. "Easy."

I sniffed tentatively and caught an odor of bitter almonds. Something cold ran swiftly up my back and I stared silently, held by the narrowed intensity of his gaze.

"Oil of bitter almonds," he said. "A solution of hydrocyanic acid."

I guess we stood there ten seconds without saying a word. Finally I asked what he intended to do.

"I don't know," he said. "But for now, let's leave it and get out of here until I can figure something."

I started to ask him if we shouldn't tell Dunbar and then I let it go. This sort of thing was more in Garlin's line than mine and if he wanted to wait it didn't make any difference to me.

In the hall, he started for his room and I grabbed him. "Look," I said, "you've got to help me. Dunbar thinks Carol killed Johnny, doesn't he?"

Garlin bunched his lips and smoothed down his mustach again.

"He's got a case, all right. Plenty of people have been hung for less than he's got right now."

"She didn't do it," I said. "Everyone here probably had some motive for wanting to see Johnny dead and—"

"You did, for one. And that medical discharge you got from the Marines doesn't help any. You were under treatment for months because you couldn't control your nerves or your temper. Some guys like you have had amnesia. For all Dunbar knows maybe you drew a blank for a few minutes."

"I'm all right now."

"Maybe. And maybe Dunbar isn't so sure. Anyway he knows your motive is pretty sweet." He shrugged. "Plenty of times a man and a woman have cooked up propositions like this one could be."

I admitted it. I walked along to his room, talking all the time. I told him I wasn't afraid of what Dunbar could prove against me but that I was afraid he would concentrate on Carol instead of looking for someone else. I said I couldn't just sit by and wait. I didn't know anything about detective work, but he did and he had to help find who killed Johnny Marshall.

We were in his room then and he shut the door. For a moment he looked at me with those narrowed eyes and his dark face was grim.

"Don't think I'm not," he said. "But you don't want me to help you. Look." He touched me on the chest with his index finger. "Johnny getting knocked off has done two things to me, both bad. One—I'm out of the best job I ever had; two—I'm going to be known as the guy that let Johnny Marshall get killed right under my nose. I was supposed to be a bodyguard. I still have a private dick's license but I might as well tear it up unless I can get the bastard that killed him."

"Okay," I said. "That's what I—"

"No, it ain't," Garlin said. "You don't think Carol killed him and you say you didn't. If you run across something that makes it tougher for her, you're going to cover up. If I find anything I'm going to crack it wide open and if it happens to hit you or Carol that's just too bad. Maybe Dunbar'll do it alone—he's a pretty smart cop—but I'll do what I can."

By that time I was a very sober guy. The way he talked you believed him and I thought it over before I said anything. I knew I wouldn't want Garlin running me down. I had an idea he'd be a cold, ruthless individual if anyone got in his way. But I hadn't done the killing and I was sure Carol hadn't so I decided there really wasn't any alternative.

"I still want to work with you," I said.

"Okay." He spread his hands. "You know how it is. What do you want to do? Come on, what's needling you?"

"I want to take a look at that chapel Penzance has."

He puckered his eyes at me. "Why?"

"How do I know?" I said irritably. "It's something to do, isn't it? And the more I know about that character the better I'm going to like it."

He thought it over. "Maybe you've got something," he said. "Let's go."

One side of the Doctor's sand-colored chapel was close to the edge of the woods and easy to reach without being seen from the main house. We came directly up the hill—it wasn't more than a five-minute walk if you cut through the woods—but when we got there the small square windows along the side were too high for us. Luckily Garlin found a couple of old packing cases around at the back and by piling one on the other, he was able to climb up and look inside.

I don't know what he did up there but he got something from

his pocket and I heard a sharp, snapping sound and then the window was open. He went through, hung by his elbows with his legs and hips inside, and motioned to me. I climbed up after him, squeezing through the opening and lowering myself until I hung by my hands in complete and utter darkness.

"Okay, drop," Garlin said. "It's only a couple of feet."

I let go and my feet hit a thick rug and then Garlin snapped on a pencil flash. We stood between the wall and a velvet curtain and when we ducked under it we were in a moderate-sized room completely draped from floor to ceiling in dark blue velvet. Near the center was a table, with a chair on each side, and a metal pedestal in the middle with what looked like a glass and metal doughnut on top.

Garlin went to the desk and ran his fingers along the under side. I heard a switch click but nothing happened and then there was a second click and the glass and metal doughnut became a circular light, with a two-inch black hole in the center.

"Tricky, huh?" Garlin said. "This must be the inner sanctum. I wonder how we get out of here."

He started one way and I started the other and we each found a slit in the drapes with a door beyond, one leading towards the front of the building, the other opposite the window we entered. We went through the front one into another room, draped like the first but much larger, and containing a pulpit-like desk and a thick rug, room size.

Garlin went to the main entrance with his flashlight, found a switch on the wall and when he snapped it a pale blue glow filled the room. This time I was the one who explored the pulpit. I found an electric switch here and pressed it and instantly the whole room was a blaze of light.

I tried to find out where all this brilliance came from but it hurt my eyes. I could hardly see Garlin and as we stood there I became aware of a faint warmth on my skin that had not been there before.

"What kind of light is this?" Garlin said.

"Sun lamps," I said, guessing aloud.

He didn't answer until we had stood there awhile, feeling the warmth of that fierce light growing on our faces. "Damned if they're not," he said finally. "Must be eight or ten of them up there in the ceiling. Boy, if this isn't something. When the sun doesn't shine he brings the suckers in here and gives 'em the business . . . Turn 'em off."

I did. He snapped off the blue light and we went back to the first room. For some reason that doughnut-shaped light on the table intrigued me and I asked Garlin for his flash, poked it into the hole of blackness in the center and snapped it on. What I saw was a metal grill, and something about the construction of this was so familiar that I began at once to explore the under side of the table. When I saw the metal pipe with the wire running through it and into the rug, I guess I got excited.

"Hey," Garlin said, when he saw me crawling across the rug. "Are you nuts?"

"I don't know," I said. "I want to find out where these wires go."

"What wires? For that light?"

I'd reached the wall by then, and by feeling under the drapes I found the hole I wanted. It was about two feet from the second door and I straightened up and opened it, poking the flashlight ahead of me.

At first this cubicle seemed empty but then, on the left, I found what looked like a large, built-in cabinet with sliding doors. I slid them back and what I found didn't surprise me because by then I expected it, just as I'd known that the doughnut-shaped light concealed a microphone of some kind.

"What is it?" Garlin asked. "A new kind of juke box?"

"A recording machine," I said. "The kind that makes sixteen inch records."

Garlin blew out his breath and in the half-light his swart face was moist and wrinkled. "A recording machine," he said in slow amazement. "Brother, what a set-up for a blackmail racket. He gets the sheep in here for a confidential talk—"

"And does what hypnotizing he can," I said.

"And it all comes out on a record." Garlin sighed and there was admiration in the sound. "What a set-up. Imagine the price the guy must get for some of those records."

I'd been looking for a play-back machine without finding any. I couldn't find any records that had been cut either, though I did find a few blanks. "Maybe he made some of Helen Bradford," I said.

"Maybe." Garlin said it slowly and then, abruptly, his voice was clipped and businesslike. "Close it up and let's get out of here."

We closed the cabinet and went back to our window. It was pretty high and Garlin said he'd boost me up. We were some acrobats. He boosted me and I went up, tipped off balance and grabbed at the velvet to save myself. I tore a piece of it down from the ceiling so that the window was partly exposed, and ended up on top of Garlin.

"Nuts to that," he said, getting up off the floor. "We'll go out the front way. It's almost dark anyway."

It was a good idea, but we didn't make it. For we were about halfway across the main room, moving in the dark with only Garlin's pencil flash boring ahead, when we heard someone at the door.

The sound of the key, the sure knowledge that we would be trapped, stopped me cold, and when Garlin's light went out the panic hit me. I was rigid all over. I might have been there yet if Garlin's curt urgent whisper hadn't ordered me into action.

"Duck! Behind the curtains!"

I wheeled and leaped towards the wall. I didn't know where Garlin was but I found the velvet drapes under my hand and pawed along until I came to an overlapping section and found an opening. I slid along the wall and pulled the curtain in front of me just as I heard the click of the opening door; then I flattened out and held my breath.

The door closed loudly and the bluish light I had seen before came on in the room and fingered the edges of the opening on my left. There wasn't a sound but the thumping of my pulse, and I waited, not knowing where Garlin was nor what had happened to our visitor. I stood it as long as I could, until I could no longer bear the tension winding up inside me; then I put my face to the edge of the curtain and pulled it aside a quarter of an inch.

Doctor Penzance stood in the doorway of the room at the rear, his massive shoulders almost touching the casings. The thickness of the rug had silenced his steps and now there was some light beyond him and he was facing away, his great head cocked, his body poised like a wrestler's. He moved like a wrestler too in that next second, abruptly, swiftly, gracefully. One instant he was there and the next he was gone, and I had dropped the curtain and started moving to my right, towards the corner, my back pressed to the wall.

I knew he'd seen something wrong. I wondered if it was the piece of velvet I'd pulled from the window, but I didn't much care. All I wanted to do was get out. I admit it, the guy scared me. He looked capable of murder, even in broad daylight, and what I wanted now was room in which to run. His voice struck at me just as I reached the corner.

"Come out!"

The hair stiffened on the back of my neck.

"I have a gun in my hand," he said.

I grew small against the wall and the perspiration was leaking down my back. I wondered if he was bluffing. I wondered about Garlin, knowing I was only about eight feet from the door, knowing also that a bullet would stop me before I could reach it.

"I'm going to count three," Penzance said, and now he had moved; now he was down at my end, quite close to the door.

Okay, I told myself, *step out while you can*. And then I thought, *Maybe he'll shoot anyway. He has a right to.*

"One," Penzance said.

And then another voice, sharp and unrecognizable, said, "Stand still! This thing in your back is a gun."

I stayed scared another couple seconds, scared and bewildered. I knew it must be Garlin, that the voice was unrecognizable because he had made it so deliberately; the rest of it was understandable when you realized what had happened, when you knew what sort of opportunist Garlin was.

Penzance had seen the curtain bulge as I moved. He had moved to the door to block me off, and since he faced me, his back was to Garlin and Garlin simply stepped out and stuck a gun against the Doc's spine.

"Who are you? What are you doing here?" the Doc said.

"Drop it!" Garlin said. "And don't turn around. Now kick it under the curtain." I heard the soft thud and the kick and then Garlin said, "Now walk to the door, go inside and close it. If you turn round you get it."

I was still moving behind the curtain and when I came out by the main entrance Penzance had passed the pulpit-like desk. He continued to the open doorway of the room at the rear and I reached for the doorknob behind Garlin while he reached for the light switch.

Penzance did as he was told. When he stepped into the other room, Garlin switched out the lights and I opened the door. We went out and slammed it behind us. We didn't wait to put away the crates under the window.

10

By the time I had cleaned up and come downstairs everyone was sitting around the living room with a drink in his hand—everyone but Carol. I went over to make an old-fashioned and Helen and Linda were standing at the end of the table talking, and I asked where she was.

"She's been in her room most of the afternoon," they said.

And then I got an idea. I knew it must be tough staying up there alone in Marshall's suite with things as they were and I asked Linda if she had twin beds in her room.

"Yes," she said. "Why?"

"I thought I might move in with you," I said, and grinned. She grinned back and I said, "No, I thought maybe it would be a good idea if Carol could move in with you."

I said maybe it would be a good thing for her if she could get out of her present room. Both women agreed.

"But there are plenty of rooms," Helen said.

"I know," I said. "But it might be better if she had company, someone to talk to at night."

"I think you're right, Alan," Linda said. "I'll ask her. Helen and I can talk her into it some way."

I tasted my drink and glanced at my watch. It was seven thirty. "Isn't she coming down for dinner?" I asked.

They said no. Carol complained of a slight headache. She was going to have something sent up later.

When I heard that the drink didn't taste so good any more, I had counted on seeing her. I hadn't even spoken to her since we had the session with Dunbar and now I wanted to very much. I put the glass down and went upstairs.

"Yes," Carol said when I knocked.

"It's Alan," I said, and waited, and presently the door opened and Carol stood there looking at me.

She wore a sort of hostess gown made of some crepe material, nice and thin, with a wide belt that moulded beautifully her young figure. Her blond hair waved softly over her ears and her skin was fresh and clear; so were her eyes, dark hazel under the darker brows. I looked for a smile in them and couldn't find any. They watched me steadily, almost defiantly. And it embarrassed me because I'd half expected to go in and now she was standing there as though waiting for me to deliver my message and go away.

"I came up to talk you into coming down to dinner," I said. She started to shake her head and I said, "All you have to do is take off that blue thing and put on a dress."

"I don't think so, Alan."

"But you shouldn't stay up here by yourself," I argued. "It isn't good for you. What you need is a drink." I gave her the best grin I could. "A couple of fast ones and you'll feel better."

"Really, Alan," she said woodenly. "I can't think of anything I need less."

This wasn't the Carol I knew, not at all the Carol I knew. It wasn't just a headache that made her like this, but I didn't know what else it could be so I struggled along in an effort to sell her my idea and cheer her up a bit.

"If you're worrying about Dunbar, don't. He hasn't got a thing but that scarf and that doesn't prove much. And listen, darling, I meant what I said this morning in the study." I paused feeling the warmth in my face, the growing thickness in my throat. "About us. There wasn't anyone else, there never was anyone and—"

I reached for her hand. She snatched it back, and I saw that her face was set, her eyes dark.

"I'm sure it's very flattering, Alan," she said with furious politeness. "It's nice to know, finally, that one hasn't the mind and character of a child."

I stared at her. I felt as though I'd been slapped back on my heels—without knowing why.

"That's what you thought, wasn't it?" she said. "It must have been to do what you did a month ago. I suppose I wasn't mature enough to be told the truth."

"But listen—"

"Of all the idiotic, stupid things. . . ."

"But I told you why."

Her eyes were blazing and her mouth was white and stiff. For another second I just looked at her, feeling the taut hard pressure of my nerves, the old shaking start in the back of my legs.

"We wouldn't be here now," she said; "none of this would have happened if only you had told me. If two people trust each other—"

"Wait a minute!"

I heard myself yell and I couldn't help it. I'd had a pretty good day until now. I'd blustered some at Dunbar and I'd been scared when Penzance caught us in the chapel and now the thing was back that had bothered me for so long. Maybe I would have been angry anyway. I had assumed that after what I had told Dunbar that morning, with Carol listening, I'd find some tenderness and understanding when I saw her. Instead the lash of her anger set off my own and we were glaring at each other.

"So it's my fault we're here," I said. "You married the guy, didn't you? You didn't have to, did you? At least what I did I did because I thought it was best for you."

She started to interrupt and I wouldn't let her. "A lot you must of cared. It took you not quite a month to go out and grab yourself a rich guy, a guy you hardly knew."

I saw her lips tremble and her face begin to break up. Her eyes, stricken now, started to fill and then she jumped back and slammed the door. And because the anger I felt was blind and unreasoning I did not think about what had happened to her face. I wanted to break the door down. A month, two months, ago I'm sure I would have. I'd have hammered and kicked until reaction hit me and then I'd have stood there weak and shaken and ashamed.

I caught myself in time. I was shaking all over and it was hard to breathe, but I turned and began to walk along the hall. I walked up and down twice until my hands stopped trembling; then I went downstairs and had the two quick ones I'd recommended for Carol.

It was just ten o'clock when I stood on the porch of Doctor Penzance's white house and looked through the screen door at the three women and a man who were playing bridge in front of the living room fireplace.

I had done a lot of walking since dinner and I'd had time to do some thinking. I was ashamed of what I'd done to Carol. Not of what I had said because, thinking of her own reaction, the way she felt, it seemed to me now that the things I'd thought and said were true. That she could have married Johnny Marshall within a month of the time we'd parted was what had made me bitter. I had hoped she might give Dunbar some explanation that morning, as I had done. But there had been none and the facts were there and that's how it was. But the way I'd yelled, the fury of my anger, were something else. I didn't like to think about it and so I recalled some of the things the doctors had told me.

Last night there hadn't been much sleep for me. Tonight had to be different. Sleep was important, the doctors said. It was nothing to worry about, providing you were tired physically and had had enough exercise during the day. But if you were tired and then could not sleep—well, that was something else again. So I was going to be tired tonight. I walked about a mile up the road and back again and when I finished thinking about Carol I got to wondering about Penzance.

Whether Carol had ever really loved me or not, I knew she hadn't killed Johnny Marshall. Neither had I, though such simple statements were not going to convince Dunbar or the district attorney. So eventually my thoughts came back to Penzance and his recording machine; and then I knew something was missing. There had to be a machine for playing the records Penzance made, and somewhere there had to be the records themselves. It was this that brought me up the hill to the house.

I had no idea of what I could do until I stood there on the porch and then I realized that at one end of this there was a window which gave on the library. The front door led directly into this big living room and the library was on the left. Two of the library windows overlooked the front lawn and this other one faced the porch, and I could see as I stood there that this window had been raised about six inches.

I watched the foursome in front of the fireplace. Two of the women were youngish—around thirty, I thought, one with a flat boyish figure and the other a busty type—and the third was perhaps ten years older. The man was small and wiry, with thin sandy hair and an angular face that looked bored and unhappy. When I saw there was no one else about, I tiptoed to the window, raised it another foot and slipped over the sill.

There was enough reflected light from the porch and the moon to see where I was going and I moved first to the door to the living room. Quietly I opened this far enough to reach the button which controlled the spring lock, fixed it, and just as quietly closed the door, confident now that no one could surprise me from that direction. I thought about pulling down the shades and this seemed like a gamble either way so I left them up and snapped on the desk lamp, which had a reflector that put most of the room in shadow.

There was a closet in one corner and I looked here first. When I found no recording machine I examined the bookcases along one wall, finding them built on either side of the two windows and much thicker along the bottom two shelves than at the top. This made a wide seat at each of the windows, with a recess under each and a grill of the type used for reflector radiators. On a hunch I tried to lift one of these seats and it came up easily from a hinge on the back and there was my record-player.

It was a self-contained unit with a turntable big enough to take those sixteen inch, fifteen-minute records, and there was a cabinet underneath. I was reaching for this when I heard someone turn the knob of the library door.

I jumped about a foot and my heart began to thump. I lowered the window seat and looked at the open window and was afraid I couldn't make it. By that time I could hear the key being fitted into the lock and the only place left—unless I wanted to argue it out with Penzance—was the closet. I headed for it, turning out the desk lamp as I passed, and then I was inside with the door open a one-inch crack.

The room light went on as the door opened. I heard someone come in and the door closed and then Penzance, apparently continuing a conversation that this entrance had interrupted, said:

"I tell you I don't know who it was. One of them could have been that hoodlum Marshall had for a bodyguard, but there was someone with him."

"But what could anyone want in the chapel, Sam?" It was a nice voice, throaty, low, intimate. Mrs. Talmain's voice.

"I don't know."

"Then stop worrying. The police can't prove anything and with him out of the way you haven't a thing to be afraid of."

"There's still a copy of that report—unless he lied to me. He said there was another. There must be one someplace."

I heard a desk drawer open, the rustle of papers. After it had closed Penzance and the woman moved into my range of vision. She still wore the peasant dress and her straight hair, pulled back to a small bun at the nape of her neck, was shiny black in the lamp light. As I watched she slid her arm through his, turned him and then kissed him lightly on the cheek.

"At least," she said, "the police do not have it. Otherwise you would have heard about it."

Then, before they passed on, she smiled. It did a lot of nice things for her face and it made me wonder what sort of status Mr. Talmain had in this place.

I went back to the window as soon as the door clicked behind them. I didn't bother with a light this time, but raised the seat, fumbled with the cabinet door and found what felt like forty or fifty records there. I pulled one out at random, closed the cabinet and window seat and went over to the window.

The bridge game had broken up and the quartet was just coming out on the porch, the women babbling and replaying the last hand, the little guy standing disinterestedly on the top step and staring down across the quadrangle. It took them about five minutes to disperse and by that time the lights in the main room

went out and I heard someone shut the door. I waited a couple of
minutes longer, then climbed out on the porch and started down
the slope with the record under my arm.

11

THE moon kept ducking in and out of clouds and I couldn't
always see where I was going so I had to take it slow until I found
the road that wound down the hill. I reached the main highway
without trouble and saw the lights of the house ahead and only
then did I begin to wonder what I was going to do with the record
now that I had it.

Obviously it was no good unless I could find a way to play
it, but there was no machine in Marshall's place with a big enough
turntable. I wasn't sure what I was going to prove even if I could
hear what was on the record, but having made off with it I was
determined to see what I had if I had to go all the way to Elmira.
Meanwhile what was I going to do with it?

I stopped on the road and searched my head for possibilities.
I could hear, faintly, the whisper of the stream that tumbled down
from the hills and passed under the highway behind me but there
was no sound from the house, none from the bullfrogs I'd heard
the night before. I glanced at my watch and it said eleven o'clock.
That meant there would be people in the house and people meant
explanations unless I could hide the record. Then I thought of
the boathouse and the sail-loft.

The sound of an approaching car moved me off the road and
I drew back in the hedge until it passed. When it was quiet again
I slid along the hedge until I came to the front gate. Circling the
house, I moved cautiously along the edge of the terrace by the
tennis court, trying to avoid the light from the windows which

spilled flatly across the lawn, and I had nearly made it when I saw someone move in the shadows of the lilac bushes near the French doors.

Something light showed against the darker background and I knew it was a woman. I stood quite still, hoping she would pass by, and then some reflection touched her face and I saw it was Linda.

"Is that you, Alan?"

I waited, still motionless, until I was sure she was coming my way; then I said, yes, it was me. I moved into what looked like a darker spot and waited until she came close.

"We wondered where you were."

"I took a walk," I said. "Down the road and back."

"Oh." Her eyes were in shadow but I could tell they were peering at me. "What's that?"

"What's what?"

"That—thing you have under your arm."

"Oh, that? Hah, that's a record."

"Did you—did you get that down the road, Alan?"

So I had to tell her. Better her than some of the others in the house and I made it clear that she was to keep it under her hat. I didn't tell her the whole thing. I made it as brief as I could. I said I got to wondering about Penzance and took a chance and searched his library. "I think he makes records of some of the things his flock tells him," I said.

"You mean he blackmails them? But how could he make records without their knowing it?"

"Maybe he hypnotizes them," I said. "I don't know. I don't even know he makes records; that's why I brought this one along. Only I'm not going to say anything to anyone else until I find out for sure. I was going to hide it in the boathouse for now."

She tucked her hand inside my arm and we went along the path to the dock. The moon was still battling the clouds but we could see pretty well and neither of us said anything until we reached the boathouse.

The front of this—by that I mean the part that faced the dock proper, the part where the doorway was—was in shadow and I gave her the record to hold while I struck a match. I had an idea the place wouldn't be locked, and it wasn't. The hasp was thrown back and a wooden stake had been thrust into the staple.

"There's a wide platform in the center," I said when we were inside. "Stay on that and you'll be okay."

"All right," she said. "But what are you going to do with it?"

"I'm going to put it up here." I reached up and felt the planking of the loft and put the record on top of some sails that rested there.

"Bert was working here today," Linda said. "Suppose he looks up there."

"That'll be too bad."

"What I mean was, he was shellac-ing the sailboat. If he's finished he'll probably not go back to it again right away and you could maybe hide it in the cabin."

"It'll be all right."

"Strike a match anyway and let's see if there isn't a better place."

"Okay—"

I never really finished that word. I heard the sudden, scraping sound come from the sailboat and turned to meet it. Beside me Linda made a hushed and frightened sound and then a voice I had never heard said:

"Don't strike that match!"

I didn't. I couldn't. I was stiff all over and Linda had hold of my arm and then light exploded in our faces and we were staring into the blinding cone of a flashlight.

"Move down to the end of the platform." The voice was muffled, barely distinct. "Keep facing me."

We began to back up and the flashlight began to move too. I shut my eyes against it and opened them again, hoping I could penetrate beyond the light. It was no good. The man held the flash out in front of him and moderately high so that I never did see anything but that light.

I watched it move out of the sloop to the platform and then begin to retreat. I took a step forward, figuring he might be bluffing.

"Stay where you are!" the voice said. "Another step and I'll shoot."

"With what?" I was flutter-nerved and tense but my voice sounded okay. "How do we know you've got a gun?"

He had it all right. He pushed the muzzle forward just enough to touch the rim of light. So we stood there, Linda hanging to my arm, though I don't know if she was clinging to it or holding me up, until the door closed. I didn't try to rush it; I waited until the hasp-slapped shut and the stake was jammed into the staple. Right after that I thought I heard something that sounded like a splash, followed by running footsteps on the planking. Then the silence closed down on us.

"O-h—" said Linda as she let her breath out. "He scared me."

"Scared you?" I growled. "What about me?"

"He was in the sailboat . . . Why? . . . Who was it, Alan?"

"How do I know?" I said. "It was a man. It could have been anyone."

"Spence Haughton? It didn't sound like him."

"Because he didn't want it to sound like anybody. Yes, it could have been him, or that guy Eddington, or Garlin—"

"Penzance?"

I had to think about that and before I finished she told me to look and see if the record was still there. It was. I said, "It could have been, I guess."

"Let's look in the boat," she said. "Strike a match."

"Let's get out of here."

"No, please, Alan."

I struck a match. I struck three of them but we didn't find anything in the cabin or cockpit of the sloop. I struck another to look about the boathouse. I went over to the door and banged my weight against it and knew it wouldn't do any good.

"Can you swim?" I said. "That's the only way we're going to get out of here."

"But Alan—" she began.

"Slip in here, swim through the piles and out to that ladder at the front of the dock."

"But we don't both have to go. You can swim. Then you can take that stick out and open the door for me."

I sat down on one of the dinghies and lit a cigarette. I didn't feel chivalrous. I felt low and frustrated and sore at everything, including myself.

"Nuts," I said. "I'll toss you for it."

"No," she protested, sounding incredulous and forlorn. "Oh, no, Alan. It'll be cold. It'll be freezing."

"Sure it'll be freezing."

"But you're a man."

"You've got less clothes on," I said. "It's a lot simpler for you. All you've got to do is take off your dress and pants."

"And brassiere."

"You don't need a brassiere," I said.

"But"—she giggled—"I'm wearing one." She came up to me and took my hand. "Oh, please, Alan."

"Ahh—"

I knew damn well I'd have to do the swimming but I had to work up to it; I had to argue, and maybe in the back of my head I even thought I might talk her into something.

"Okay, sissy," I said, and got out of my clothes.

I thought I'd lost both feet right up to the knees when I hit that water. I couldn't feel a thing below that and the hole above my knee began to ache before I could even start to swim. I don't know what happened to my breath but I couldn't find it until I'd pushed between the pilings.

It took me about two seconds to make the thirty feet to the ladder. I went up there like a monkey on a stick and was almost to the top when something above me caught the corner of my eye. It was black and didn't belong on the dock and I thought maybe it was some cloud shadow. I climbed another rung and looked up and then I nearly fell off the ladder; for there, squatting in front of me, was a man. He had a gun in his hand and the muzzle of it was about six inches from my nose.

I was looking up and this guy was looking down and for a moment I couldn't see his face. I don't know what I thought, or if I thought at all. Maybe I was too cold and scared to be anything but furious.

"Take that damn thing out of my face and get out of my way," I said.

The man moved. He started to straighten and that gave me a better perspective and I saw it was Earl Garlin. He started to put the gun away and I saw he had a flashlight in his other hand.

"What the hell do you think you're doing?" I fumed.

He snapped on his light and looked at me but he didn't say anything so I went over to the boathouse, still fuming, still freezing and wanting my clothes badly.

"What gives?" he said. "I saw lights in the boathouse and when I got down here I heard someone swimming. I couldn't figure it but I was taking no chances."

"I'll say you weren't. I guess you didn't meet a guy on the path. A guy with a gun in his hand."

My fingers were so cold I had to fumble to get the stick out of the hasp and open the door. Then, for the first time I remembered Linda—and Garlin's flashlight.

"Hey," I yelped. "Turn that out, will you?"

From out of the darkness inside came Linda's giggle.

"The laughs can wait," I said. "Come on, will you? I'm cold."

I stepped behind the door and Linda came out. "Earl," I heard her say, when I ducked into the boathouse. "I wondered who was out here. If you'd only come sooner, Alan wouldn't have had to swim."

I found my clothes and knew it was going to be no fun getting dressed. I figured the sooner I got a drink and into bed the better off I'd be so I dried as best I could with my underwear and struggled into my trousers.

Garlin came in. His voice was cold, remote.

"What was that about a guy with a gun in his hand?"

I told him.

"Who was it?"

I said I didn't know, nor did I know what he was doing in the sloop. Garlin inspected it with his flashlight while I put on my coat and buttoned it. I rolled my underwear in my shirt, pocketed the tie, tucked the socks in the shoes and stuck them under my arm with the other bundle.

"What were you two doing in there anyway?" he asked when we joined Linda.

"Maybe we went in there to neck," I said.

"Umm," Garlin said. "Funny place for it."

"I'll tell you something else that's funny," I said. "Last night I get slugged; tonight a guy waves a gun at me and locks me up. Both times when I come out of it I find you. What would you call that, coincidence?"

"Anyway, Alan," Linda said, and there was still a smile in

her voice, "you were sweet to swim."

"Oh, sure."

I was ahead of them on the path now, and walking fast. Before I outdistanced them I could hear Garlin starting in on Linda. Was she sure she didn't know who it was? Couldn't she tell anything by his voice?

As for me I still wasn't convinced of Garlin's apparent innocence. It could have been him for all Linda and I knew. It could very easily have been him. . . .

It was a good time to run into Carol and I guess I made quite an entrance. Eddington was there in the living room, looking plump and comfortable and well-fed and so was Helen and Carol, and you should have seen them stare at me with my bare feet and my shoes and things under my arm.

"Why, Alan," Helen Bradford said. "Wh—what happened?"

I marched over to the stairs and put my bundle and my shoes down. I came past the doorway on my way to the dining room. "I went for a swim," I said and marched on to the cellaret. I poured three ounces of Scotch into a glass and added a little water. I took a big gulp and went back to the living room where Garlin and Linda were embellishing the story of my swim.

Carol's eyes avoided me. Eddington wore a grin which he did not seem to care about hiding, and Garlin's glance kept sliding towards me and he kept pulling it back. I lit a cigarette and stood listening while the water trickled out of my hair and down my neck.

"I saw the lights from my window," Garlin was saying, "and went down the backstairs. Has Haughton been around lately?"

Helen Bradford shook her head. "Not in the last half hour. He went to bed, I think."

Garlin looked at Eddington. "Have you been here long, Mr. Eddington?"

"Why, no." Eddington's smile went away. "As a matter of fact I came down about five minutes ago. I'd been working on some papers in my room and—" He broke off abruptly and his cheeks got pinker. "See here—You're not insinuating—"

Helen stepped into the breach. "What I don't understand," she said hurriedly, "is why you happened to be there in the first place, Alan."

I was going to tell her that Linda and I had been talking and found the boathouse door open and stepped inside to see if everything was all right. It wasn't good, but it would have passed. Except that Garlin didn't give me a chance. I think he was still sore from the way I needled him.

"According to Alan," he said flatly, "they could have been necking."

Linda didn't like it. "Really, Earl," she said. "If that comes under the head of humor—"

She didn't finish and neither did I. I was going to but I happened to look at Carol. Her glance took me in from my bare feet to my wet and matted hair, and it was a cold glance, definitely withering in intent and annoyingly superior. *Oh, what the hell,* I thought and said:

"I can think of worse places to neck than a boathouse," and I took my drink and gathered my things from the stairs and went to bed.

12

CAROL, Linda, and Spence Haughton were at the table when I went in for breakfast the next morning, and in the hall I could hear Garlin talking on the telephone. I said Good-morning, and everybody said Good-morning, even Carol. She waited until I had my orange juice before she said anything more. She smiled

with about the same amount of warmth you'd get from your in-
come tax collector and said:

"No ill effects from your swim, Alan?"

I smiled back at her. "No," I said. "As a matter of fact I feel
like a million for a change. It tones you up, a swim like that, im-
proves morale and sweetens one's outlook on life. You should
try it sometime."

"Alone?" she said with a brittle laugh. "Or with you, darling?"

I had a quick, uncontrolled desire to hurt her, to strike back. I
couldn't let it drop.

"You ought to try it too, Linda," I said. "Only next time I keep
my clothes on and you perform. Maybe we should start a club . . .
The Boathouse Necking & Moonlight Bathing Society." I might
have had more to say if Garlin hadn't come in.

"One of Marshall's lawyers'll be here in a half hour," he said to
Carol. "I think you'd better figure on spending some time with
him."

Linda left the table when I did. Without saying anything we
strolled through the living room and out on the terrace. It was
another nice morning, warm and bright, but I didn't know it then
because I was still brooding about Carol. I didn't even know where
I was going until I had passed through the front gate and was out
on the highway.

"You weren't very nice at the table," Linda said. "To Carol,
I mean."

"I know it."

"You just make things worse."

"I was all right until she started needling," I said. "Did she
sleep in with you last night?"

"Yes. I doubt if she wanted to after that scene but she'd already
said she would and she kept her word." She hesitated. "I told her
about the boathouse. I said we found the door open and went in

to see if everything was all right and surprised whoever it was that was hiding there." She touched my arm. "You know, Alan, I think you could get her back if you tried."

I wanted to say, "You wouldn't think so if you heard her bawl me out yesterday afternoon," but I didn't. We had reached the bridge over the stream from the hills and I stopped and leaned across the concrete rail. I watched the clear, blue-green water rushing headlong over the rocky bottom and tried not to think about Carol and I must have succeeded, for presently I was thinking about Penzance and the record in the sail loft.

"Did you ever go see Doctor Penzance?"

Linda gave me a quick, strange look and when she saw I meant it her brown eyes grew thoughtful. "Once." She turned, took two steps and came back, slim and vital and with that same lovely figure that had made her a model in the first place. She leaned beside me on the rail. "Why, Alan?" she said.

"I wondered if you knew whether he really could hypnotize anyone or not."

"Johnny said he could. He and I went up there early this Summer. He'd found out then that Helen had given the Doctor a lot of money the year before to build that chapel and he wanted to find out why?"

"Why should Johnny care?" I said. "It was Helen's money, wasn't it?"

"Yes but—" She hesitated and now her glance was troubled and remote. "Johnny had to turn over Helen's share of the estate two years ago when Helen was twenty-five, but there was something in the provisions of the original will that said that control of her share would revert to Johnny if she proved to be incompetent."

"Proving Penzance was a phony wouldn't prove that Helen was incompetent, would it?"

"Not in itself. But Johnny knew Helen had given Penzance thirty thousand for the chapel. For all he knew she might have given Penzance a great deal more. If he could get enough on Penzance he thought he might also find out more about what Helen had been doing with her money. If he could, he could force an accounting. That was what he wanted. Once he had that he'd know what to do next. He wasn't sure he could prove her incompetent, he just hoped he could."

A lock of hair fell in one eye and she pushed it back. "He spent months having Penzance investigated. Before we left he said he thought he had enough for a showdown. He said he had a report that would chase the Doctor out in the open. He told Helen she'd better come along."

I thought about the bit of conversation I'd heard between Penzance and Mrs. Talmain, and then I remembered Eddington. "So that's why Helen asked Eddington to come? He was supposed to protect her interests in case Johnny got tough with her."

"I suppose so."

A car came along the road from the direction of Hammondsport and I watched it pass. It had a taxi license tag and there was a lone man in the back seat. When it turned into the Marshall driveway I said:

"That must be Johnny's lawyer. They ought to have quite a session—he and Eddington and Helen and Carol."

She made no reply and presently I came back to my original idea. "What's all that got to do with Johnny going up to see Penzance—Johnny and you?"

"Doctor Penzance had never seen Johnny. Everything had been done through Johnny's lawyers—the lease and all that, I mean—and Johnny hadn't been up here in two years. So we pretended we wanted help."

"The kind Penzance had for sale?"

"Yes. We stayed a week and cooked up a story and finally Johnny got the Doctor to try to hypnotize me and cure me of this mental trouble I was supposed to have."

"And did he hypnotize you?" I asked.

"Johnny says he did, but I never really believed it. Johnny said I was in a trance for fifteen minutes, but if I was I don't remember. I think Johnny just liked to think that because it helped to prove what he wanted to prove."

"But you're not absolutely sure?"

"Well"—she smiled and made a little face—"no."

I was willing to believe that Penzance could hypnotize her, having seen his eyes at close range and listened to his voice. I said I wished I could see the Doc in action sometime.

Linda flipped her cigarette into the water and watched the current snatch it towards the lake. "You might be able to see part of it," she said. "The outdoor part."

She looked up at the sky. "It's warm and the sun is good. They might be out this morning." Her eyes danced mischievously. "Do you want to try? Johnny and I spied on them once."

I told her sure I'd like to try and we started back along the road. About a hundred feet past the house she started to cut up into the woods and someone hailed us from behind. It was Earl Garlin and we waited for him.

"The legal wizards are busy," he said. "Where you bound?" Linda told him.

Garlin grinned. "That's for me," he said. "Let's go."

It took us about ten minutes because there wasn't any path and we had to take it easy climbing through the woods. When we came to the last ridge Linda pointed below to a cleared space a hundred yards or more from the back of the chapel, a rectangular grassy plot enclosed by high shrubs and bushes.

We approached it quietly from the rear and when we were

fifteen or twenty feet from one end of the thi
tioned us to stop. We were still unable to see anythin, da mo-
line of bushes, but when she stretched out on the groud that
lowed her example and then, because the stems wer'e fol-
near as good a screen as the foliage, we could get a pretty far view.

Inside that rectangle the ground was flat and the turf look a
soft and green. At the far end, the Doctor faced us. Slightly to
one side stood Mrs. Talmain and with their back to us were
fifteen of the faithful, twelve women and three men.

It was something, all right, and I've got to admit that the Doc
was a pretty good testimonial for what he had to offer, at least
insofar as the physical part. He was really built. He reminded me
of the body-building advertisements I'd seen. He wore the briefest
of trunks and he was bronze all over, with a small hard waist and
a deep, upward-arching chest. From where we were we couldn't
hear what he was saying, but presently he began a bending exercise and the flock followed as best they could.

I think Mrs. Talmain was there chiefly to give the women confidence. With her there exercising beside the Doctor she was in
effect both chaperone and model student and as for the men, they
watched her too. They did unless they were crazy.

Without the peasant dress she would have been a good model
for Petty. Her ankles were good, her thighs rounded but not
heavy, her hips solid but not bulging. She had the same even
bronze color the Doc had and she wore brief white tights and
above that a handkerchief or scarf was knotted across her breasts
and she had what it took to keep it there. The grace with which
she did this exercise was exciting in itself; she made it look so
easy; she was so poised and sure of herself.

Suddenly the Doctor stopped and everyone waited while he
explained something else. Mrs. Talmain looked straight ahead,
her head up, her straight black hair glistening in the sun. Her

was impassive and remembering how she
strongly mo   unbar questioned her the day before, I knew
had looke   in had a lot to say about what went on in the
that M d of Horus.

Eventually I got around to looking at the flock. They were
exercising again and they looked pretty good, much better than I
had expected. The women were of various sizes and not all were
graceful, but they had nice color and they looked healthy. They
all wore shorts, some brief, some baggy. A few that could get
away with it, wore handkerchiefs across their breasts like Mrs.
Talmain, the others wore halters.

Of the three men, one was tall and thin and gray, with mahogany skin and hard stringy muscles. One was plump and bald
and bulging at the middle; the other was the little guy I had seen
playing bridge. He looked more out of place than the others for
some reason, possibly because he apparently had the sort of skin
that tans the hard way, if ever. The others were brown or tawny;
he was pink. I was thinking that maybe Penzance had something
to offer in the line of physical conditioning when I heard the
thick, low voice behind us.

"Get up!"

I rolled to one elbow. Mr. Talmain stood watching us, squat,
and powerful in his khaki trousers and undershirt.

"Get up!" he said again and his eyes under the heavy black
brows were mean.

We got up. I was ready to go and so was Linda. Garlin was in
no hurry. He moved his shoulders to hitch up his coat collar
and took out a cigarette.

Talmain's brows screwed down and his fingers twitched at
his side. "Get going," he said. "Come on, move."

"When we're ready," Garlin said.

"This is private property."

"So we're trespassing. Why don't you call the Doc?"

Talmain took a step forward. He was a tough-looking character and his face was getting darker by the second. Garlin waited. He was as thick-bodied as Talmain and half a head taller; he didn't scare very easily. He lit his cigarette, watching Talmain over the flame.

"Oh, come along, Earl," Linda said impatiently. "Why do you have to start something?"

Garlin looked at her and then at the thicket. Apparently we had not been heard because nothing happened in that direction. He looked at Talmain and grinned with one corner of his mouth.

"Okay . . . Be seeing you, Junior," he said to Talmain and started along behind us.

When we were halfway up the ridge I looked back. Talmain was standing where we'd left him; he still looked as if he wanted to tear us into small pieces.

After lunch I looked up Bert Donelly and asked him if I could take the station wagon to Bath. He said it was all right with him, but that I'd better ask Helen. I caught her just as she was going into another huddle with the legal departments and she told me it would be perfectly all right. So I got an old newspaper and went down to the boathouse.

What I'd seen at Penzance's place and what Linda had told me about the guy, made me want to do something about that record and I wanted to do it before Dunbar and Corrigan came back and started snooping around. I didn't know how else to sneak the disc out so when I took it down from the sail loft, I put it between the pages of the paper. It might look funny if someone saw me, because I couldn't fold the paper properly, but it was the best thing I could think of.

Earl Garlin was waiting for me when I came off the dock with the paper under my arm and the moment I saw that narrowed, knowing look in his eyes I knew what the score was.

"What're you going to do with it?" he said.

"With what?"

"That thing you got in the paper—that record."

"Been watching the boathouse, huh?" I said irritably.

"When I wasn't watching you and Linda." He grinned. "You don't have to go into any boathouse to neck," he said. "I knew damn well there was a good reason and I looked around till I found it. Where the hell did you get it, anyway?"

I told him and he shook his head. There was an undertone of admiration in his voice. "Well, I'll be damned. For an amateur you do all right. Now how you going to find out what's on it? There's no name on the label; nothing but a number. Number 41."

"I'm going to Bath first," I said. "And if I can't find a record-player big enough there I'm going to Elmira."

I started to walk towards the garage and he kept pace. He rubbed his mustache with the knuckle of his index finger, glanced sideways at me a couple of times and finally said:

"Okay, I think I'll go with you. I'd like to hear what number 41 has to say to old Doc Penzance."

13

WE had gone about a mile down the road when we saw this man walking along. I slowed down slightly and when I did he turned and gave me a half-hearted gesture with his thumb. It was the little guy I'd seen playing bridge in the Penzance drawing room the night before. I stopped and he came running after us and climbed in.

"Thanks," he said. "Thanks a lot. I was going to Hammondsport but I wasn't sure I'd make it. Tough, getting rides these days, I guess. This'll be a big help."

He had a straight, sharp nose and a sort of pointed face that made me think of a terrier. He looked to be about forty and he had a touch of carrot in his hair, which explained why he burned in the sun while others tanned.

"This is the Marshall station wagon, isn't it?" he asked. "Terrible thing, that accident. Tragic."

I glanced at Garlin. I hadn't known until then that Dunbar had not officially announced the death as murder. I said yes, it was most unfortunate.

"Just goes to show you," he said. "A champagne bottle. Think of it. A splinter in the throat, huh? Severed his juggler."

"You're up at Doctor Penzance's, aren't you?" I said, after we'd gone along another couple of miles.

He said, "Yes," and he said it disgustedly.

"Alone?" Garlin asked.

"With my wife—and her sister. Vernon's my name. George Vernon . . . From Scarsdale . . . I'm in the real estate business there."

We introduced ourselves and Garlin asked him if he'd been here long.

"Ten days," Vernon said. "Four to go. It's murder. Imagine spending your vacation in a place like that. Exercise half the day and listen to a lot of hogwash about the cosmic this and esteric that, and after dinner you play bridge or go to bed. No booze. Hell, it's getting so I'm almost ashamed to smoke."

As though that reminded him of the fact, he took out a cigar and bit off the end. I asked him how come he was here if he didn't like it.

"Hah! The wife wanted to come. That damn sister of hers got her started. It was her fault, and then when they decided they're coming they have to have me along. Because they're a little scared they'll get raped or something."

He thought it over. "That guy could do it too, I guess. Have you seen him? What a brute."

I glanced at Garlin and he winked. "I understand," he said, "that there is a Mrs. Talmain up there who is pretty nice."

"You can say that again." Vernon rubbed his hands. "She's terrific."

He had more to say about Mrs. Talmain but I wasn't listening just then; I was thinking that here was a chance to find out a little more about Doctor Penzance.

"How did your wife's sister happen to run into Penzance?" I asked.

"Somebody told her about him. He's got a place in Westchester. Nothing like this. Just a big house where he lives in the winter and gives consultations to anyone with the dough to pay him. This damn sister-in-law of mine—Eunice—is thirty-two and there's nothing wrong with her that a good husband couldn't fix. Now she thinks she's all nerves and neuroses and worrying about the war and her health, so she goes to this Penzance."

He stopped to light his cigar. "That would be okay if she didn't start sellin' my wife the idea. What the hell does my wife need with a guy that talks about cosmic truths and the secrets of the ancient Egyptians?"

"You think he's a phony?" Garlin said.

"Certainly he's a phony," Vernon said. "He has to be with that kind of racket. Fifty a week a piece for board and room with private consultations extra. Phui! I'd like to get something on the big bum, chase him out into the open. Then maybe I'd get some peace and comfort in my own home instead of always, 'Now, George, Doctor Penzance says you shouldn't do things like that.' I tell you, the guy's a menace."

I agreed, though not in the way George Vernon meant. I got more and more excited about the record and when we got to Bath I found a place that sold sheet music and records and inquired about a record-player. There was, according to the proprietor, none in town. When I asked him what was the nearest place likely to have one he said there might be something in Elmira.

I drove back to the railroad station and parked. Vernon was still with us. When we went through Hammondsport I asked him where he wanted to get out and he said if we were going on to Bath he'd go along.

"I'm just beginning to feel normal again," he said. "And the rest of the day I'm playing hookey from those screwballs."

I went into the station and Garlin went with me. The ticket agent gave me the bad news: There were no more trains until evening.

"9:02 is the first to Elmira," he said. "Course you can get a bus."

"How far is it?"

"About thirty-six miles."

"What about trains coming back from Elmira?"

"One at 4:02 and one at 11:10."

He said there was a bus in twenty minutes and I thanked him and turned away. Garlin touched my arm and peered at me. "You're not going to bounce thirty-six miles on a bus just to hear that record, are you?"

The way I felt I'd have gone all the way to New York if I'd had to. "You don't have to go," I said.

"I suppose I can hang around here and pitch quoits."

I told him to take the station wagon, that I'd get back to the house one way or another. He was a suspicious guy, this Garlin. He half closed one eye, studied me, shrugged.

"Okay," he said. "I'll go along for the ride."

George Vernon was waiting outside. We told him we were catching a bus for Elmira. I said I was with American Broadcasting and the record was an audition I had to hear. I said I was sorry I couldn't drive him back.

"Oh, that's all right. He looked up at me with that terrier's face, pushed his lips out; pretty soon his eyes wrinkled. "Tell you what," he said. "I'll go with you."

I told him we wouldn't be back until late but it didn't make any difference. He'd made up his mind, and having reached the decision, he was eager to be off. We were his pals. He was going to stick with us, and he was such a likable little guy that I had to laugh at his answer.

"All right, so I'll be late," he said. "It don't make any difference, I'll get hell anyway."

The Elmira *Star-Gazette* was housed in a two-story building that stood on a downtown corner, a brick and stone affair with big, ground floor windows on one side so you could see the presses work. The editorial rooms were on the second floor and as soon as I went in I spotted Kiley, the demon photographer.

He recognized me right off and limped over and shook hands. "Hi, Mr. Wallace," he said. "See your picture in yesterday's *Star?*"

I told him I hadn't and he said, "Wait a minute." He went out into the hall and came back a minute later with an eight by ten glossy print of Helen Bradford and me standing on the Marshall dock. "Here," he said. "You can have it."

While he rolled it up and snapped an elastic around it I told him what I wanted. "Just keep the Marshall part out of it," I said. "I'm just a guy that works for American Broadcasting and they mailed this to me and I'd like to hear it . . . I've got two other fellows with me. They're waiting outside."

He told me to sit down, and presently he was talking on the telephone. "All right, I think," he said when he hung up. "Wait just a second, will you?"

He went over to a desk in the corner by the windows and spoke to the man behind it. I knew they were talking about me because I could see them glance my way as they talked. Finally Kiley came back and leaned against the desk.

"I was just thinking—" He paused and looked at the floor. He seemed embarrassed and his face was flushed so that the freckles were more prominent. "Maybe you don't want to talk about it, but I wondered if you'd give us a little story. You know, about your experiences in the Solomons. Any little personal thing."

I just stared at him.

"I found out you were Captain Wallace," he said. "We read a little about you some months ago. When you were wounded. It was the leg, wasn't it?"

He glanced down at his own legs and I saw then that one foot was twisted in a way that even the shoe could not quite hide. It made me feel bad—not the leg so much but the wistfulness in his glance, the boyish envy for one who had done the sort of fighting he could never do.

I had to lie to him because I didn't know how much time I had. I told him my experiences were old stuff now and that I didn't like to talk without a public relations officer along.

"There'll be plenty of local boys coming back," I said. "They'll have stories as good as mine or better."

In a way he seemed a little relieved. He smiled and reached for a battered hat. "All right," he said. "I wasn't sure how you felt about it . . . Let's go see Ben Parks."

This Ben Parks had a music store a couple of blocks from

the *Star-Gazette,* and when we walked in he stopped talking to a blonde who sat at a desk halfway down the store and came to me us. Kiley introduced Garlin, Vernon and me as being connected with American Broadcasting. "The gentlemen I told you about over the phone," he said.

Parks, a genial sort of fellow, with five-o'clock shadow sprouting from his jaws, and a lot of gray-black hair, shook hands and said he was glad to meet us. He glanced at the record under my arm.

"There are only a couple in town that will take that," he said. "I wanted to be sure of the size before I called. Stick around and I'll see what I can do."

Kiley and Garlin leaned against one of the show cases and lit cigarettes. I hit a couple of chords on a piano near the entrance and when I looked round, George Vernon was talking to the blonde. He was doing all right, I guess, because she was laughing and he was leaning stiff-armed on the desk.

"Okay," Parks said when he came back. "We'll go up to Ned Yager's place," he said to Kiley. "My car's around back."

"It's very kind of you," I said, "but couldn't we just go up to this place and tell Mr. Yager you sent us? I don't like to take you away from your work?"

"What work?" Parks said, and belched. "Between the shortages and this Petrillo, business is sort of tough. Come on."

We went to a place called Strathmont on the West side of town, a big, Tudor-type house on a hill. A maid let us in and Parks led the way as if he owned the place. He took us into a big living room and walked over to this record-player and while he was fooling with it Ned Yager came in and was introduced.

Yager was a big man, ruddy-faced, hearty-voiced. I told him we were very grateful for his kindness and he said, "Glad to have you. What about a drink?"

George Vernon hardly gave him chance to finish. "That would be very nice," he said. "Thanks very much."

Garlin looked at Vernon and then at me, and winked. Yager found out what we wanted and went out. "Hold the record," he said to Parks, "I'd like to hear it."

We waited for Yager and the drinks and by the time I was getting pretty damn jumpy. I couldn't figure any way I could have avoided the audience—after all, I couldn't ask all these favors and then chase everyone out—and now I didn't know what was coming. I didn't know if there'd be names mentioned or what to expect, so just before Parks started the machine I tried to give myself an out.

"I don't know what this is," I said. "It'll probably bore you stiff but they sent it up from New York and asked us to listen. It's probably just another turkey some advertising agency cooked up."

Well, the record started and the sweat pores opened up a little more on me and then I heard Penzance's voice. For three minutes I held my breath and stared at nothing; then I began to breathe and my muscles loosened up and I drank greedily from my glass.

What we heard was terrible, but it was all right in a way. It was a question and answer sort of thing between a Mrs. Alingbrook and the Doctor, and sounded like something from the Domestic Court Hour, with a lot of the emotional calisthenics of a radio serial added. It couldn't possibly make much sense to an objective listener but Garlin had his ears pricked up and so did I when we got some of the content.

It seems that this Mrs. Alingbrook was a most unhappy woman. Her married life was not as it should be, her husband did not return her affection in the manner she thought essential and as a result she was starved for affection and understanding. Because of this she had turned to other things, among them a man she had known before her marriage. She had, in some moments of weakness, been indiscreet and she wondered now what she should do. . . .

I didn't wait for all of it. I'd heard enough to realize just how good Doctor Penzance was when it came to extracting secrets painlessly. That sonorous, understanding voice was the thing that did it and though I could not tell if this woman was under any hypnotic influence, the quiet monotone in which she spoke told me such a spell was quite possible. I glanced round at the others. George Vernon seemed interested only in his drink. Yager and Parks were looking at me doubtfully now, wondering probably, if I was in my right mind. Only Earl Garlin remained attentive.

I got up and shut the record off. Yager said, "What is it supposed to be? One of those things you call soap operas."

"It's pretty bad, isn't it?" I said.

"Anybody who'd buy that belongs in Valehaven," Kiley said.

"Pure corn," Parks said, and belched loudly.

Yager insisted we have another drink and it was nearly six o'clock before we could get away. Parks asked us what our plans were. We told him we were going to hang around until we could get the 11:10 train for Bath, and how about having dinner with us.

"Where's a good place to eat?" I asked.

"There ain't any," he said. "The hotel's as good as any."

He said he couldn't join us, but that he'd go along and have a drink. We had the drink. We had a couple more and Parks called up his wife and came back to tell us it was all right, he'd have dinner with us.

Apparently it had been quite a while since George Vernon

had been out and he'd made up his mind to enjoy himself. He had four drinks at the bar in addition to the two he'd had at Yager's house; he had another Scotch and soda with his dinner and called for brandy with his coffee. Parks was doing all right too. He got a lot of laughs out of Vernon, who long ago had insisted that we call him George.

"What time is it?" he wanted to know while I was waiting for the check. "Eight thirty? That gives us two hours and a half, huh? Where can we go, Parks, old Pal?"

"Oh, there are places," Parks said. "This is quite a town."

"All we need," said Vernon, "is a bottle and some women." He gave the table a bleary-eyed grin and began to count by stabbing the air with his index finger. "Five women," he said.

"Not for me," Kiley said. "I got work to do."

"Four then," Vernon said.

Earl Garlin grinned at him. "Not tonight, Georgie," he said. "We got a train to make. Come on, let's get out of here."

Ben Parks took us around. We went into a couple of places on Lake street after Kiley left us. One was big and noisy, with tables at the back and a three piece orchestra and a girl who sang and played the piano.

George Vernon insisted on buying the drinks here. In fact it was with some difficulty that we restrained him from buying for the house.

Garlin shook a finger at him. "Georgie," he said. "I'm afraid you're getting cocked."

Vernon grinned and patted Garlin's shoulder. "Yeah," he said. "And I love it."

Parks shook his head. "What a guy," he said. "Come on, you want to go somewhere else."

We did. To a place on East Water Street, with a small bar in the front and a big back room with a four piece orchestra and three or four acts and a twenty-five cent cover charge. Parks took charge of us. Everybody knew him and the proprietress bought us a round of drinks and Vernon followed her out to the bar to return the favor. We went to one other place, similar in character but smaller and farther from the center of town and by the time we'd had our drink there it was ten minutes of eleven.

We came out and piled into Ben Parks' car. I still had the record in one piece and I had a nice glow so I didn't particularly care whether it got broken or not. Garlin was nicely mellow. He didn't get tough with anybody and he didn't start any arguments. But it was George Vernon's evening. He was as likable drunk as he was sober and he knew he was drunk and he was glad.

"Now," he said, as Parks drove towards the station, "we get the women, hunh?"

"Sure," said Garlin.

"When?"

"When you get home."

"When I get home," Vernon said, "I won't care." And he snuggled contentedly in the corner of the car and went to sleep.

14

THE train was on time getting into Bath and as it pulled out and we climbed into the station wagon a clock somewhere in the town struck twelve.

Vernon had slept all the way on the train. He woke up long enough to get off and climb into the station wagon, long enough to chuckle and ask where the girls were, and then he was asleep again and Garlin and I sat watching the road sweep up at us in the car's headlights. We didn't say a word until after we'd passed through Hammondsport; then Garlin sighed heavily.

"What a guy?" he said.

"Vernon?"

"The Doc. Jesus, what a racket! Did you hear what that dame said on the record? What do you think a woman would pay for a thing like that?"

"She'd pay what she had to pay."

"Maybe there *is* something in that hypnosis business."

I said it would probably depend on the subject. "And anyway he didn't sell that record."

"Yeah. You mean otherwise he wouldn't have had it on hand. I thought about that. Maybe he hasn't got around to collecting yet or maybe the woman didn't scare. That's what makes me think she was hypnotized, partly anyway. If he played that back to her when she was all right, she could deny it."

"Some would rather pay and have the record," I said. "That's probably how he figures. If he runs across one that won't, he wouldn't risk doing anything about it, would he?"

"I doubt it. He's got a good thing. If he tried anything and the person was willing to risk the publicity to bring charges the Doc could be put away for quite awhile." . . .

The lights were still on in the lower part of the house when I swung the car into the driveway and coasted into the garage. Garlin yawned and tapped the record he had been holding in his lap.

"What do you want to do with this?"

I didn't know. I said so.

"We could put it back in the boathouse where it was," he said. "I'll take it out for you if you want . . . And what about him?" he said, and jerked his head towards the sleeping Vernon.

I felt tired and logy. The effects of the alcohol had about worn off and I wanted to get to bed; yet when I thought about George Vernon I had to grin. I decided I owed him quite a lot. For several hours I hadn't thought about the murder or Carol or worried any about whether I was all right again or not. I was relaxed and I'd had a lot of laughs and Vernon was responsible for most of them. I didn't envy him when I thought about what might happen when he got home, but I did have a real affection for the little guy.

"Leave him here," I said. "When I get a drink I'll come back and take him home."

Spencer Haughton and Douglas Eddington were talking in the living room when I walked in. They looked sort of surprised to see me.

"Lieutenant Dunbar was looking for you," Haughton said.

"I don't doubt it."

"Helen was asking about you too," Eddington said. "She said you had the station wagon."

"Yeah," I said. "We took a little trip, Garlin and I." I flopped into a chair, too tired at the moment to make a drink or to do anything. "Anything happen here?"

They shook their heads. Dunbar, they said, had been around asking more questions but that was all. I said that was good and would Haughton do me a favor.

"Make me a drink." The door from the terrace opened and Garlin came in. "Make Earl one too," I said.

I watched Spence go over to the table and start to fix those drinks. He had his back to the room and you couldn't see what he was doing, and like that, it hit me. I don't know why. I don't know what made me think of it, or why I hadn't thought of it before; all I know is, I had a very weird feeling come over me that left me empty and gone and strangely shocked inside when I remembered that bottle of poison I'd seen in Haughton's bag and realized how easy it would be for him to use it if he wanted to.

Not here, in front of people, but somewhere, sometime when he wouldn't be caught. I glanced at Garlin and wondered if he had told the police about that bottle of Hydrocyanic acid solution. I was sore at myself for thinking so much about other things that I had neglected to be more sure of this possibility. I decided there were two things I could do—find out from Garlin what, if anything, he had done about it and take another look in Haughton's room.

The idea was all right but it didn't work out. Garlin took a swallow of his drink and said he was going up to bed. He looked at me. "Will you take care of Georgie?"

I said I would. Then Haughton yawned and stretched and smiled at us through those horn-rimmed glasses. "Time for me to get to bed, too," he said. "See you in the morning."

I watched him go out. Eddington stirred in his chair. He rubbed his plump hands, took off his glasses and began to polish them. Without them his eyes had an owlish, peering look.

"Who's Georgie?" he said.

"A fellow we picked up this afternoon. He's a little drunk," I said. "I've got to get him home."

I finished my drink and stood up. I told him to leave a light on so I could find my way around when I came back; then I went out to the garage and found George Vernon still asleep in the station wagon.

"Come on," I said, shaking him. "Time to go home."

He mumbled something I couldn't understand but presently he woke up and I spoke to him again.

"Yeah," he said. "That's right. Good Ol' Alan."

Until then I'd figured on driving him up to his place and now

I saw it would be better if I could walk him home. The car would make noise going up the hill and turning around and I figured some of his neighbors would hear us. It would be tough enough on him with just the wife to worry about—and her sister—but if the neighbors were in on it, it would be that much worse for him the next day.

"Come on," I said, and pulled his arm. "We're going to walk. Quiet now."

"Yeah," he said. "Shhh!"

He could stand pretty well, and by leaning on me and letting me guide him, he could walk. He didn't make a bit of trouble. He didn't argue, nor question my right to help him. He was completely tractable, talkative now, but ready to quiet down when I told him to.

"Yeah," he'd say. "Shhh."

We went up the curving road to the Penzance colony and the main house was white and glaring in the moonlight, the chapel somber and spooky-looking at the edge of the woods. I asked Vernon if he knew which house was his and he said he did. He said his was the left-hand one in a group of three that stood at one corner of the quadrangle and when we were about fifty yards away he lurched to a stop. What he said then corroborated my former opinion that here was a very nice little guy.

" 'S far enough," he said. "I've had a wonderful time. 'Preciate your taking me along. It was great, everything was great." He leaned against me and I could see his grin in the moonlight. "Everything but the record. That was bad, huh?"

"That was bad," I said.

"Now I'll go the rest of the way. I'll get hell anyway and tha's okay. No use in you getting dragged into something. You go ahead home. Gertrude—tha's my wife—won't know who I've been out with."

See what I mean by being a nice guy? "Sure you can make the door?" I said.

"Poshitive."

I watched him go. He weaved a bit but he kept to the general line and made the door without trouble. When I saw it open and Vernon lurch inside, I turned and started back down the road. . . .

I think I was about halfway down the hill when I heard the shots, two of them in quick succession and off to my right. They weren't loud—just a couple of sharp cracks in the stillness that sound like the .25 calibres the Japs used on us at first—and they weren't very close.

I stood still and listened and there wasn't anything else. I tried to tell myself that they weren't shots, but a car down on the road that had backfired. The trouble was I'd heard too much gunfire to believe any such thing and besides, the direction wasn't quite right. *Maybe it's a farmer taking a shot at a skunk that was prowling around,* I thought. After that I thought about Johnny Marshall and the murder and then I knew I couldn't go home without having a look.

I stepped off the road into a stand of pines, heading in the general direction of the shots. The moon was high and clear and the tall pines cast a patchwork of highlight and deep shadow on the ground. Because of the covering of needles I did not make much noise as I moved carefully ahead, eyes straining and every sense alert.

With no idea of what was ahead of me I kept going in what I hoped was a reasonably straight line. The terrain sloped gently to my left now and I kept working slightly uphill, staying in the shadows when I could and keeping away from tree trunks that seemed thick enough for someone to hide behind.

I had covered perhaps a hundred yards like this when it happened. I didn't see anything but the flash. I had no warning of any kind. One moment the woods were quiet and the night was still, and the next something exploded up ahead and I saw a brief bright flash in the center of a patch of shadow and then I heard the slap of a slug in a tree trunk a few feet from my head.

I was moving before the echoes died away. Without knowing it I was turning the other way and in the same motion I was running—running the hell out of there.

15

NEAR the road that led down the hill to the main highway, but not too near, there was a stump. It was damp on top but I didn't care. I sat down on it gratefully because my knees were weak.

My head was pounding and my lungs were tight and I had the shakes. My legs still quivered and inside everything was vibrating. I could think all right, but that only served to tell me that I was not quite cured yet. Such things had happened to me before —in the jungle—and in those days you didn't run. You stepped behind the nearest tree and knew there was a guy up ahead behind another and you worked something out so you got him before he got you.

It wasn't smart to run, it wasn't smart at all. Even without a gun it was best to locate your man first before you turned your back. Someone had shot at me and if I could stalk this someone and find out who it was I might know who murdered Johnny Marshall. But first I had to sit here and demobilize myself until I could face this thing calmly.

I told myself that perhaps if I waited this person would come past and while I waited I turned my thoughts deliberately away

from what had just happened. I began to think about the murder
and the people involved.

It was a good idea. It was interesting, once I got started, because
heretofore I'd never taken the time to consider the possibilities
objectively. I started with myself. I had a very good motive for
wanting Johnny dead and I had the opportunity; that's why I
was high on Dunbar's list.

Carol was next. I knew she couldn't have done such a thing
but that was my heart, my emotions, talking. The mind said she
had the best opportunity of anyone and she had two motives, one
planned—with the idea of financial gain—and the other a spur-
of-the-moment crime done in rage or passion. The method of
murder did not cancel this possibility since she could have struck
him and, still in the grip of this blind rage, smashed the bottle for
a murder weapon.

Linda? Linda, too, had no alibi that I knew of. I didn't know
what the motive could be but that did not mean there was none.
She was Johnny's secretary. She might have the opportunity to
falsify accounts, for instance. Over a period of years she might
have accumulated considerable money. If this was so Johnny
might recently have found her out and if she faced prison she
might kill. I had to admit this theory did not fit in with the
twenty-five thousand dollar check Johnny had made out to Linda,
but it was a possibility.

Haughton's motives was well known. He had come to get back
his contract, and he had come with a bottle of deadly poison.
Someone with glasses on had been searching Johnny's room that
first night, and Spence was the only one with glasses. Also someone had searched the study desk. It could have been Haughton.

Helen Bradford had no alibi. Her motive might be the strongest
of all. She had been to Penzance. Johnny was out to prove
Penzance was a crook and a phony and he might therefore prove

Helen was incompetent. Certainly he had scared her to the extent of bringing her lawyer along. . . .

All of a sudden I was sitting up and thinking harder than ever. What about Eddington? He apparently had been handling Helen's affairs, several million dollars worth. Suppose he had appropriated some of those millions for his own use, possibly with the intention of putting them back? Suppose he'd been speculating? He was safe enough so long as he was the boss. But if Johnny could force a sudden accounting—and that had been his intention, according to Linda—Eddington would be out on a limb. And like Haughton, Eddington wore glasses. A man with glasses had searched Johnny's room . . . Without realizing it I was talking to myself.

"Only Eddington wasn't here then . . . or was he?"

"He wasn't on our train."

"But suppose he took a morning train out of New York. He'd be in Bath in the afternoon. If he was bent on murder he might have got off in Elmira, come up here in a hired car, done the job and driven back. He could spend the night there and still get the morning train, arriving in Bath as though he'd taken it in New York the night before."

The idea excited me. It presupposed several things but it was new and it was possible. It almost made me forget I still had Doctor Penzance to consider.

I didn't waste much time on Penzance. He already impressed me as a guy who could murder if he had to, and he had many things to protect. Also, here I was on his land, and those shots had come from this vicinity. I stood up, feeling calm and poised and ready to try again. I crossed the road and started through the pines.

My headlong flight had brought me back to the road about a hundred feet from the spot where I had originally entered and

I angled down that way and then started slanting upward and to the right in an effort to keep close to my first line of search. With all that confusion of light and shadow and trees looking alike, it was hard to be sure, but about fifty yards farther on I did come to a spot near a fallen tree that seemed familiar.

I still felt okay. I was keyed up but I wasn't afraid and I kept thinking how wonderful it was that I had had the advice of those psychiatrists in the hospital. Ten minutes ago I was in a panic; now I was ready for the job and tingling with anticipation. I was almost a Marine again, remembering the tricks I had learned.

I don't think I made a sound, nor did I once pass through a spot of moonlight. I kept to the trees and the shadows and I kept going until the ground fell sharply away in front of me and I saw I was at the edge of a ravine or gorge that looked sheer and black and bottomless.

I backed away and tried to orient myself. A short distance to the right I saw where the ground projected into the wall of the gorge in an inverted U. Moving up to this, I cut back into the woods a few feet and then I knew why I had been shot at.

Whoever had the gun had apparently been coming down along the edge of the ravine, had heard me moving up and realized that if I kept coming there would be no retreat except the inverted U. Once there, this person would be trapped and . . .

"Oh-oh," I said, half aloud, and suddenly I was damn glad that I had been spotted coming through the woods. I did not know what the first two shots proved but it was not difficult to imagine what might have happened if I had backed this person up against the ravine. If this was the killer and I had got close enough to see him, I would have been a dead pigeon by now. The thought shook me and I moved quickly back into the friendly shadows of the woods.

I stood there a few seconds, thinking hard and getting more

exasperated. I had, possibly, been close to death; yet, if I had been more careful, if I had practiced the jungle lore I had learned in the Solomons in the first place I might easily have seen who this gunman was.

"A fine damn detective you'd make," I thought, and then I started up the gorge, keeping my distance and always staying in the shadows, knowing somehow that it was too late to do any good but continuing on sheer stubbornness.

I don't know how far I followed this gorge. It was all uphill, though not particularly steep, and my enthusiasm for the hike cooled rather quickly. Perhaps I continued another hundred yards, perhaps two, but in the end I turned away, aware now that my hunch—that I was too late—was right.

Not bothering about stealth, I cut directly to my right and came out of the woods at the edge of the quadrangle a few minutes later. What happened then was nothing but luck. I just happened to be looking in the right direction at the right moment; the moon happened to be bright and high and the spot near the edge of the white house was highlighted vividly.

There was a patch of this illumination between the trees and one corner of the house and as I watched, someone crossed it, walking fast. Two steps and he was gone and though I saw the figure clearly I was too far away to know who it was. I could not, in fact, tell whether the figure was big or small, nor even if it was a man.

Still stubborn, still smarting from my lack of success, I circled towards the spot, keeping to the edge of the woods and watching the house. I crossed the bright patch, swiftly, as the other had done, and slid along the back of the house.

One room on the ground floor was lighted. The curtain was drawn but there was a one-inch crack at the bottom from which brightness streamed and I went up to it, stooped and got my eyes to the crack.

What I saw was a big bedroom. Doctor Penzance, in slacks and sweater, was pacing up and down, talking vigorously to Mrs. Talmain. She sat on the arm of a heavy chair, swinging one leg from the knee. She wore a quilted robe, buttoned at the throat, and fur-trimmed slippers. She was watching Penzance pace, her dark eyes speculative, her red mouth smiling but somewhat sullen.

Penzance looked sore. Those horizontal wrinkles in his forehead were tightly folded and his jaw was like a rock. He swung his hands as he talked and apparently he was talking fairly loud—but all I could hear was a rumble. I tried putting my ear to the pane. It didn't do much good except to make the rumble louder.

I watched awhile longer. I saw him quiet down and finally I saw that Mrs. Talmain was talking. She got up and moved over to him and kissed him. She smiled and said something and went over to the door and opened it. Penzance watched it close. I couldn't see his face then but when he began to pull off his sweater I moved away from the window and started down the hill.

I kept to the road after I'd crossed the quadrangle. I didn't see anyone or hear anything but I did a lot of thinking. Actually all I knew was that I'd heard two shots and been shot at. I didn't know why. I couldn't identify the person I'd seen move to the edge of Penzance's house. But what troubled me most at the moment was Dunbar.

Should I phone him now or not? Looking back it is easy to say that I should have called him; it was not so simple then. I was a suspect in Marshall's murder and had been found under suspicious circumstances by Garlin. Suppose now that someone else had been killed? I didn't know that anyone had but if such was the case how could I prove I hadn't fired the shots and then fired another into a tree to substantiate my story that I had been shot at? Unsubstantiated, my story wasn't worth a damn; it would in fact, make things worse for me since to tell it all would be to admit that I had been on the spot.

So that's how it was. Maybe I'd tell Dunbar in the morning, maybe I wouldn't. Meanwhile what I needed was sleep and I knew that tonight I was going to get some. . . .

Eddington had left a light burning in the living room. I could see its glow as I opened the gate and moved round to the left with the idea of going in from the terrace rather than struggle with the heavy front door. I was just rounding the lilac bushes when I saw something move off to the left, in the direction of the tennis court.

I stepped back into the bushes where I could watch. For a second or two I could see nothing but darkness; then there was a tiny red glow which brightened momentarily and then faded again. When it moved I knew it must be a cigarette, and it seemed to be coming closer.

I stayed where I was. I was still keyed up from what I had seen before and I didn't know who it was and I decided I'd find out who else was up at this hour. The trees along the edge of the plot put the lawn in deep shadow and even when I realized there were two people, when I could hear faintly the drone of their voices, I did not know who they were.

But they were moving towards the terrace doors and I could differentiate between the voices enough to know one of them was a woman. They passed by about fifteen feet from me. I could not seem to penetrate the darkness but I did catch a snatch of the hushed conversation as they passed up on the terrace—a man's voice saying:

"I still think you should pay if you have to. Until you know what is in that report no one must know about Valehaven . . ."

The voice passed out of range. I moved away from the bushes so I could see the French doors and not until they walked into the patch of light that filtered through from the living room did I know for sure who had spoken. It was Douglas Eddington and beside him, in a dark, flowing robe of some kind, was Helen Bradford.

I watched them go through the doors and cross the room to the hall and I was thinking, *Valehaven, Valehaven*! It had a familiar sound. I'd heard it somewhere but I could not remember when or anything about the circumstances. I sat down on the stone step and lit a cigarette. I waited about ten minutes to give them time to get into their rooms before I went upstairs. I was still thinking about Valehaven when I dropped off to sleep.

16

I awakened with the sun streaming across my bed, and for perhaps five seconds I examined the turning leaves of the maple tree that screened the sky; then I was thinking of Valehaven.

I gave it perhaps two or three futile but intensive minutes of speculation and went progressively backward from there—to Mrs. Talmain and Doctor Penzance and the hurrying figure I had seen but could not identify. I remembered the gorge and my headlong flight after the shot and the two shots before that. Which brought me back to the house and Spencer Haughton and his vial of poison.

That was all I needed to bring me out of bed. I grabbed slippers and robe and glanced at my watch. It was eight forty. Breakfast time for Haughton, I hoped. I didn't wait to wash. I ran a comb through my hair and went downstairs with the idea that if

Haughton was eating I could come back and search that Gladstone bag.

Eddington was the only one at the table and I said Goodmorning and beat it back to my room. I washed and shaved and dressed. When I got back downstairs Haughton still hadn't appeared so I sat down opposite Eddington and started on the melon. I'd taken one spoonful when I heard the front doorbell ring.

Bert Donelly scurried down the hall and then there were voices and a lot of steps. They stopped by the stairs and I heard Dunbar giving orders to Corrigan.

"Take a look," he said. "I'll be back."

I was listening for more when he poked his head into the dining room and beckoned to me.

"Let's take a ride," he said.

"I haven't finished breakfast."

"Then let it wait," he said. "Come on."

He wasn't mild-mannered any more, nor patient. His voice had a bite in it and I decided I'd better humor him. When we got in his car and started up the hill towards the Doctor's place I could feel a lot of very small goose pimples growing on my forearms.

"I don't get it," I said finally.

"You will."

He gave the car wheel a twist and we bounced off the road about halfway up the hill and not far from the stump where I'd done my "demobilizing" the night before. He stopped under the pines behind two other cars, got out, waited for me to catch up with him. We started through the trees, moving silently over the carpet of needles and saying nothing until we came to the edge off the rocky gorge where a state policeman waited.

This gorge looked different by daylight. It was perhaps fifty feet deep at this point and the stream that made it was the one that emptied into the lake close by Marshall's house after passing under the highway bridge. It was a pretty spot in the morning sunlight and reminded me of the ones they have around Ithaca, except this gorge was smaller and not so deep.

Across, on the other side, the land was cleared and there was a wire fence with a vineyard beyond. There were five people standing at the fence looking down: a man, two women, and two teen-aged boys. They had wooden trays under their arms for picking grapes but I guess they didn't pick any that morning; they were too busy looking at what was going on at the bottom of the gorge.

Dunbar took my arm and pulled me to the edge. He pointed down to a flat ledge that was probably under water in the spring but was perfectly dry now. Three men—Tait and Whelan and Ryder, the coroner—were squatting around the body of a man who lay stretched out beside the stream. When one of them moved I saw the man's face and knew who it was.

"Earl Garlin!" I said in a voice I did not recognize.

"Yeah," Dunbar said.

It took me awhile to add anything. My knees were uncertain and my heart was hammering. It was not the murder, as such. I think I expected that on the ride up and it explained much of what had happened the night before. No, it wasn't the murder, it was the victim. I hadn't even considered Garlin. I don't know why exactly, unless it was because he had not been around for breakfast, but somehow I had expected to find Spence Haughton. When I tried to swallow my throat was dry, and if what I said sounded silly it was because I was stalling.

"He fell. He stood up here and"—I looked round at Dunbar and those gray eyes stared back at me—"somebody pushed him."

"Yeah," Dunbar said. "But first somebody shot him twice in the chest."

"I heard it," I said, but not until I heard the sound of my voice did I realize what I'd done.

"*What?*" Dunbar grabbed my arm and his mouth was hard. "You what?"

I had to go through with it then. I don't know whether I had intended to tell him or not; I do know I had no intention of telling him then. What I had hoped to do was get a little more information. I had wanted to appear casual, maybe even dumb, and in the stress of the moment up jumped the devil and I told the truth.

"I heard the shots last night," I said.

He opened his mouth and got ready to blast. It must have taken quite an effort to close it again but he did. He closed it and I watched him tighten against his anger.

"When?" he said, his voice thin.

"Around one, maybe a bit later."

"What were you doing up here at that hour?"

I told him about bringing George Vernon home and how I'd heard the shots and what I'd done and how I'd been shot at.

"Show me," he said, and beckoned to the trooper. "Come on."

For once I was lucky. I wasn't sure I could come close to finding the right spot but I went down the gorge until I located the inverted U, and cut diagonally into the woods from there. The trooper found the tree about ten minutes later.

"This looks like it," he said.

We inspected the tree and the hole, which was about six feet from the ground. Dunbar got out his knife and cut around the hole until he could see the metal.

"Okay," he said to the trooper. "Dig it out—and be damn sure you don't scar it up." He turned back to me. "Now what were you and this George Vernon doing, anyway? Garlin was with you, wasn't he?"

Well, there it was again and maybe it gives you an idea how

tough it is to hold out on the police once you've said more than you should. If I explained why we went to Elmira I'd have to bring in the record. If I did that Dunbar'd want to know where it was and there would be no point in lying about what was on it because he'd surely find a way to play it. But if I told him about the record, I would also have to tell him I stole it from Penzance's library, and for all I knew, considering the way he felt now, Dunbar might slap me into jail for breaking and entering.

"Yes, he was with me," I said, "and the three of us went to Elmira and got a little drunk. Why? What's your trouble anyway? You've had three days. Why don't you solve the case?"

"We will, brother. We will."

"Who do you think did it?" I said when I got my temper pushed back where it belonged.

"Probably the same one that killed Marshall." Dunbar spat viciously and tugged at his hatbrim. "And don't get the idea it couldn't have been you."

"You're nuts," I said.

"Yeah? I'm the one that's nuts now, huh?"

That one hit below the belt but maybe I had it coming. "Plenty of people had a motive for wanting Johnny out of the way. I'm one of them. All right. But Garlin—"

"Garlin knew something," Dunbar said. "He must have. That's the trouble with these private snoops. They want to horn in on everything but when they get something themselves they like to play it cozy. Either Garlin saw something that first night and held out, or he found out something later and tried to cash in on it. Whichever it was, he must've made a date for last night and sneaked up here after he left you—if he didn't come with you—and the guy let him have it after kidding him along. He outsmarted himself and it cost him his life and me a lot more grief and—"

He broke off suddenly, as though realizing he was just wasting his breath. He sighed and gave his hatbrim another tug. He looked me up and down and shook his head disgustedly.

"Go on back and get your breakfast if you want," he said. "And be damn sure you stay there till I get back."

I could hear voices in the dining room when I came into the main hall and one of them was Haughton's. I didn't think I'd been heard, and having a one-track mind I beat it upstairs and down the hall to Haughton's room. I looked over my shoulder, like you see them do in plays—though it was no joke to me—and palmed the knob. I went in on tiptoes, shut the door quickly and started for that Gladstone bag.

When I got it open I reached for the soiled sox and shook them. Nothing came out. There was no bottle in the bag at all and after five minutes of frantic search through the chest, bathroom and the spare suit hanging in the closet I knew the oil of bitter almonds wasn't there.

In the hall I mopped the perspiration from my face and tried to figure it out. To me it seemed that Doctor Penzance was still my number-one boy but I knew that when Dunbar got here all of us would take a verbal beating. Until last night when I remembered the poison vial, I had let Garlin handle our original discovery. I did not know if he had advised the police or not but I could understand why, if Haughton was the killer, he had got rid of the poison. He had not used it but that meant nothing.

Assuming that Haughton had come to kill, but not knowing exactly how or when, the poison would certainly be a good method. The exploding champagne bottle that first afternoon gave him an idea that made the poison unnecessary. He had followed Carol and Johnny to the wine cellar in the hope of finding the opportunity and one had been presented to him. Carol and

Johnny had an argument. Carol had run out, losing her scarf, and when Haughton finished the job he left it behind.

Why hadn't he disposed of the bottle immediately he returned then? There was, I saw presently, a reason for that too. A quick-acting poison was certainly preferable to months in prison ending in the electric chair; therefore Haughton could quite understandably hold on to that vial a while longer. The following day, when Garlin and I found it, Haughton had not been sure. Then, assuming that Dunbar was right in his theory that Garlin had seen or found out something, Haughton saw he had to kill again. He had done so last night—with a gun. Whose gun I didn't know or care. . . .

It was all conjecture. All I knew was that Haughton could have killed both men and disposed of the poison sometime after Garlin and I found it. I knew, further, that I was getting jumpy. I could feel my nerves winding tighter and tighter and I remembered what the doctors had told me. I went to my room and picked up the play Marshall had wanted me to read. I'd never finished the first act but I sat down and read it right then.

I felt better when I got up. I wasn't really relaxed but I was all right and I thought of one more place to look for that vial. Only Garlin and I knew about it. Suppose Garlin had taken it after we'd come back from the Doctor's chapel?

It was worth a try and I went to Garlin's room and opened the door. I took two steps inside and stopped dead, and it was a good thing I took time out to do that reading. For sitting in the chair, his legs crossed and a cigar in his mouth, was old red-face Corrigan.

"Hi," he said. "Looking for something?"

So, I thought, *he searched the room. That's why Dunbar left him behind?* But all I could do was stare and back out.

"No," I gulped. "Wrong room."

When I got downstairs Linda Jordan was just coming out of the dining room and Haughton was still eating. Linda stopped in front of me. She wore a tweed skirt with a green pullover and cardigan and her face had a fresh, healthy glow that matched the sparkle in her eyes.

"Where were you yesterday afternoon and evening?" she asked.

"We went to Elmira," I said. "We got a little drunk."

"Oh." She pouted, though the smile remained in her glance. "I think you might have taken me."

I told her about George Vernon. I said it was a good thing we didn't or she'd have had to fight him off all the way home. She said something about being able to do that too, and then I was past and moving towards Haughton. I sat down next to him.

"I hear Dunbar was here earlier," he said. "Corrigan was snooping around too."

"Yeah," I said, and told him about Earl Garlin.

He stopped eating. He passed a hand over his thinning hair and the worried look was back on his angular face again. I told him Garlin had been shot and I gave him Dunbar's theory and then I got to what I had in mind.

"There's more," I said. "You can get it from Dunbar but the point now is this: I think I've covered up for you long enough."

He put his coffee cup down and turned slowly. He wet his lips and behind his horn-rimmed glasses his blue eyes were veiled, wary, so was his voice.

"In what way?"

"You were searching Johnny's room the night he was murdered," I said. "I nearly caught you at it, and I did see your glasses. Who else wears them?"

He shook his head and smiled but nothing changed in his eyes. "You're mistaken, Alan. I don't know about the glasses or what you saw—or think you saw—but I wasn't there."

"You came up here to get a contract from Johnny. You searched his room and you probably searched the study—somebody did. You were in the boathouse the night Linda and I surprised you." I paused and lied deliberately. "I recognized your voice."

He sighed. He took out cigarettes and offered them and when I refused he lit one.

"No," he said. "You couldn't have. I wasn't there."

His calm, complete denials irked me and I leaned closer.

"Also, you brought a bottle of oil of bitter almonds with you. Some hydrocyanic acid solution, at least. It was in your Gladstone bag."

He studied the ash on his cigarette and I said, "I think I've covered up enough. Dunbar will be getting tough. Right now I could be his number one suspect and Carol could be number two."

Mrs. Donelly came in with some bacon and scrambled eggs. He waited until she had gone.

"I don't know anything about oil of bitter almonds or any bottles. I'm sorry, but you're mistaken."

I watched him but he kept looking at his cigarette, turning it slowly in his fingers. Then I saw it was no good pressing the point about the poison. There was only one other witness to the fact and he was dead. I could argue all day with Dunbar but a simple denial from Haughton would make such arguments legally worthless.

"Okay," I said. "I just wanted you to know. I'm telling Dunbar about you searching Johnny's room, and about the boathouse." I remembered something else and threw it in with the rest of the bluff. "That time, after you'd locked Linda and me in, there was a splash. I think Dunbar will want to check over the bottom of the lake around the dock. I think he'd like to find the briefcase and the gun that were missing from the study desk."

Haughton pushed back his chair and stood up. "I'm sorry about

Garlin," he said. "It will probably make things more difficult for all of us."

He went out and left me there and since there was nothing more I could do, I ate my eggs and bacon.

17

ALTOGETHER it was a bad day. Dunbar and Corrigan stalked through the house that morning questioning us separately and together and I'm pretty sure he worked hardest on me. He gave it to me first right in front of everybody—with the idea, I suppose, that I might say something someone would refute—and when that did not give him what he wanted he got me in the study an hour or so later and went to work with Corrigan.

It's no fun trying to match wits with a good detective like Lieutenant Dunbar, not when you know he thinks he has a good chance of pinning two murders on you, not when every admission you make leads to other admissions you don't want to make and everything you say is twisted to get the meaning that he wants the statement to have. He was good, all right, and I think part of his success was due to his change in tactics. Up in the gorge he had been angry and threatening and blustery; now he was mild and patient and shrewdly confidential, like he had been that first day only more so.

Part of what I told him was my own idea—like my theory about Spence Haughton's searching Johnny's room and possibly the study; the rest of it he got out of me one way or another. I told him I thought Spence had thrown something into the lake after he'd locked us in the boathouse and somehow I mentioned the record in the sail loft and Dunbar sent Corrigan for it.

Then, little by little, it came out. I told him how Garlin and I had found the recording machine in the chapel and how we had gone to Elmira to hear the record. I told him about seeing someone hurrying from the gorge to Penzance's house a few minutes after I'd been shot at. When I got that far, Dunbar told Corrigan to send for Penzance and the Talmains, and after that I balked at just two things—how I'd got the record, and the story of the poison.

"Now just between the two of us," he said, "how did you get the record?"

He was leaning back in his chair, smoking, smiling faintly, sounding casually interested and pretty friendly. I wasn't having any. I'd seen him pounce on my statements too many times and I had the idea he'd toss me in jail in a minute if he thought it would help his case.

"How do you think?" I said.

He spread his hand. "You must have searched his library and taken it."

I smiled at him. This was the second time we'd gone over this and now he smiled back.

"You know people can be arrested for having stolen property in their possession," he said.

"So I understand."

"And Penzance is probably going to say this record was stolen."

You see what I mean? Now it was having stolen property in my possession, or breaking and entering—if only I'd admit it. I let the stolen property one ride.

"I'll worry about that when I have to," I said.

The poison was a little different. If, instead of letting Garlin handle this information, I had told Dunbar that first day I would have been all right; now I had nothing to back up my story. There was no poison and Haughton would certainly deny there ever had been. Furthermore the story I had already told was wild enough without complicating it with an unsubstantiated tale of poison. It sounded too much like something a man might dream up to throw suspicion away from him and I was afraid Dunbar might consider the reverse was true.

"You know you've done some pretty good work," he said while we were waiting for Penzance. "We could use a guy like you in our outfit."

"I'll bet," I said.

"What did you say was on this record?"

"I told you," I said. "A lot of questions and answers between Penzance and some woman."

"Why do you think he made it?"

I told him I hadn't the faintest idea, and because this casual, confidential act of his had me worried I thought of something else and asked him about it.

"Marshall's lawyer was up here yesterday," I said. "Does Mrs. Marshall get a third of the estate? Like you thought she might?"

He thought it over and the smile went away. "No," he said with some reluctance, "she doesn't."

I felt better. "How much does she get?"

He ground out his cigarette and pushed the ashtray away. "This Marshall thought of nearly everything," he said. "He added a codicil to his will the day he got married. She was to get a flat fifty thousand, or, if she contested it, nothing."

I felt a lot better. It was a relief to be able to feel a bit smug about something.

"That sort of cuts the props from under that motive you had for her, doesn't it?"

"Some of the props."

"It certainly doesn't help your theory that she and I cooked up a plot to knock him off and split the inheritance."

He waved one hand idly. "It isn't as good," he admitted. "But people have done murder for less than fifty grand. Also there is the question of whether Mrs. Marshall knew what was in the will. Quite obviously she didn't or she would have said so."

Just the same the room seemed brighter to me, and not only because Dunbar's theory about Carol had been weakened. There is something formidable about a woman with six million dollars; fifty thousand was something else. In good years I'd made half that much, so I didn't consider her what the papers call "an heiress," and more.

And then I thought of something else. "Did she sleep in with Linda Jordan last night?"

Dunbar pulled his nose and looked up through his brows.

"Last night and the night before."

"Then she's got an alibi," I said.

"Like hell she has. Neither of them have an alibi."

Gradually I got the story out of him. I don't know if the original idea had been male intuition, foresight, or pure fool luck on my part, but my suggestion of two nights ago helped. Carol had said she went to bed at the same time Linda did. She insisted she had not left the room at any time thereafter, nor had she heard Linda leave, enter, or even move around. Linda was just as positive. She had not gone out; she was sure Carol had not. She was a light sleeper normally and she did not think Carol could have dressed and left the room and returned later without waking her.

Dunbar wasn't happy about it. He had told them, and he told me now, that they had no alibi. Technically he was right, but he was also aware that what the girls had said would carry considerable weight with a jury. Carol's alibi wasn't perfect but it was good enough to cause doubt, a lot of doubt, and the thing that made me feel so good was that he had been unable to add anything damaging to the case he already had against Carol.

We were still talking about this when the door opened and Corrigan herded Penzance and the Talmains into the room. Dunbar stood up and waited until the woman was seated. He asked them if they had heard about the murder and they nodded. He said:

"There are a few questions I'd like to ask. First"—he picked up the record—"is this yours, Doctor?"

Penzance wore dark slacks and a silk sport shirt with half sleeves and a broad collar, open at the throat. You could see those powerful muscles in his chest and shoulders bulging against the soft fabric and some of the bronze coloring of his torso seemed to show through. His face was impassive, superior, and his dark eyes had about as much expression as two marbles.

"In case there is any doubt," Dunbar said when the Doctor hesitated, "we will assume that if your voice is on the recording the record is yours."

"Yes," Penzance said in his deep sonorous tone, "it is mine. May I ask where you got it?"

I waited to see Dunbar squirm but he fooled me. "We found it in the boathouse," he said. "How it got there, I don't know."

"I see," the Doctor said.

Dunbar pretended he was consulting his notes and I glanced at Mrs. Talmain. She wore another peasant dress, a blue one this time, so that there was only a hint of the magnificent figure beneath it. She held her head high and her olive skin was smooth and vital. She looked relaxed, composed, and there was no sign of worry in her glance; instead it seemed to me that her eyes were amused in a disdainful sort of way. Talmain, on the other hand, was like a lump in his chair. His black-browed scowl was a component part of his face and though he said nothing you had the idea that should such a thing be necessary the voice would be sullen and resentful.

"Do you have many of these records, Doctor?" Dunbar asked. And when Penzance hesitated, "You make them on that recording machine in the chapel, I suppose."

The Doctor cleared his throat softly. "Yes."

"And what is the purpose of these records?"

"They are made in strict confidence—"

"Naturally."

"—and for the purpose of showing the student the mirrors of his mind."

"Oh."

"When the records are played back, the student is able to trace his progress and growth, to know exactly the reason for certain reactions, to find the source for—shall we say, any complexes or phobias that may be bothering him."

He patted gently the thick mane of black hair and smiled indulgently. "It is difficult, Lieutenant, to explain to the layman. There are so many things involved. Many of those who come to me are troubled individuals—frequently sick in mind and body—and under my supervision we try to give the subconscious mind a chance."

"This supervision," Dunbar said dryly, "might consist of some form of hypnotism?"

"If you like to call it that. I prefer to call it—"

"Mental suggestion," Dunbar said.

"Thank you . . . yes. Of course this is only a part of the value of these individual recordings. You understand of course, that I am unable to be with many of my students more than a week or two a year. Some of them come great distances, and in the months when their studies are limited to letters and lessons by mail it is of tremendous help, as you can imagine, to be able to hear one's voice—and mine—and to remember certain truths, to hear revealed certain secrets of one's own inner self . . ."

He kept talking in that easy intimate way and I was taking it all in and liking it. Underneath it all you felt a subtle menace and yet there was a fascination too, that made you want him to go on. It wasn't what he said, which was pure hoke, it was the way he said it and that quality of voice or personality that had you practically believing it. I felt comfortable and rested and I rather resented it when Dunbar broke it up.

"All right," he said. "Very interesting."

He moved around in his chair and made a great show of consulting his notes again and when I saw the flush in his face I grinned. I was thinking that for a couple of minutes even old Dunbar might have been under the Doctor's spell.

"Right now," he said, "I'm more interested in what you were doing last night about one o'clock."

"I was in bed," Penzance said.

"No," said Dunbar.

"I beg your pardon."

"Around one o'clock or shortly after, you were down by the gorge. You were seen going home."

"By whom?"

I spoke up, figuring if Dunbar wanted to throw his bluff I'd go along. "By me," I said.

Penzance turned those depthless black eyes on me. He inspected me at length.

"You are mistaken," he said.

"No." I shook my head. "Furthermore, you weren't in bed. You were in a downstairs bedroom arguing with Mrs. Talmain."

For a long five seconds no one spoke; then there was a throaty sound on my left and I looked round and it was Talmain. He was sitting up, watching the woman through narrowed lids. She turned towards me, her full red mouth half smiling, half sullen.

"Yes," she said. "We were discussing plans for closing up the camp. That is why I know the Doctor could not have been at the gorge. There was much to talk about. Since eleven o'clock we talked."

"Hmm." Dunbar's look was deceptively sleepy. "And how about you, Talmain?"

The man seemed startled, so intent was he on the woman. "Me? I was also at the house. What they say is true."

"In other words," Dunbar said, "you two"—he glanced at the couple—"are prepared to swear to the Doctor's alibi?"

"Of course," the woman said.

"All right." Dunbar measured his words. "Let's see if you'll stick to that when we get around to that Chicago business."

He pulled that one out of the hat. I didn't know what he was talking about but I could tell he meant it. So, apparently, did the Talmains. The woman's smile was gone and there was a white-ness at her cheekbones that had not been there before. The man's stare wavered; he looked down at the hat he carried and began to turn it in his hands.

Penzance's voice was just the same. "Was there anything else, Lieutenant?" he asked.

The door opened before Dunbar could answer. Corrigan stepped over to see why and two women and a man were crowd-ing through and nothing Corrigan could do would stop them. The woman in front, a busty, solid-looking woman of forty or so, just pushed and Corrigan fell back sputtering, and the other two followed in her wake.

They marched up to the desk, the busty one flanked on one side by the tall, mahogany-skinned man I'd seen exercising the pre-vious day, and on the other by a straight standing, mannish woman who had several thousand dollars worth of rings on her fingers and a firm, pointed jaw.

"I'm Mrs. Mortimer Varden," the busty one said in loud tones.

"I—we represent the group now studying at the chapel, and we demand to know why you and your policemen should persecute Doctor Penzance and upset the privacy of our lives."

Dunbar blinked and got red in the face. He stood up and took a breath and tried hard to keep control of the situation.

"This is a murder investigation, madam," he said. "There is no question of persecution and if we have upset—"

"Exactly," said Mrs. Varden. "A murder investigation. Then why should you bother the Doctor at all? Do you have the temerity to infer that he—or Mr. and Mrs. Talmain—could have any possible connection with murder?"

"All we're trying to do right now is—"

"The Doctor's rights will be protected. Our rights will be protected. We will hire the best lawyer in the country . . ."

"A dozen lawyers if necessary," the mannish one added.

"All right," Dunbar said. "All right. Hire them. Call Washington . . ."

"We demand that he be released at once," Mrs. Varden cut in.

I started to move towards the door. No one paid any attention to me. I was going to laugh, and loud, in another minute and I didn't want to do it in front of Dunbar. I heard him say: "But madam, the Doctor is not even arrested," and then I was in the hall.

With the study door open you could still hear the strident tones of Mrs. Varden, and Dunbar's rising voice. Spence Haughton and Helen Bradford came into the hall to ask me what it was all about. I stopped laughing long enough to tell them the Doctor's flock was up in arms over the police investigation and then seeing Helen, I thought of something else. I left them in the living room doorway and went down to the boat house in search of Bert Donelly.

He was working with the varnish again, on the speedboat this time, and there was nothing in his manner to suggest that there had been a second murder. He took his empty pipe out of his mouth long enough to acknowledge my Good-morning and went on with his work. I asked him about the performance of the speedboat.

We talked intermittently for five minutes or so but what I was thinking of was the word I'd heard Douglas Eddington say last night, the word that was so familiar to me and yet so obscure. Valehaven.

"Do you know of a place around here called Valehaven?"

Bert waited until he varnished the corner of the coaming. "Yes," he said. "Seems like I do. Yes. 'Taint around here exactly but I know of it."

"What sort of place is it?"

"Well—kind of a place for crazy people."

I knew then. Even the words were clear and I could see the setting in Ned Yager's Elmira house after I'd shut off the record we had been listening to. And Kiley saying, "Anybody who'd buy that belongs in Valehaven."

I felt something tighten up inside me and a curious tingling ran along my nerve-ends. I realized I was holding my breath, that Bert Donelly was watching me. I made my voice interested but matter-of-fact, or tried to.

"You mean an insane asylum?"

"Not exactly." He grinned at me. He took off his sweat-stained hat and scratched his head. "Course I never been there, but from what I've heard tell it's more like a sanitarium."

"Oh," I said. "A private place."

"I guess so . . . Why?"

Why indeed? I told him I'd been in Elmira the day before and heard a couple of fellows arguing as to whether it was a State institution.

"Where is it from here?" I asked.

"Other side of Watkins Glen. Between there and Trumansburg, I think, just off that highway."

"Oh, yes. And about how far is that?"

He picked up his brush and went on with his work. "Can't tell you that either, not very close anyway. Ain't been over that way since they started to ration gas. Maybe forty miles more'r less."

I went back to the house and asked Helen Bradford if I could take the station wagon again.

18

IT was after two thirty before I could get away. From the middle of the morning until nearly two o'clock the highway was blocked with reporters and photographers now that the news of Garlin's murder was out. Dunbar and the district attorney could no longer pass the case off as another accident and when the police finally left while we were having lunch, the press followed them.

I had hoped to get away without being noticed and got as far as the garage before Linda Jordan came out of the house and headed my way.

"Where you going?"

"How'd you know I was going anyplace?"

She smiled. She arched her brows prettily.

"The way you walked out," she said. "I mean, you just looked as if you were going someplace special. You looked so grim, Alan. You still do, actually."

"I'm going to Bath," I said.

"Can I go?"

"No."

"Please?" she pouted good-naturedly. "I haven't been away from this house since we got here."

"No."

"You didn't take me yesterday. You went off and had fun. I should think you might at least—"

"Oh, all right." I was grumpy about it and my reluctance was ill-concealed. On purpose. I thought maybe she'd be offended and refuse, to show her displeasure. I hoped she'd say, "Oh, all right, if that's the way you feel about it, I'd rather stay home." Instead she uttered a delighted little cry and said, "Oh, wonderful. Wait till I get a coat."

I backed the station wagon out and she came running down the driveway with the coat slung over her shoulder. She climbed in and closed the door and she looked so completely content when we started off that I was ashamed of my boorishness; in fact, it was not long before I began to see that perhaps her coming along with me might be a good thing.

I didn't know what I was going to find at Valehaven, nor even what I expected to find, but I knew what I was going to try to do and I realized that Linda could help to dress up my act. To begin with she probably knew more about the affairs and history of Johnny Marshall and his sister than anyone else, now that Garlin was dead. She could supply information I might not be able to get otherwise, and I had not forgotten how she cried over Johnny's check nor what she said to me that first morning. I knew how she felt about Johnny and I was pretty sure she would do what she could to pay back for his death, just as I wanted to be sure that Carol and myself were cleared of suspicion—and quickly. So by the time we got to Hammondsport we were getting along so well that I felt I could tell her where we were going.

Her eyes got big and round when I told her the sort of place Valehaven was. "But why, Alan? I mean, why are we going there?"

"All I know," I said, "is that Helen and Eddington were talking about it around two this morning—out by the tennis court—and I'd like to find out why."

It was a perfect afternoon for a ride and even though I was doing a lot of thinking and talking I could see it was nice country, with the green hills and valleys and the leaves just beginning to turn on the maples and beeches. After we'd cut round the end of the lake we were on a secondary road that carried us through farm land that looked fertile and productive; at one point we had a lake on each side of us, and Linda was so impressed she dug a map out of the glove compartment and identified them.

"That one's Lake Waneta," she said, "and that one"—she pointed to the right—"is Lamoka."

Watkins Glen seemed like a good place to get further directions and while I got out at a gas station to ask an attendant, Linda skipped across the street to a drugstore to get cigarettes.

"How much farther?" she asked when she came back with cigarettes and a package of gum.

"About fifteen miles. Come on, get in," I said and gave her a slap on the fanny when she stooped.

She jumped unexpectedly and cried out. "Oww," she said.

"Oh-oh," I said. "Are you always that touchy?"

"No, you dope." Her annoyance vanished quickly and she tipped her head. "Only I have a boil there and you had to smack it . . . Don't you ever get in trouble doing that?"

"Not often." I grinned at her. "I only do it to girls I like."

"You'd better not let Carol catch you."

"I won't," I said, and then I didn't feel like grinning any more. . . .

We crossed south of the lake and started up the east side. Our road turned off the main highway and presently we started climbing. We drove through Burdett and Reynoldsville and then, just beyond Perry City, we came to a private road marked by two square stone gateposts. A metal plaque on one said: *Valehaven*. The road went straight across a field to a stand of hardwood and then circled gradually upwards for a quarter of a mile until we came to a clearing. There was another gate here, and a fence which ran round the clearing and its buildings. This gate had a watchman.

I asked him who was in charge and he said Doctor Gaylord. I said we would like to see him about one of his patients. I said the name was Bradford. He went into his little house and spoke briefly into a telephone. When he came out he motioned us on.

"That building on the right," he said.

The grounds inside the fence covered perhaps four acres and there were four rectangular two-story buildings of stone and stucco, one on each side of the central rectangle.

I stopped where the guard had told me to and as I did so I noticed a man with a fishpole in his hands sitting beside a round pool with a fountain in the center. He was an elderly fellow, very clean and neatly dressed. He was sitting on a canvas camp stool holding an expensive-looking bamboo bait-casting rod and dangling a line in the water. There was a big tackle box on the ground beside him and as I stepped closer I saw there was about six inches of water in the pool.

"Any luck?" I asked.

He turned and frowned at me. "Shhh," he cautioned. "You'll scare 'em."

"Sorry," I whispered back. "I forgot . . . Any luck?"

"The wind isn't right," he said. "It may swing when the sun goes down."

I heard steps behind me and when I turned a jut-jawed husky in a white suit was moving up and eyeing me suspiciously.

"Who do you want to see?" he asked.

"Doctor Gaylord."

"Didn't the guard tell you where to find him?"

"Why, no," Linda said. "Will you show us?"

The attendant looked at her, his suspicion tempered with approval. "This way," he said, and took us up the steps and across the porch to a reception room with ivory-colored walls and wicker furniture. On the left an office door stood open and the attendant spoke to a nurse who was busy at a desk.

"The man at the gate phoned about us," I said.

"Oh, yes." The nurse looked Linda over first and glanced at me. "Just a minute, please."

She opened a door behind the desk, closed it. When she came back a moment later she smiled. "Go right in," she said.

Doctor Gaylord was a slender, moderately tall man in his fifties with graying hair, pince-nez and a neatly-trimmed Vandyke. He rose, bowed and motioned us to chairs.

"I want to find out about a cousin of mine," I said. "She was a patient here some time ago, I think, and she has recently disappeared. I came here on the possibility that she might have come back, or been in touch with you."

Gaylord thought it over. He did not seem suspicious like the jut-jawed fellow but you knew he was sizing you up when you watched his eyes.

"The name you gave the gateman was Bradford," he said finally.

"Yes."

"We have had no one here by that name."

"I doubt very much she came here under her own name. Her first name was Helen but—" I broke off deliberately and reached into my pocket, offering silent blessings to Kiley, the *Star-Gazette* photographer, and the circumstances which brought him to Marshall's house and took me to Elmira. I took out the picture of Helen and me he had given me and unrolled it.

"This is my cousin," I said, "and myself. It's not the best likeness of course but I'm sure you can identify her if she's ever been under your care."

Gaylord accepted the picture but continued to look at me for a moment before unrolling it. When he finally gave the photograph his attention nothing changed in his face and I could feel my heart begin to pound.

Linda was leaning forward slightly now and I could almost see the tension holding her there, as it held me. Gaylord rolled up the picture and handed it back and still nothing changed in his face.

"We knew her as Helen Brainard," he said.

I tried to let my breath out easily. I leaned forward to take the picture and kept my eyes on it lest they reveal my thoughts. I took my time putting it back in my pocket. As part of the act I looked at Linda.

"I told you they'd be able to recognize her," I said.

"I know you did, dear," she said.

"She was brought here by a Doctor Gleason," Gaylord said. "With offices on Fifty-eighth Street in New York, as I remember."

"A big fellow?" I said. "Powerfully built, with dark eyes and a lot of thick black hair?"

"That's the man."

"Helen told us she was coming," Linda said. "She said that Doctor Gleason thought it would do her good. Of course, she never told us what the matter was nor how long she stayed—"

"It was about six months," Gaylord said.

I had to keep him going. I had to do some fishing and I took a chance. "She came voluntarily, didn't she?"

"Oh, yes."

"I don't know the ethics of such things, Doctor," I said, being properly hesitant, "but I wonder if you couldn't tell us what she was like as a patient. You see, we're pretty worried about her, and if you could give us some clue as to her behaviour it might possibly give us a lead in our search. She's been pretty much alone. She lost her husband shortly before she came here—"

"She told us."

Bullseye, I thought.

"She was never violent, was she?" Linda asked.

"Ah—not at first." Gaylord leaned back in his chair and built a steeple with his fingers and his manner was no longer quite so reluctant. "Doctor Gleason used to visit her once a week and for the first month or so she was a model patient. Later she did become somewhat violent. A most peculiar case really. She was definitely not a paranoiac, in the usually accepted sense; there was no consistent manic depressive psychosis apparent, nor could I say that she had the schizophrenia that one associates with dementia praecox. It was most puzzling because her behavior followed no set pattern.

He went on. "As I remember she had some complex about mistaken identity. One day she'd insist that her name was not Helen Brainard, but Helen Marshall, and then again she would tell us her name was Helen Bradford. As often happens there were times when the persecution complex manifested itself in other ways, such as her insistence that she had been tricked into coming here and that she was victim of some strange hypnosis. At times she could not even recognize Doctor Gleason. She called him all sorts of strange names. I don't remember them now but one always reminded me of a Gilbert and Sullivan opera."

I almost said, "The Pirates of Penzance." That near-slip scared me and I changed the subject fast. I asked him how long the condition lasted.

"Well—Doctor Gleason seemed to have an excellent effect on her even when she was at her worst. After he left she might be all right for a day or so and then it would break out again and she would be screaming at her attendants. But—well, I should say that at the end of three months there was a definite improvement, and she continued to improve steadily."

"Whose job was it, Doctor," I asked, "to say how long she should stay?"

"Oh, Doctor Gleason's. This is a private institution, you understand, and he could at any time have her removed." He allowed himself a smile. "Naturally there was a period when there would have been no point in removing her unless Gleason was dissatisfied with us. A woman in that condition needed expert attention and care and if it was not here, it would have to be in some similar institution. When she began to improve it became just a question of time. When Doctor Gleason thought it wise—and we agreed that she seemed quite normal at the time—he took her away."

I nodded and looked impressed. I was plenty impressed, actually, but not in any way the Doctor could understand. I was impressed by a guy named Penzance and the terror and the frightfulness of the ordeal that Helen Bradford had suffered.

"It's very good of you to tell us this," I said.

"Yes," Linda said. "We do appreciate it."

"If only we could get a few more definite details," I said. "Perhaps we could talk with the doctors who were closest to her here. I mean, as the head of Valehaven, you wouldn't know her idiosyncrasies as well as a man who had daily contact with her. Perhaps—"

"Unfortunately," Gaylord said, "the two men who had most to do with your cousin are now helping out in the battle zones."

"Then possibly there would be something in the records," I said.

The Doctor's smile went away. He looked grave, a little puzzled, and I wondered if I had pulled a boner.

"I'm sorry," he said. "There are no records."

He must have seen my surprise because he went on hurriedly.

"Oh, we keep records, of course. Naturally. Extremely detailed and complete records. But in the case of your cousin—" He broke off and looked embarrassed. "It must have been someone here," he said. "We try to be most careful of our patients but now and then one of them will perpetrate some bit of deviltry that is entirely new to his behavior pattern and then we have trouble. I say it must have been some one on the grounds because I have never been able to see how an outsider would have any interest in such clinical material."

I should have seen it coming but I didn't. I had the feeling something was strangely wrong but my brain told me nothing so I sat there waiting for him to finish.

"You see," he said. "A few months ago Miss Hennig—the nurse you met outside—discovered that the records of five of our patients were missing . . . Helen Brainard's was one of them."

I didn't say anything to Linda until we were back on the highway leading to Watkins Glen. It took me that long even to want to talk. The enormity of our discovery held all my interest and I had to go back over each point of Doctor Gaylord's story before I was ready for anything else.

"Did Johnny hire someone to swipe that folder?" I said finally.

"No," Linda said.

"How do you know?"

"I—just do. I would have known somehow. Last October Helen was supposed to have gone to New Mexico. She must have come here. But Johnny didn't know. Don't you see? This was just the sort of thing he was trying to prove. If he had known he could immediately have proved that she was incompetent."

"He asked her on this trip. He told her she'd better bring her lawyer."

"It was something about her connection with Penzance," Linda said. "He hoped to prove she was incompetent, or to force an accounting but— No, I'm sure he didn't know."

I watched the road and my thoughts were pounding.

"Then it was Penzance."

"But why? He already knew she'd been here. He was the one who brought her."

"That's not the same as having the records."

She put her head back against the seat and when she spoke again her eyes were closed.

"How could he do it?" she said dully. "How could he make Helen agree? He couldn't keep her hypnotized that long."

"He wouldn't have to. I don't believe she was hypnotized. She'd lost her husband and she was emotionally upset and she turned to him and he helped her, or she thought he did. Stay around him very long and listen to him talk and he could convince you of almost anything. He must have convinced her that a rest in this place would be good for her, and once he got her to go voluntarily, under an assumed name, and maybe sign the necessary papers, he could do as he liked."

"You don't think Gaylord was in on it?"

I considered this. "No," I said. "Penzance said he was Doctor Gleason and gave some Fifty-eighth Street address. Maybe there is a Doctor Gleason at that address—in case Gaylord looked it up in a directory—but the thing is, Penzance said he would stop in every week. Often enough so Gaylord would never have to call him. Hell," I said, "I'm only guessing. We don't know what sort of story Penzance gave Gaylord but it must have been a good one because the way he acted today—unless he *was* acting —shows he believed what Penzance told him."

"And now," Linda said, "someone has a folder with all of the records. . ."

We stopped in Watkins Glen for a drink. It was dark when we came out of the tavern and I drove along until, somewhere beyond the two lakes we'd passed, I noticed a place on the side of the road that had a neon sign. When I saw it said: *Wines and Liquors,* I turned in.

Linda didn't offer a thing. She got out of the car and we went into this place. There was a small bar and booths along one wall and at the end, a tiny dance floor and a big juke box. There were three men at the bar and about a third of the booths were occupied. I ordered two old-fashioneds at the bar and carried them over to the booth Linda had picked.

We drank them and I got two more. When I came back Linda had a greasy menu in her hand. I asked her if she wanted to eat here and she said we might as well, we'd be late getting back anyway.

A girl came to take our order. She said the pot roast was good. There was no steak or chicken tonight. There was pot roast, roast pork, vegetable plate and lamb stew. We took the pot roast and had a bottle of beer with it.

We didn't talk much. I'd never seen Linda this way before. There was no sparkle in her eyes, no enthusiasm in her voice. It was listless, subdued, like her spirits. I suppose I was no better. I couldn't seem to think about anything but Helen Bradford and what Penzance had done to her. And yet I didn't want to talk any more about it. I wanted to get out of this place but I didn't want to make the effort.

Maybe the pot roast helped Linda. When we had finished our

coffee she put her hand palm-up on the table and said, "Have you any change?"

I dug down and showed her what I had and she picked out a quarter and went over to the juke box. She took her time making her selections and when she came back the thing was booming. A couple got up to dance and then another. Linda looked at me.

"Dance with me, Alan."

I danced with her. My leg bothered me a little and I had to stick to fundamental steps but with Linda it did not matter. Her body felt firm and rounded in my arms and her auburn hair was soft against my chin. I remembered the spilled perfume I'd smelled on the train because it was here again. I liked it much better now; it seemed just right for Linda.

We danced two numbers and went back to the booth. I asked her if she wanted another drink before we left and she said she guessed not. I was looking for the waitress when a man and woman passed the booth, going towards the back of the room. The man was swart and stocky, the woman taller, with straight black hair worn in a bun at the nape of her neck, and nice legs.

I glanced at Linda. She was staring vacantly out past the bar and I covered her hand with mine.

"Did you see them?"

Her eyes came back to mine. "Who?"

"The Talmains. They just walked past our booth."

"Oh?" Linda looked as though she wasn't sure just who the Talmains were for a moment; then she said, "Oh," again, with interest. She started to peek around the corner of the booth but I stopped her.

"Wait a second," I said.

I was facing the rear and by sliding over slightly on the seat I could see the corner booth and that was where the Talmains were. Already they were ordering from the waitress and when she went away Mrs. Talmain began to talk.

From the way her attention was centered on the man beside her I knew she had not seen us. So I nodded to Linda and she had a look. "Well, what do you know?" she said. "The Brotherhood of Horus is slipping."

The waitress came back with a highball for Mrs. Talmain and straight whisky for the man. He called the waitress back as she turned away, tossed off the drink and apparently ordered another. When it came he let it stay on the table. He watched it, his dark face scowling and truculent, and listened to the woman.

She sat close to him. She had her hand up under his upper arm and occasionally she would shake it slightly to accent some point or demand some answer. Whatever she was saying she was obviously oblivious of her surroundings, and the intensity of her manner suggested she was trying to sell something important.

We watched them fifteen minutes and nothing else happened. "Shall we go?" Linda said. I got the check and paid it. We stood up and went out without looking back. I don't know whether the Talmains saw us or not.

It was after ten when we came into the Marshall living room and found a bridge game going; Carol and Eddington playing Helen and Spence.

Immediately she saw me Carol became interested in getting a cigarette out of a case and lighting it. But that first glance took in me and Linda and I could see the eyes get stony and the softness leave her mouth.

"Well," Helen said, "what've you two been up to?"

Her voice was pleasant and she was smiling and because of that her classic beauty was softened and lovely to see. Linda said something about having dinner down the road and then something came over me that said I couldn't let it go at that.

I was angry with Carol. The way she was acting I had no hope of ever getting anything more than a civil answer from her, and yet I knew she was no murderess. I remembered what Dunbar had said that morning he announced Marshall's death was no accident. I still had my money on Penzance but I could be wrong. One of us might easily be the killer and you couldn't cover up for people, not if you expected to clear yourself—and Carol. I felt like hell but I had to do it, to find out if I could what would come next.

"Yes," I said. "We took a ride over beyond Watkins Glen. We stopped at a place called Valehaven."

19

AT first when I opened my eyes I thought I had not been asleep. It seemed as though I had been lying there for hours trying to sleep and had never quite dropped off. I turned on my back and stared up through the darkness, conscious now of a certain heaviness in my body, a thickness in my brain. I felt lazy, drugged, and it was such a familiar feeling that I knew finally that I had been asleep, that something had wakened me.

I wondered what it was. A truck going past the window, perhaps, or some restlessness on my part. My mind began to clear as I thought of this and I was annoyed now because I was afraid it might be hours before I dropped off again.

I closed my eyes and tried to relax and breathe lightly and then suddenly I realized that I was not trying to go to sleep. With no conscious thought on my part I was listening, holding my breath and listening.

My eyes came open and some odd inner chill began to spread through my body. I lay perfectly still, feeling the urge of some instinctive warning that I could not explain. At first there was nothing but the pulsing of blood at my temples and then I thought I heard something and listened again, my nerves tightening and every sense alert.

I tried to tell myself it was nothing but imagination but I could not stop listening nor could I deny this instinctive warning, this premonition of impending danger. Finally I heard the sound again, some shadow of a sound, a faint, softly brushing bit of movement; then I knew that I had been awakened not by some sound out on the road but by something inside this room.

Very slowly, still telling myself I was crazy, I slid my hands from under the covers. I began to lift my head, feeling the strain in my neck as I held it off the pillow. The room was dark. The moon, if there was one, was on the far side of the house and only by the windows was there any relief from the blackness.

Here the sky beyond was dark blue and I could make out the curtains, the shades. The windows themselves were as I had left them and when I saw there was nothing here I let my straining eyes move on until, between me and the door, I saw some vague form which had no size nor shape and might have passed unnoticed had it not been lighter than the shadows.

Somewhere in the room I heard the sound of breathing and I listened and it was not my own. It came from the direction of this thing I had seen near the door and now, staring as hard as I could, I saw it move and knew at last that someone had opened my door and closed it and was moving quietly towards the bed.

I stifled the impulse to cry out. I was scared but I was not panicky and, curious as it may seem, there was time for me to realize this, to feel good about it. Surprise was what I wanted now and I slid one leg to the edge of the bed and then out from under the covers so when I finally threw them back and leaped out I'd have something to stand on.

I waited until that slowly moving form was nearly to the foot of the bed. I still could not identify it but it did not matter now. I took a breath and in one continuous movement threw back the sheet and bounced to my feet. I took one fast step, arms outstretched, hearing the sudden gasp, the hushed and frightened voice.

"*Alan!*"

I couldn't stop. I knew who it was now, but I was moving too fast. I bumped into her and for a moment as I grabbed her arms above the elbows to steady myself my body was hard against her.

"Helen." I stepped back, still holding her arms. "Good Lord! Do you know what you're doing? You scared the hell out of me."

It was the reaction. Such overwhelming relief brought anger. I wanted to shake her to let her know just how badly I had been scared. I heard her breath come out in a long sigh. She stood perfectly still and then I could feel her begin to tremble. I let go of her arms. My anger went away when I realized what I must have done to her.

"What is it, Helen?" I said. "What's wrong?"

"I'm sorry," she said, her voice nothing more than a whisper. "I—I had to talk to you."

"Oh."

"I was afraid to knock. I thought if I could come in quietly and wake you up it would be all right and no one would know I was here."

I could see more clearly now. She wore a soft satin robe, open at the throat, and her hair framed darkly the oval of her face. My hand trembled as I took her arm again, gently this time, to lead her to a Boston rocker that stood a few feet from the bed.

"Here," I said. "Sit down, Helen. I'm sorry I frightened you.

You must have wakened me when you closed the door but I didn't know who it was and—"

"I know. I was afraid but I didn't know what else to do."

She sat down and I felt around for my robe. I belted it around me and thought about the bedside light. When I reached for it she stopped me.

"Couldn't we—I mean, wouldn't it be better—"

"I guess you're right," I said. I found cigarettes and my lighter and sat down on the foot of the bed.

I think I knew what was coming. I'd watched her face when I made my announcement in the living room. I'd seen Eddington too. No one questioned me then and I supposed Carol thought Valehaven was some nightclub. But I knew Helen and Eddington couldn't let it go; only I expected them to wait until morning. Helen was silent until I had my cigarette going.

"How did you know, Alan?"

"About Valehaven?"

"How *could* you have known?"

"I heard you last night. I heard something Eddington said, to you," I said, and told her how I had come down from the hill and stepped into the lilac bushes when I saw them coming from the tennis court.

"But you couldn't have known what it was then."

So I told her about Kiley and my questioning of Bert Donelly. And then I realized I'd have to tell her why I had reason to wonder about her in the first place. I said I knew what her brother had been trying to do.

"Yes," she said. "He's been trying for a long time." She paused and I wanted her to go on in her own way, so I waited. "No matter how much money he had, he wanted to control more. By the terms of Dad's will I received as much as Johnny and I don't think he liked it. I don't know why but from the things he did I'm sure he must have felt that way. He had control of my share until I was twenty-five. He wanted me to sign some things that would have continued that control. I wouldn't do it. By then I wouldn't do anything that would give Johnny any satisfaction."

She put her head against the back of the chair and stared up through the darkness. "I don't know what changed him. Until after Dad died and Johnny came into the money he seemed— well, like any brother, I suppose. I was never so very close to him but he was never mean. Even Carol can tell you the sort of boy he was when he was in college."

I heard her voice drone softly on. Somewhere out on the highway I heard a car. I heard it go past the house and suddenly I didn't hear it any more and wondered if it had stopped. Then I had forgotten it and was sitting up straight and feeling the sudden pounding of my heart.

"What did you say?"

She stopped and looked at me.

"About Carol?" I said. "What about Carol and Johnny?"

"I said she could tell you that Johnny wasn't always this way."

I wondered if I could be hearing right. I looked at her another moment, still holding my breath.

"When did Carol know him? How?"

"Why—when she was nine and ten. When Johnny was in his last two years of college. Her grandfather was the caretaker on Dad's Long Island place. I thought you knew."

I hadn't known. All I knew was that Carol's father was a school teacher in some upstate town and that she had come to New York to be an actress. She'd worked on some shows at American Broadcasting and that was how I met her. Now Helen was telling me how Johnny Marshall, at twenty-one had taken a fancy to this child who had come to spend the summer with her grandfather. He had taken her riding and bought her ice cream cones and teased her and it was all so new and wonderful to Carol that she tagged after him like a grateful puppy.

"I wasn't there the first summer," Helen said. "I was with my Aunt, but the second summer I knew Carol. Once in awhile we would play together—I was three years older and at that age felt so superior we were never really good friends—but I knew what she thought of Johnny."

I listened, incredulous, yet so utterly relieved that I wanted to hug Helen. I wanted to jump up and shout and find Carol and make her tell me the rest of it. There was enough now to understand that Carol's marriage to Johnny was not the thirty-day affair it appeared to be. It was this belief—that Carol had married a man she hardly knew—which had so embittered me and now, to know that I had been wrong, was so exciting that I had a hard time sitting still. I wanted to hear the rest of it, to question Helen and keep her talking about Carol; then, as she went on, I saw that what I wanted must wait. I forced myself to remember that for now there was something more important, that there was still a murder to be solved.

"That's why it was so hard to understand the change that came over Johnny," she said. "Dad died when Johnny was twenty-four. I was in school. I seldom saw him during the next two years, but each time I did there would be a little more of the dictator in him. There was an arrogance beneath the charm, and suspicion, now that he had the responsibilities of that fortune."

She went on in the same wooden tone. "He wasn't a brother any more, he was a guardian and not a pleasant one. He didn't like the boys I liked and always he would find some way to make them stop coming to see me. Once I tried to run away and he threatened to have me put in some home."

She said, "He would have done it too. He could have found ways to make people testify to whatever he wanted to prove. He had the money and influence, and I was dependent on him then and—well, I suppose I was too young, too weak really, to know what to do about it. It was all right for him to chase around with chorus girls and marry whom he liked and get divorces and pay alimony. But always he could think up some scheme to prevent me from doing what I wanted to. The men I liked were all fortune hunters, or their families weren't good enough, or they had no prospects. . ."

There was more of this and as I sat there listening to her quiet monotone I wanted to believe her. It sounded fantastic until you remembered Johnny Marshall and thought of that mean sadistic streak. The way he had tricked me into coming on his honeymoon, his contract with Spence Haughton, his determination to ruin Penzance and his belief he could prove Helen incompetent—all these things bore out the story she told me now.

"It was different when I came into my share of the estate," she said. "Different at least in that I had something to fight him with now. He tried every way he could to make me sign over the control to him; he tried to break up my marriage to Larry Bradford but that was one thing he could not do . . . We had four months together before Larry went to sea. And then he was lost. . ."

Her voice trailed off in a small choking sound. I put my cigarette out and took plenty of time doing it. I didn't say anything. I knew there was more and I waited until she was ready.

"I told you I was weak. I was. It seemed for a while as if I could not possibly bear it. I think I was a little afraid that I *was* losing my mind. Perhaps it seems strange that I could be lonely, that anyone could have my background and advantages and money and be lonely. But it was true. I had no real friends and I knew finally that there had to be someone to talk to, that could understand and tell me what to do.

"I knew of Doctor Penzance. I went to him, I think, because I was desperate, not really believing he could help but simply because I could not think of anyone else. Well, he did help. He gave me things to read and study and talked to me once a day. Johnny didn't know anything about it and I spent most of last summer here alone, and the Doctor did help. He was kind, and while I couldn't believe all the things he wanted me to, I—I trusted him."

That part was not difficult to believe. I'd heard the Doc enough to imagine what he could do with the right sort of prospect and Helen was in the proper emotional state to make her pliable and grateful for almost any sort of understanding.

"You gave him the money for the chapel," I said.

"Yes. When I first went to him he told me there would be no fixed fee. When I finished, if I thought he had helped me, I could do whatever I thought was right. At the end of the season I asked him what I should do and he told me about the chapel he wanted to build. He told me how important it was to him and to the others who like myself came to him for help. He said whatever I would like to pay to help in its construction would be all right."

"So you gave him the whole works," I said. Just thinking of the way Penzance had sold his proposition made me angry. "Of all the ways he might have handled you, he chose the one that would pay off the best. He made you grateful—"

"But I *was* grateful."

"I know," I said and I was still angry because the Doctor was so clever. "What about Valehaven?"

"I left here in August," she said. "I wanted to do something

for the war effort. I found there was a large estate for sale—
John Granvill's place—for taxes. It was next to ours on Long
Island. So I bought it and made it into a home for wounded
merchant seamen."

"Oh."

"Johnny was furious. He said it would ruin our own place
. . . That may have been what started him to checking up because no one could ever hurt Johnny—even an imaginary hurt
—without him getting vindictive about it. But it didn't matter
then. For two months I hardly left the home. I worked with
the nurses and helped to entertain the men and I guess I over-
did it. I had a breakdown and my doctors told me I had to get
away. I needed rest and a change."

"So you went back to Penzance?"

She looked at me and said, "Yes. In Westchester. I intended
to talk with him awhile and see what he advised. He told me to
come back in a few days and when I did he told me about Valehaven."

"You didn't know it was for mental cases?"

"I thought it was a rest home."

She was silent for a moment and I watched her. The darkness did not seem so thick now and I could see the fine line of
her cheeks and her mouth, the darker pools of her eyes, the warm
column of her throat that lost itself in swelling roundness in the
V of her robe.

"Did he hypnotize you into going?"

"No."

"Did he ever hypnotize you?"

"He may have at times during last summer. I— I think he did."

I thought I knew the rest of it but I had to be sure. "He talked
you into using an assumed name, and took one himself, because
that way you could not be traced."

"I had told him about Johnny. It seemed best."

So then I told her what Doctor Gaylord had told me. How she acted, how she tried to get him to believe the truth.

"Yes," she said. "I suppose I was what you'd call violent when I realized what had happened and what Penzance was doing. But he had planned so well there was nothing I could say that anyone would listen to. They simply considered me what Penzance had told them I was—a mental case. When I saw it was hopeless I did what he told me. He said I would not be released until it seemed that I was cured. He promised that when three months passed in which I made no trouble he would take me out . . . I was there nearly six months altogether."

"When did he start to collect?"

"How did you know?"

"Why else would he spend all that time and effort on you? Why would he dream up such a plot?"

"I had been out about a week when I had a telephone call from him. He asked me for ten thousand dollars—as his fee. I sent him a check."

I said that wasn't very smart, that even though she now had the cancelled check, that check could have been photographed.

"A month later," she said, "he telephoned again. This time I went to see him. You see, by then Johnny was doing what he could to show I was incompetent and all Doctor Penzance had to do was tell him where I'd been a patient."

"He stole the records," I said.

"Yes," Helen said and now her voice was spent and weary and I had to lean close to hear at all. "That was because Penzance knew that Johnny also had detectives checking up on him. He'd found out about the chapel some way and he suspected there was something wrong. And I think Penzance was afraid.

I don't know why, or what else he had done, but he seemed to think that Johnny could eventually break his lease. He said in that case he would be ruined and that to offset this possibility he must have more money. He said he'd give me the Valehaven records for one hundred thousand dollars."

"If he gave, or sold, them to Johnny you would have lost control of your estate?"

"Yes."

"But now," I said, "Johnny's dead."

"I—I would still lose control." She turned in the chair so that her knees were inches from mine. She put her elbows on them and leaned towards me. "Dad's will covered that. He had a rich man's fear of having his fortune dissipated. We were to use our money wisely or lose control. There are two trustees who have the power to judge what shall be done."

I thought it over, remembering the snatch of conversation I'd heard the night before.

"That's what Eddington meant when he said, 'I think you should still pay if you have to.' He knows all about it."

"Yes."

"But he knows Penzance framed you."

"He says under the circumstances it might not make much difference. I was at Valehaven and they know there how I acted. The rest is only my word against Penzance's. So—when Johnny told me I'd better come along I brought the money with me . . . You see, I must have those records."

I just stared at her. "You brought a hundred thousand—in cash?"

"Fifty thousand. I hoped to—well, I hoped to bargain with him. Even fifty thousand will be hard to account for; a hundred thousand . . ."

She broke off and I sat there trying to digest what I had

heard. Having already been to Valehaven, nothing she told me about that phase of her life was any surprise. If she had been weak it was because she had accepted early the domination of her brother; she had lost tragically the man she loved and she had suffered emotionally more than her share.

The things that Johnny had done to her and his persecution of her rights were understandable, if you knew Johnny. That he had done worse things to her than she admitted, I was sure; I also saw that no matter what she said now she had a very excellent motive for murder. I didn't want to believe it, but the facts were there. She still feared the information Penzance had, but it was Johnny who had been behind most of her troubles.

I kept on figuring until I came again to Eddington. I remembered the fleeting suspicion I'd had, the theory that came to me before. Eddington was interested in what happened to Helen and, indirectly, to himself. If an accounting had to be made of this estate he handled he would be responsible for any shortages. What I had to do now was check on train times and be sure he could not have been here that first night . . ."

I don't know just when I first became conscious that the room was getting colder. There was a draft playing around my ankles where none had been before. I looked at the window and for a moment the curtains at the bottom bellied outward in the opening.

Outward, I thought, and glanced quickly at the door, and there was no door there, but only a yawning blackness in the frame. I came to my feet and the creaking of the bed was a loud and fearful noise. Helen sat up, startled by the suddenness of my reaction.

"Alan," she breathed. "What—is it?"

Something moved against the blackness of the open doorway and the tension hit me hard. The draft on my ankles moved swiftly up my legs and now it spread along my back and I could not look at Helen or even answer her.

I reached back of me, feeling for the bedside lamp, knowing that someone had opened the door and stood listening, waiting. I didn't reach the lamp. A hoarse voice, quietly violent, said: "Don't move!"

20

I DOUBT very much if I could have moved if I had wanted to. But Helen did. She jumped up and faced the door and she was closer and must have seen more clearly. Her little cry was a tortured, frightened whisper and one hand flew to her throat, gathering tightly the collar of the robe.

"Stand where you are," the voice said again and now I could see the door begin to close. I heard its soft click, the familiar sullen cadence of that voice. It rang a gong somewhere inside my head and I remembered it before the man crossed to the windows and pulled down the shades.

"All right," he said, "you can put on the light."

I put it on but I could not see until I had blinked back the brightness and let my eyes adjust themselves. He was standing by the windows, a squat, dark figure with an ugly-looking automatic in his hand. He seemed to be figuring out what came next.

"Oh," Helen said weakly. "Oh . . . Mr. Talmain."

He was motionless as we were. His swart face was like a leather mask but the eyes were bloodshot when he opened them against the light. Faintly the smell of liquor reached across to me and then I remembered the car I had heard. That seemed hours ago until I tried to measure what had happened since

then. Probably about twenty minutes, I thought, and this thinking helped me. The stiffness in my back and legs went away.
I tried to make my voice casual.

"You were in that car I heard," I said. "It stopped down the
road."

"Keep your voice down," Talmain warned huskily. "Keep it
quiet and you won't get hurt."

Helen still held the collar of her robe and she had backed up
until now she stood almost beside me. I glanced at her and
though her cheeks were pale, she no longer seemed afraid.

"You're a little drunk, aren't you, Talmain?" I said. "Why
don't you shove off before you get in trouble? How'd you get
in here anyway?"

"From the terrace," he said. "Those French doors were a
cinch . . . Don't get the idea I'm too drunk to handle you."

I didn't know what the score was, but I knew it wouldn't do
any harm to keep him talking—if I could.

"Who were you looking for?"

"Her." He waved the gun towards Helen.

"How'd you expect to find her in the dark? Penzance tell
you which room she had?"

"I found out."

"Oh—he sent you, huh?"

"Nobody sent me. I went to her room and nobody was there
and I came down the hall and heard someone talking. But
there wasn't any light showing so—"

"So you had a look."

He watched Helen a moment and his hand went to the pocket
of his topcoat. I saw then that he had a manila folder which had
been folded again lengthwise. It looked bulky. He tapped it.

"Do you want this?"

"What is it?" Helen asked.

"You know what it is."

She took a step forward. "May—I see it?"

"Sure." Talmain pulled the folder out and offered it to her. "Go ahead. Take a look. And don't get the idea you can try anything funny."

Helen took the folder and sat down in the rocker. The cover was crammed with papers and her hands shook as she started to leaf through them. While she looked, I watched Talmain, wondering how many steps it would take me to reach him. He still held the gun, but carelessly now and he had backed to the windows again. I decided it was too far unless I could work a lot closer. Maybe five long steps in all. I took one of them by pretending to glance over Helen's shoulder.

She spent three or four minutes with that folder, until Talmain said, impatiently, "Well, what about it? It's all there."

She looked up at him. She moistened her lips. It seemed to take quite an effort for her to speak.

"Yes," she said.

"The Doc wanted a hundred grand. He told you to bring it." Talmain waited. When she did not reply he said, "I'm selling it to you for half price. For fifty thousand it's yours."

I watched her and right then I saw she was going to say yes. I could see her lips start to form the word and then I spoke up.

"Wait a minute!"

He let his lids come down. "You stay out of it."

"I'm already in," I said. "You swiped that folder from Penzance."

I thought he was going to deny it; instead he said, "Okay, so I swiped it. What difference does that make? She wants the records and—"

"Oh, yes," Helen said.

Talmain almost grinned. "Well, there they are."

"Not for fifty thousand," I told him. "To Penzance maybe. He's the one that figured it out and stole them from Valehaven."

"No," Talmain said. "I stole them . . . Me and Della."

"Della? So that's her name." I was thinking fast now. About this woman whose first name I had never heard before, of the scene in the roadside tavern earlier and the steady aggressive way she had talked to Talmain. And remembering the latent power her personality suggested, and that striking face and figure, I knew why Talmain was here. "So she's the one who sent you," I said.

Talmain's brows bent. "Listen," he said.

"You listen." I don't know why I argued. It wasn't my money, nor hardly any of my business. "Those things might have been worth fifty thousand when Penzance was the only one that knew what was in that folder; now it's different. He knows and you know and I know. It's not exclusive stuff any more."

Helen stood up. "Please, Alan—"

I ignored her. I said, "Ten thousand or nothing, Talmain."

"Ten thousand?" He choked a little on the word.

"And no argument," I said. "You can have the cash right now, or you can take your records back to Penzance."

He took a step and the gun came up. For some reason it didn't scare me. I told him so. I said waving that automatic around wouldn't get him the money.

"Make up your mind," I said, "before people start waking up. If you get caught here all you'll get is a couple of years in the clink and—"

"Shut up!"

I had him going and I rode my advantage. "Get the money, Helen," I said. "Ten thousand. Don't let anybody hear you. We'll wait."

She hesitated, then stepped out bravely, the folder still in her hand.

"Leave it," Talmain said.

"Nuts," I said. "And have you hold us up again? She'll bring the money, just to get rid of you. Go ahead, Helen."

Talmain turned and watched her open the door. I thought he was going to say something so I said:

"Shhh."

He was getting the habit of obeying. He watched the door close and not until then did he get angry. He started my way, switching the gun so he could club it.

"All right, you smart bastard," he said. "You loused this up for me—"

I reached for the carafe on the bedside table.

"Go ahead," I said. "Make a lot of noise."

He stopped.

"You're getting ten thousand and you're getting away with it. If you really want to get caught, start something."

I grinned at him and let go of the carafe. "Della," I said. "She's nice. Whose woman is she, anyway?"

"She's my wife."

"That wasn't the question."

"We know what we're doing."

The door opened quietly before I could say anything more. Helen came in with the money and Talmain counted it. "Just stay quiet," he said, and went out.

We stood there watching the closed door for quite awhile. Finally Helen turned. "Thank you, Alan," she said. She took a step and then seemed to stagger slightly. She reached for the bedpost and clung to it to steady herself and I stepped to her side and slid an arm about her waist.

"Easy," I said. "It's over now."

I could feel her tremble, the shaky sound of her breathing. I led her to the chair and eased her into it. I got cigarettes and matches and this time she took one.

We sat smoking until we heard the car start. When the sound of the motor faded into silence, Helen rose.

"You'd better burn those papers before you go to bed," I said.

"Yes."

She wasn't afraid any more and when I opened the door she moved quickly, surely, down the hall. Under the nightlight at the head of the stairs she looked tall and graceful and confident.

21

I awoke late, thinking of Carol and what Helen Bradford had told me. I bathed and dressed hurriedly, all the things I had to say on the tip of my tongue, and then when I got downstairs I found she had gone to Bath to sign some papers that had to do with Johnny's estate.

It was awhile before I remembered Eddington. In fact I didn't remember him until I saw him on the terrace with Helen, and when I saw how pink and plump and self-satisfied he seemed I went to the telephone and got the station agent in Bath. I wrote down what he told me and took the paper into the study.

According to Eddington, he had taken a train from Hoboken at 1:05 of the night Marshall was murdered, arriving in Bath at around ten the next morning. He could just as easily have left Hoboken at 9:20 of the morning we arrived at Bath. He could have arrived at Bath at 4:46, and if he had had murder in mind he could have left the train at Elmira at 3:55, hired a car to bring him up to Marshall's place that night, murdered Johnny and driven back to Elmira, staying overnight at a hotel. Then when the train he *said* he took came through at 8:45, he could have climbed on and got to Bath when he said he did.

It was such good information it excited me and I went to the telephone again and called the Elmira *Star-Gazette*. When I got Kiley I asked him to check the hotels for me and see if anyone by the name of Eddington had registered there the night of the 14th. I had to admit that if Eddington had done this he would probably have used another name, but at least I had to try.

It was around eleven o'clock when I finished with this, and because I wanted to do some more thinking, I went down the road to the bridge and hung over the railing watching the tumbling stream. Presently a car came along behind me and stopped just beyond. When I turned I saw it was a taxi, and George Vernon was leaning out the window.

"School's out, kid," he yelled, his freckled terrier's face one big grin. "And the Talmains blew—so gossip has it."

I could see then that there were two women in the back seat with him and one was tugging at his arm and talking hard.

"Even the Doc is not his cheery self," he said.

His face vanished and the car started up. There was a bit of a struggle in the back seat and then his face re-appeared and I could just about hear him yell:

"Remember . . . Scarsdale . . . George Vernon—real estate."

I waved and grinned and then the grin went away. I decided I wasn't surprised that the Talmains had fled. It seemed now that they had some such idea in mind when Talmain came to the house with the papers. They knew somehow that the police were closing in—on what I was not sure—and they apparently decided to cash in the best they could, which explained Talmain's eventually accepting the ten thousand instead of fifty.

But I needled Dunbar when he arrived with Corrigan a few

minutes later. I told him I understood the Talmains had run out on him and what kind of business was that?

"Or maybe," I said, "they weren't considered suspects in these murders."

Dunbar looked me over with those gray eyes. He wasn't sore; just sardonic.

"They won't get far," he said. "We'll pick 'em up."

"And what about the Doc?"

"He's staying."

I took Carol to the bench on the end of the dock right after lunch. She didn't want to come. She argued with me when I told her I had to talk to her. The listlessness and resignation that had marked her manner the past two days was still discouragingly evident. She said she really didn't think we had anything to talk about, but finally, reluctantly, she came.

She wore a brown-and-white checked skirt and a blue Shetland pullover and her hair was like half-ripe cornsilk in the sun. She was lovely. She was somber and unhappy but she was lovely just the same. She sat down and looked across the lake.

"This time we're going to talk about you," I began. "What I did to you was a stupid, idiotic thing—just like you said. Why I did it or what was in my mind isn't important now. I did it and I'm sorry and I guess that's why you wouldn't tell me—or Dunbar—that you knew Johnny when you were a child."

She looked at me, her eyes round, her lips parted. "W-who told you?" she whispered.

"Helen. I know all about it but I think Dunbar should know too."

She glanced down at her hands. She didn't say anything so I went ahead.

"I guess I don't blame you for not telling me. You were sore. You had every right to be. I'd done a rotten thing and I'd confessed in front of Dunbar and was feeling pretty noble. I was willing to forgive you for your mistake with Johnny and you couldn't accept such forgiveness because I didn't know the truth, because in a way I was accusing you of marrying a guy for his money just the way all those other dames did . . . That was it, wasn't it?"

She nodded, still not speaking. I wanted to ask a lot of things. I wanted to ask her why she hadn't defended herself, why she could not have been frank, if not with me, at least with Dunbar. I didn't ask her. Who was I to understand women? I said:

"The Johnny Marshall you married was the one you remembered. He must have been a pretty nice guy once."

That did it. The tightness in her face broke up muscle by muscle as the walls of her resistance crumbled. She wouldn't look at me but her eyes filled and then the words came tumbling out. It put a thickness in my throat that hurt but I was glad because these things inside her had been bottled up too long; there had been no one to talk to and the self-imposed silence, brought on by pride and loneliness, had eaten deeply into her strength.

It was just like Helen said, except that now I got the details, and the thoughts and hopes and dreams that had gone with them in this girl of nine. Because at twenty-one Johnny Marshall had apparently been a pretty nice guy, just like I said. Perhaps he had been bored that first summer; perhaps it was simply that Carol was the sort of child that people liked; whatever the reason Johnny let her tag along with him sometimes and kidded her about being a tomboy when she wanted to learn to ride and sail a boat. But he had taught her and took her in his car to the village for ice cream, and Carol, who had never known any-one quite like him, adored it.

By the end of the second year she had the idea firmly fixed in her young mind that some day when she grew up she would marry Johnny Marshall. It was a deep secret with her of course, and it was revived the next Christmas by a present from him. Then the idea faded as she grew up and Johnny Marshall was just a pleasant memory, or a name in the newspaper, until about two years ago when she met him at some party. Perhaps because he wanted to keep alive the impression he had once created in this girl, he turned on the charm and was on his best behavior. In all she had seen him perhaps a half-dozen times between then and our break-up, and each time he was the same nice guy she remembered.

She'd read about his marriages and troubles of course, but she'd never really believed they could have been his fault. She blamed the women and thought they had taken advantage of him because that was what she wanted to believe. And think-ing this, what chance had she when he finally started to rush her?

To begin with she was on the rebound emotionally, for I'd made her believe what I wanted her to believe, and here was a man with all the money in the world and all the charm he needed. He knew how to please women; the right things to say and do were old stuff and he had been attracted not only by her youth and freshness but possibly by the memory of those summers long ago. There was one other thing that helped make her accept him; a strictly feminine reason. Call it stubbornness, pride, ego or what ever you like—and it was this same thing that prevented her from telling me the truth when we had our fight the other day—but it boiled down to the belief that she had the necessary requisites to make a go of a marriage that heretofore had failed. When her friends warned Carol it served only to strengthen her determination to prove they were wrong. She believed in him and in herself. His other marriages had been failures because of the women; hers would be a success because she had the qualifications to make it so; because to her he was the Johnny Marshall of twenty-two.

Oh, it was easy enough to understand, and it was wonderful to hear. I wanted to shout and hug her hard but I didn't; I slid my arm gently around her waist, not holding her, just letting it rest there until she finished.

She said she was sorry she had been so stubborn and blew her nose and presently she put her head on my shoulder like a tired little girl. It was wonderful just to sit there, and the remembered fragrance of her hair, so much sweeter than the perfume Linda used, made me think of other days we'd spent together.

I told her it was wonderful. I said it was especially wonderful because Dunbar hadn't been able to further his case against her. The fact that Johnny had cut her off with fifty thousand had been the first thing and the partial alibi for the time of Garlin's murder was the other. Her head moved and I glanced down. Without lifting it she was shaking it from side to side and her voice was small and desolate again.

"It isn't enough, Alan. I didn't hear Linda go out that night and she didn't hear me, but it doesn't prove anything. Not really."

"But you would have heard her," I said. "She would have heard you . . . Anyway, it stopped Dunbar. At least it slowed him down. Maybe it doesn't prove anything but it's a lot better alibi than I've got."

She didn't say anything and I sat silently until I realized she was looking at me. When I glanced up I knew she had been staring at me for some time, and it was such a strange

look that it scared me. Then, as she dropped her glance, a horrible
thought scared me more.

"Good Lord!" I said. "Carol, listen. You don't think I killed
them?"

She shook her head, not looking at me. "N-o," she said.

I let my breath come out. Then, before I could add anything,
she said.

"They've got to find out who did it."

"They will."

"They've got to. Unless they do I'll always be—I mean, how
can there be any happiness for us while any doubt remains in
anyone's mind? Always people will wonder why the murder
wasn't solved, and they'll look at us and we will know what
they are thinking and—"

"Wait," I said, and because she was so right, because I hadn't
thought of this before, my buoyancy at being back with her
again, was withered and gone. "Please, darling, don't think
about it. Dunbar is smart. He'll find out."

But I wasn't as sure as I sounded. Dunbar wasn't saying much.
He knew a lot of things I didn't know, but did he know enough?
I tried to think of something I could do to analyze the things
I knew. Finally I thought about one thing which had never
been clear to me.

"What happened that night in the wine cellar?" I asked.
"What made you run away?"

She sat up, staring straight ahead now, her voice wooden. "I
tried to love him. I wanted to because—"

"I know," I said.

"I didn't mind his getting drunk the first night, not really.
I was a little afraid because just in that short time something
seemed to happen to Johnny so that he became a different man
from the one I knew. I wouldn't admit it but I couldn't help

wondering just a little about the things others had told me. Then, when you came into the stateroom, when I found out what he had done to you, I guess I knew I had been wrong all the time."

She sighed gently. "There were other things. They aren't important now. I don't know what I thought the day we arrived. Perhaps if he had tried to explain or apologize I could have believed him, but instead of that he made it worse. He thought it was a wonderful joke; he took everything for granted, including me, and the things he said, his complete callousness, made me know it would never work out for us. I went to the wine cellar because I didn't want a scene in front of you. If it had been anyone else—" She paused and tried again. "I couldn't let you know how I felt. I couldn't be ashamed nor admit I was wrong while you were there."

"Sure," I said.

"I was going to tell him when we got back, but by that time he was tight and when we got to the cellar he told me about a room he had fixed up off the office—a private room that no one else could use. He wanted to take some champagne up and spend the night there."

She glanced down at her hands and her voice was barely audible. "With someone you loved it might have been fun, but then—I don't know what I said exactly but I knew I was coming back to the house. He grabbed me. He tried to carry me and I got away and ran down another aisle—"

"I wondered how he happened to be lying in that particular place," I said, but she did not seem to hear me.

"When he caught me again he held me by the scarf and somehow I got free and pushed him. The floor must have been slippery because he fell backwards. I didn't wait to see what happened. I ran to the car and he didn't follow me. The Lieutenant says there was a bump on the back of his head so Johnny must have struck his head on something when he fell but I didn't know, I didn't wait."

"Yeah," I said. And I thought, *Somebody came in and found him there alone and did the job. . . .*

I got my call from Kiley, in Elmira, later in the afternoon. He said he couldn't find where anyone by the name of Eddington had registered at any hotel the night of the 14th. Nevertheless I phoned Dunbar just before dinner and told him my idea.

"We already checked on him," he said.

"What did you find out?"

He was very cooperative. He said, "Nothing that helps you any," and hung up. . . .

Dinner was a little earlier than usual and it couldn't have been much after eight when I went out and started up the road. I wasn't going anywhere, I just wanted to be alone. It was a swell night, with the moon big and mellow, and I guess I was hoping that if I did enough thinking I might be able to pull something out of the hat that would help Dunbar. I'm not sure how long I was gone—quite awhile, I suspect—but I was on my way back when I saw someone running towards me. I could see it was a woman, but I wasn't sure who it was until Carol called to me.

"Alan!" she said, her voice tight, "Alan!"

I ran up and pulled her to me. I could feel her tremble and I was shocked and frightened by her tone, her breathlessness.

"It's Linda," she said. "She's gone to see Doctor Penzance. We've got to go to the chapel!"

"What?" I said. "Why—"

"Oh, please, darling." She struggled free and pulled my hand. "I don't know why."

I checked the other questions that were battling it out in my head. I began to run, still holding her hand, and when we came to the path in the woods that Garlin and I had taken that second afternoon, we started up. Then Carol told me some more.

"She talked to him on the phone," she said. "There wasn't anyone else around and—"

"What about Spence and Helen?"

"Eddington decided to go back to New York. They're driving him to Bath."

"Does Dunbar know?"

"Oh"—her tone was pleading, exasperated—"how do I know? I just know Linda and I were alone in the house and I heard her talking on the phone when I came downstairs and she asked me to find you, to bring you to the chapel. She said she had an idea."

"But what about the police?"

"She said you could get them later if she was right." Carol stopped to get her breath and gasped out the words when she could. "She said our only chance was to make Penzance think she was alone, but she wanted you somewhere near in case she needed help."

Climbing up that path, holding Carol's hand, I still didn't know what it was all about but I could understand Linda taking such a chance if she thought she could prove anything. She'd always had plenty of assurance and confidence in her own ability, and she never was the kind that scared easily. But Penzance was different. She must have had reason to believe he was the killer and if she was right, he could certainly kill again.

I pulled Carol to a stop when we reached the edge of the clearing. The side wall of the chapel was just ahead and I could see a shaft of light blazing from the window Garlin had used, the one where I'd torn the velvet.

There were no packing cases where we'd left them underneath the window but when I went round back I found them right where they had been in the first place. The trouble was Carol wouldn't stay where I told her to stay. She came out and pretended to steady the crates and told me to be careful. I climbed up cautiously and peered through the window. The drapes had been torn down just enough so I could look down at the table and what I saw then I'll never forget.

They were seated on opposite sides of the table, that doughnut-shaped lamp between them, Doctor Penzance leaning slightly forward and Linda Jordan sitting ramrod straight and staring sightlessly into the man's unblinking black eyes.

I could see his lips move and in fancy I could hear that deep sonorous voice droning on. I thought of what Linda had told me. Helen Bradford had admitted that perhaps Penzance had used his hypnotic influence on her several times, but Linda had never believed that Penzance had done such a thing to her. Johnny had insisted that she was wrong, but she had not believed that either. Now, in my own mind, I was sure, and something cold and terrifying snaked into my chest and coiled there.

It took a tremendous mental effort to take my eyes from those two figures in the weird half-light of the room below, but I finally knew what I had to do, and climbed down to Carol.

"What is it?" she whispered.

I told her. I took her arm and drew her into the woods. I told her she must go back to the house and phone Dunbar. "It shouldn't take him long to get here," I said. "If he hurries they may still be inside."

"But if they're not," Carol said. "W-what will you do?"

"I don't know," I said. "I'll wait. If they go outside I'll follow them."

"Then how will we know where to go?"

I made my voice curt and abrupt. I told her we'd worry about that if it happened. I said she was wasting time and making things worse by arguing and I gave her a gentle push towards the path. I turned deliberately away and went back to the box; when I glanced round, she was gone.

My hands were icy and the back of my neck was stiff and cold as I climbed back to the window. Nothing had changed inside, nothing moved except the Doctor's lips. His head seemed enormous now, his dark gaze inhuman and deadly. And Linda— Linda stared straight ahead, her small face waxen and immobile, her hair almost red in the unnatural glow of the room.

And I stared too, morbidly fascinated and listening to the whisper of my fears. It was clear enough now. Linda had learned or guessed something, and not believing she could be hypnotized against her will, had come here to trick Penzance into some move that would trap him. *Instead of that the Doctor was going to use her*.

For what? What could he do?

Suddenly I knew that this macabre scene could not end here, inside this chapel. There had to be something more! The thought jarred me and I pushed away from the window and scrambled to the ground. I put the crates away and went to the front corner of the building where I could watch the door.

There had to be something more.

And I had nearly muffed things by standing there looking into the room when I should have been getting ready for that something. Now it was all right. If they came out I'd know what to do; if Dunbar should come first he could do as he liked.

I don't know how much longer I stood there, but finally the light I had been watching went out and Dunbar hadn't come. I drew back against the side of the building, my heart pounding and my lungs tight because I kept holding my breath. After awhile, there was a loud metallic click and the rasp of wood as the door opened. I heard it close and, faintly, the sound of footsteps came to me as they crossed the gravel path.

I peered round the corner. Linda walked slowly across the grassy quadrangle, her slim body erect, her hands at her side. Behind her, and bulking huge in the moonlight, Doctor Penzance kept pace with steady deliberate steps.

When they were about fifty yards ahead I started to move. I could not follow them directly because there was no cover, but to the left a line of trees marched along the quadrangle and spread thick shadows across the grass. I reached them safely and then moved on diagonally behind the others, ready to freeze instantly should Penzance turn.

But not once did he glance round. He seemed supremely confident in what he was doing. He followed Linda across the quadrangle, through a stand of oak trees to the road, down the road about a hundred yards and then across it and into the pine trees that stood between the road and the gorge.

My scalp began to prickle again. I knew where I was. Not far from here I had come running from these woods after someone had shot at me. I had explored them later that same night—the night Garlin had been murdered.

I moved in cautiously. Here among the pines, the moonlight and shadows made the same bewildering patchwork upon the ground that I remembered and I hesitated, seeing the two of them move one moment and losing them the next. Then, as I stood there wondering how close I dared go, something, some whisper of a sound, made me turn.

Two men and a woman were moving up behind me. They were coming fast—Carol and Dunbar and Corrigan—but they made no sound and I saw that they had their shoes in their hands.

"Which way?" Dunbar said, his lips close to my ear.

I pointed. "He's got her in some kind of a trance," I said. "I don't know what he's going to do."

"Stay back," Dunbar said. "If you make a sound I'll brain you." And he started through the pines with Corrigan at his heels.

I kicked off my shoes and Carol put her face close to mine. "We saw you coming across the quadrangle but we didn't dare come too fast. Oh, darling, I'm so glad you—"

I put my fingers on her lips. "You stay here," I said.

I could see Dunbar and Corrigan and I started after them and Carol started after me. There wasn't anything I could do about it, though in the end it didn't matter because the pine needles were like a carpet under our stockinged feet and not once did I hear a sound. Nor, apparently, did Penzance.

At first I was sure he was going to the edge of the gorge where I had stood one morning and looked down at Garlin's lifeless figure, but when he was nearly there he and Linda swung left and continued down the hill, parallel with the stream.

They came to the U-shaped promontory I had noticed before, kept going. By this time Dunbar and Corrigan were about forty or fifty feet behind them and, having reached this point, had slowed their pace and now kept their distance, moving from tree to tree, keeping to the shadows but silhouetted against the lighter patches beyond.

I was not more than twenty feet behind Corrigan now and I knew Carol was right behind me because now and then I heard the soft flow of her breath. For myself I moved like a stealthy automaton, not thinking, not daring to think, just staring, trying not to breathe, wondering why the thumping of my heart didn't give everything away.

At last, when it seemed that Linda was right at the brink of the gorge, she stopped. There was a little clearing there and the moonlight was white upon her face as she turned. I saw the shadows that were Dunbar and Corrigan stop and finally I remembered to stop too. Penzance stood close to Linda, towering above her but not hiding her face. Somewhere above us a wandering breeze played briefly with the pine trees and there was a faint musical whispering through the silvered tips. Then it was gone and there was silence again.

It probably lasted no more than a second or two, that silence, but it was so absolute, so terrifying, that I wanted only to break it. I wanted to yell, to tell Dunbar to do something. I dared not even look at Carol. I stood rigidly, aching all over from the strain until, from out of the silence, Doctor Penzance spoke.

He did not raise his voice, he did not need to. It was deeper, more gentle, more commanding than anything I had remembered and there was no doubt about what he said. He said:

"You will get that gun. You will do as I told you."

Very slowly, Linda turned. She was not looking at Penzance. She was not looking at anything on this earth. She stepped away from him and knelt beside the base of a tree and when she straightened I saw the gun gleam darkly in her hand. Then, without hesitation, she lifted that hand and put the gun against her temple.

It happened before the gun stopped moving. We all knew with horrible clarity what was coming and our reaction to the strain and suspense we had been under was identical. Nerves and muscles, too long confined, snapped free. Without knowing it, I moved. My mouth was open but all I heard was the combined outraged cries of Carol and Dunbar and Corrigan.

The result was one tremendous shout that split the night wide open and broke the spell that Penzance had created. The effect on Linda was immediate and deadly. Her body jerked and stiffened. She looked at Penzance and he, startled into immobility and caught flat-footed by what had happened, wasted a second before he grabbed for her, and now it was too late.

Standing there with a gun in her hand, seeing only this huge and frightening figure reach for her, she did what anyone else would have done. She pulled the trigger—twice.

I was running when I saw the twin tongues of flame and heard the gun blast and blast again. I saw Dunbar and Corrigan break into the open, still shouting. I saw Linda look at them. I don't know what she thought, or if she thought at all, but instinct must have told her to stop, for she dropped the gun as Penzance folded up at her feet. She put both hands to the sides of her face and began to scream.

Somehow I was beside her, and Dunbar and Corrigan were leaning over Penzance. Carol tried to get her arm around Linda. She kept saying, "Linda—Linda!" but Linda didn't know it. Linda was crying and sobbing hysterically and the words that came out did not make sense.

She said something about Penzance wanting to kill her, and why she was here, and then she began to say, "I shot him," over and over. I tried to stop her. I shook her and she struck at me. Then I slapped her hard across the face.

That stopped her. She caught her breath and shuddered but the hysteria was gone. She leaned against Carol, not trying to say anything more and Carol said, "There, there. It's all right, darling. It's all right."

Dunbar straightened up and I asked how Penzance was.

"Washed up," he said. "Right over the heart, both of them."

"It ought to save the taxpayers a lot of dough," Corrigan said.

Dunbar stepped back and looked at the two women. "Can you get her back to the house?" he said, indicating Linda.

"I—I'm all right," Linda said.

"Yes, sure we can," I said.

"Go with 'em," he said to Corrigan. "Phone in. Get Ryder and

Whelan and tell 'em where to come and then come right back. I'll wait."

He gave Carol and Linda a chance to start off and then said to me, "Get her to bed. I'll talk to her later."

22

SERGEANT CORRIGAN was at the telephone in the lower hall when the rest of us reached the house. He was talking loud and fast and we stood there listening a moment until Carol told Linda to go upstairs and lie down.

"I'll help you undress as soon as I've called a doctor," she said.

"Doctor?" Linda smiled weakly. "I don't need a doctor, Carol. Really. I'm not even going to undress. I'll just rest awhile."

"You go upstairs and stop arguing," Carol said.

Corrigan went out in a hurry and Carol went to the telephone. When she hung up she was frowning. "I got him," she said, "but he hasn't been able to start the car. He says if I'll drive to Hammondsport he'll be glad to come."

"She doesn't need a doctor," I said; "not that bad."

"I most certainly don't," Linda called down the stairs.

Carol hesitated uncertainly, still frowning. "Well—"

"Let's wait and see," I said. "The main thing is to keep her mind off herself. Let's go up and talk to her."

We went up and Linda thanked us for coming. Yes, she said, she would like to talk. She stretched out on one of the beds and Carol and I sat down. I offered cigarettes and paced about and then I knew I had to know what had happened.

"Why did you go up there alone?" I said.

"Alan!" Carol eyed me reproachfully. "She doesn't want to talk about that, can't you see?"

"It's all right," Linda said. "Maybe it's better if I do." She looked at me. "I went up alone because I couldn't see how else we could ever prove he was the murderer."

"You knew something," I said. "You held out on Dunbar."

She watched the burning end of her cigarette. "Yes," she said. "Earl Garlin told me. He—he saw Doctor Penzance come out of the wine cellar that first night."

"What?" I said.

"Oh, I know how it sounds," Linda added hurriedly, "but wait until you hear the rest of it and then you'll understand. Earl didn't mean to tell me. We were talking about Penzance that night after the police first came, and he made a slip and when I caught him he had to admit the truth."

She sighed and her red mouth was sultry. "He had a story to go with it and I—like a fool—believed him. You see, he heard you come back alone," she said to Carol, "and when Johnny didn't turn up right away, he went to the cellar. He saw Penzance come out and then he went in and found Johnny."

"And me," I said.

"But after he'd made his slip to me, he convinced me that see-ing Penzance did not actually prove he had done the killing. Earl said he was in a spot. He was a bodyguard and he'd let Johnny get killed and the only way he could possibly redeem himself would be to have a hand in catching the killer. In fact he said he hoped to do it alone. If I told the Lieutenant about the slip he made, he'd be in a spot. If only I could wait, Earl thought he could do the job.

"Well, I swallowed it. I know that wasn't the real reason now. He'd seen Penzance and he knew Penzance had some money and being Garlin, he wanted all he could get. Johnny was dead and Earl was out of a job. He could tell what he'd seen to the police and maybe Penzance would be arrested, but there would be no money in that. I think now that he tried blackmail . . ."

"Yes," I said. "He must have. Even Dunbar figured it out the same way."

"And once he was killed," Linda said, "where was I? I was sure then that Earl had lied to me about why he wanted to keep quiet, but the point is I *did* keep quiet, and now I couldn't go to Dunbar. How could I when the only man who had seen Penzance was dead?"

"I guess you couldn't," I said; "not then."

"I could say Earl had said he'd seen Penzance and Penzance could say Earl was crazy and he had two people up there—those Talmains—to back him up in anything he wanted to say."

Carol cleared her throat. "You thought if you went to the Doctor alone he'd have to do something."

"I hoped he would," Linda said. "If I went alone and perhaps exaggerated what Earl had told me—-" She broke off and looked embarrassed. "Oh, I suppose I was a fool, but the police weren't getting anywhere and I had to do something. I thought if you could watch and see what happened, Alan, it would be all right."

"It was," I said, and grinned.

The grin seemed to help her. Her answering grin was a bit sheepish still, but her voice seemed better.

"Yes," she said, "but not the way I expected. I thought he might try to hypnotize me and I was going to pretend to let him. Instead of that he really did hypnotize me. I can't remember a thing after we'd sat down at the table in the chapel. Oh, I can remember telling him what Earl had told me, but after that I can't seem to remember anything but darkness and a gun going off and seeing him grab for me."

She shuddered and some of the color slipped from her cheeks. Carol glanced at me and motioned towards the door with her head. I nodded.

"It's easy enough to figure now," I said. "Penzance was waiting outside the house that first night after his quarrel with Johnny. He knew then that Johnny had enough dope in that report to ruin him and he had to stop it some way. He must have followed the station wagon down to the wine cellar and hung around with the hope that he might get a chance to kill. What happened then was made to order."

I glanced at Carol. "You pushed Johnny and he fell and hit his head with your scarf in his hand. Only you didn't know it."

"I kept on running," Carol said.

"And when the station wagon moved off, Penzance moved in. There was the guy he wanted to kill waiting on the floor unconscious. Penzance had been here three summers and he must have been in that wine cellar dozens of times. He'd know all about champagne bottles exploding. It was just luck that the rest of us happened to witness such a thing the same afternoon. That's what threw Dunbar off. He was figuring one of us as the opportunist. Instead here was a guy who knew a lot more than we did, and unless he carried a gun, he had three choices—strangle Johnny, beat him to death, or use something that might get by as an accident. He dropped a bottle and got a piece of glass big enough . . ."

"And he used my scarf," Carol said thickly.

"Sure. To keep his fingerprints from the glass and to keep from being cut."

"Then he hid it among those bottles," Linda said. "Just enough so that it wouldn't be obvious and yet be found by the police."

"Why not?" I said. "He didn't know whose scarf it was but it didn't matter. It was exactly what he needed to throw suspicion on the owner, and away from him."

Everything about that picture was engraved indelibly on my brain. I could see each detail. I could almost feel the dampness of the cellar and the cold musty air that hung over everything as I stood there with that scarf in my hand, realizing how it had been used and why it had been left. I sat still, thinking, listening to Carol ask about Earl Garlin.

"He would be alive now if he had told the police," she said.

"He was a fool," Linda said. "So was I when I believed he wanted to solve the case alone. He was never interested in anything but money."

"He made a date with the Doc," I said. "Up by the gorge. When we came back from Elmira that day he had even more to sell. He knew about the record then. I told him about the others in the library."

"He probably tried to get more money," Linda said. "And Penzance shot him because he had to. Maybe he intended to all the time. He must have known he'd have to keep on paying a man like Garlin forever."

She had raised herself on one elbow. Her face was feverish, her eyes unnaturally bright. I stood up.

"You know what I think? I think you need a drink." I nodded to Carol as she had nodded to me—towards the door. She rose and started that way.

"All right," Linda said. "I think I could use one at that."

"Get undressed and into bed then," I said. "We'll give you five minutes."

Carol and I went into the hall. As we went down the stairs I said, "I think you're right about the doctor. She's pretty worked up and Dunbar'll be along after awhile with a lot more questions. It might be a good idea to have someone here to give her a sedative in case she needs it—that is if you still want to go."

"Of course I do," Carol said. "I should have gone in the first place."

She got her coat from the hall closet and went out the back

way. I stepped to the telephone. I heard the station wagon back down the drive as the operator connected me with Quinn, the assistant district attorney.

I didn't have to tell him what had happened; he already knew. So I asked him my question. I said the morning after Marshall's murder a trooper by the name of Whelan had been looking for a missing piece of the bottle the killer had used. I said:

"Do you know if the police have found that piece yet?"

"No," Quinn said. "Why?"

"I'll call you back."

I hung up before he could answer and went quickly up the stairs. I stopped in front of Linda's door and glanced at my watch. I figured it hadn't been much more than two minutes since I'd left. I grabbed the knob and went in fast.

It was a good guess. I caught her just right. She was halfway between the dresser and the bathroom door, heading that way, and she was stark naked.

I suppose her reaction came quickly when measured in time. Yet in such instances time is relative and it seemed then that there was a minute or two before anything much happened. She had stopped abruptly at the opening of the door and she was glancing back over her shoulder, her face surprised but nothing more, her weight on one foot as she took a step.

For that next second which seemed so long, she was frozen by the blank, physical shock of seeing me. Light burnished brightly her auburn hair, and her tan was smooth and even on her shoulders and along her legs and thighs. In between the skin was milky white and softly modeled and everything in that moment was smooth and round and slender.

I heard the door slam behind me. The sound jarred us and then she moved, the muscles in her legs and back tensing first to break the smoothness, and then the eyes, and finally the symmetry of her face had atrophied into something white and hard and terribly twisted.

I must have moved when she did, for I was racing across the room to catch her before she reached the bathroom. I grabbed her before she could go through the doorway and she whirled and struck at me.

She had a hairbrush in her hand I hadn't seen and it cracked glancingly across my head. I pinioned that arm and caught the other. But she was strong, with the strength of desperation and madness, and it took a bit of doing to get my arm around her and still keep her hands from tearing my face.

There was none of this, "Let me go," business. Nothing shocked or modest. She knew what I wanted and the things she said, vicious and half-strangled by her efforts, were animal noises rather than words.

She kept it up until I lifted her, until I turned her and held her tight against me so that I could see her thigh. What I wanted was there. I had seen it fleetingly as we struggled and now I could see the bluish two-inch circle of swelling and infection, the gauze taped over the center.

Suddenly she was limp in my arms, her ribs rising and falling spasmodically under my hand. I realized then how hard I was holding her and eased up, still not letting her go because I did not know what she would do until she spoke.

"All right," she wheezed. "You win."

"Do you want to take it off," I said, "or will I?"

Without answering she freed one hand, reached down and ripped the tape and gauze away. What was underneath was no boil, no carbuncle. I've had both and this was different. There was an angry hole, badly infected, but no head, or sign of one.

I let go and stepped back. I told her to get a robe and walked to the door while she did so. I was trembling all over. I was breathing hard and my hands and face were damp and perspiration trickled down my sides.

When I turned she was in front of the closet, belting a robe about her. Her face was shiny but no longer stiff and immobile; it was slack and resigned. She put her hands behind her neck and lifted her hair that had been caught by the collar of the robe.

"How did you know?" she said thickly.

"I wasn't sure," I said. "This was the only way I could think of to find out. That story of the boil you gave me when I slapped your leg in Watkins Glen was all right so long as I didn't suspect you; when I did, there was something else that made me wonder."

She came slowly to the bed nearest the door and sat down on the edge. I saw she was waiting for me to go on.

"There was a piece of bottle missing," I said, and told her how the trooper, Whelan, had been looking for it the day after Johnny had been killed. "I just called the District Attorney. The police are still looking for that piece of glass, Linda. I had to find out for sure."

She sat with her knees together, her feet flat on the floor and still bare. She was staring at the rug.

"The champagne bottle seemed like a good idea," she said. "It was a very bad idea. I dropped the bottle to get a piece for Johnny but I didn't jump back quickly enough. Champagne bottles that are aging really do have a terrific force when they explode." She took a big breath and swallowed audibly. "That one piece cut my dress but fortunately my leg didn't bleed enough to stain anything but my shorts and I washed them that first night. I guess it didn't bleed much because it went so deep. I tried to dig the glass out. I couldn't."

I went over to the door. I felt about a hundred and three years old. I should have felt exultant—at least that's the way it seemed —because I'd been right, because I'd found out who killed Johnny and Earl Garlin, because now everything was cleared up and never would there be anyone to point his finger at Carol, or me.

But I didn't feel that way at all. It does something to you when you realize that what you have done is going to put a person in the electric chair. When that person is someone you know and have liked it makes everything worse. I felt rotten. Linda had killed three people and each one of them deliberately. She'd gambled, knowing that she might have to pay. She didn't act sorry for herself. She knew what would happen eventually and she was not asking me to cover up for her. Maybe that's why I felt so rotten.

I didn't know if I wanted to cover up for her or not, but even if I had, I knew it would be a futile, useless proposition. If what happened was as I thought, Doctor Penzance probably had a record on his recording machine when he and Linda had their talk. Dunbar would certainly check back to see.

"I sent Carol for a doctor," I said. "And now I'm going down and phone the D.A. again. I'm going to tell him where the missing piece of champagne bottle is. I'm going to tell him now because I may be a little drunk when the police get here. Do you still want that drink?"

She looked up and nodded. "Very much, Alan. Very, very much."

I went downstairs and asked the telephone operator to get me the District Attorney's office. Then I got some Scotch from the dining room and three glasses, one filled with ice.

23

LINDA was on the bed when I came back, in pajamas and robe now, with a quilt spread over her. I put the bottle and glasses down and she handed me the carafe. She asked me to fill it in the bathroom and to let the water run until it was cold.

She had three drinks poured when I came back, and had divided the ice between the three glasses. She added water from the carafe to one and handed it to me, and boy, how I needed that drink! I wasn't being polite or waiting for anyone and I took a long pull and the glass was half empty when I put it down.

"What's the extra drink for?" I asked.

"I forgot Carol wasn't here. I'll save it for her." She managed a smile. "I imagine she can use one too."

Something about that smile got me. When I saw how white and drawn her face was I knew how much effort was behind it. And suddenly I couldn't talk any more about the murders or Penzance. Eventually we'd get around to what was going to happen to Linda and that I couldn't face. I wandered about the room, embarrassed, still feeling lousy, wanting to pretend that nothing had happened because I felt that was the way she would prefer it. I stopped in front of the dresser. It was covered with bottles and jars and I asked if it took all that to keep beautiful.

"Most of them," she said.

Then I recognized the perfume bottle I'd seen in her bedroom on the train. I picked it up. It was empty now and I turned and grinned at her, remembering how I'd smelled it all one night because she'd spilled a little. It was all an act, the smile, the corny thing I said; yet I couldn't think of anything else.

"Don't tell me you spilled the rest of it?"

"What? Oh—yes." She tried to chuckle but the sound was strained and brittle. "This morning—all over the rug."

"You always were an expensive wench," I said, and started to put the bottle back. Then it hit me.

I don't know how to explain it. One moment I was grinning and thinking about what I'd said and the next, my grin was frozen and my stomach was a vacuum.

I looked at her, hard. She was watching me and what I saw in her eyes made the skin crawl on the back of my neck. I reached again for the bottle and my fingers were cold and stiff when I took out the stopper.

"No, Linda," I said. "You didn't spill it on the rug this morning or any other morning. It would take a week to get that odor out of a rug." And then, slowly, incredulously, I held the bottle to my nose.

For long seconds I couldn't move, I couldn't even think. I looked at the two glasses on the bedside table—both untouched—with an inch of whisky in each, and my scalp tightened. For blending with the distinctive odor of Linda's perfume was the unmistakable smell of bitter almonds.

I dropped that little bottle and reached for my glass on the dresser, half-crazy with fear and smothered by a sudden horrible weakness. I found the glass, but in that moment there was no strength to hold it. I tried to steady myself, to make the effort, and then, somehow, reason cut through my panic and helped me.

I let go of the glass. I didn't smell it. I didn't have to. I knew there had been no oil of bitter almonds in my drink; if there had been I would have been dead. I could not understand it but I was alive. I pulled myself together and faced Linda.

"Garlin told you," I said hollowly. "You're the one who took it from Haughton's bag. You emptied the perfume down the drain and filled the bottle with poison—in case you needed it. That's why you poured a drink for Carol, and why you're saving your own. You split your poison two ways and—"

I started towards her as I spoke and something happened to her face. Suddenly it was a flat gray mask with the lips pulled back hard and something in the eyes I had never seen before, something crazed and brightly burning.

"Damn you!" she said through clenched teeth. "Oh, damn you!" And then, when I kept coming, "Don't come any closer!"

She grabbed one of the drinks and lifted it. I stopped. Then the mask fell away and the glaze slid from her eyes.

"Yes," she said. "Two ways. If you hadn't phoned the police about the glass in my leg I might have tried some on you, though I don't imagine I could have got away with it, but since I couldn't stop you—" She grunted softly, disdainfully.

"You never were important, Alan. If I'd had enough poison for three I might have used some on you. But I didn't. I wasn't sure I had enough even for two. I thought I did, but I didn't dare split it three ways, just for the chance of paying you off for trapping me. I'm not even sure I hate you for it. You had to try and my luck had run out. You did what anyone else would have done, and I guess that's all right. No, with the amount of poison I had, I couldn't afford to waste any on you, Alan."

I went over to the door and locked it and then I sat down not far from the bed.

"You put the poison in the glasses while I was filling the carafe," I said. "I suppose you emptied it while I was downstairs. But you didn't get out of bed while I was in the bathroom."

Very slowly, her gaze never leaving me, she reached down under the bed and brought out a small glass she had taken from the bathroom.

"While you were phoning I emptied the poison from the perfume bottle into this. I was afraid if I waited it would take too long to empty it with that small opening. The poison was in here when you came back"—she tapped the glass—"and it was easy to do the rest while you were getting the water."

I heard her vaguely. I was remembering the things Dunbar had said that first morning when he told us Marshall's death was murder. He had warned us then against our friends, had said a killer would never stop at a second murder. He had urged us to remember this, to forget our prejudices. And there I was, ten minutes ago, feeling rotten because I'd trapped Linda, because I had to turn her in. It was silly. I'd liked her but I wasn't important. She would have killed me if she'd had all the poison she wanted, but since she was not sure, since she herself must be considered, she preferred to kill someone else as her last gesture.

"One drink for you," I said, "and one for Carol." And even as I spoke, knowing it was the truth, the shock and numbness still made everything out of focus. "You hated her. That's why you killed Johnny. Was it your gun you used on Garlin?"

She nodded. "An old one I'd had for years. It could never be traced."

"You knew you were going to kill Johnny when you came," I said. "You must have hated him too."

"I did. I told him I'd probably kill him if he married again. He laughed. It just didn't occur to him that anyone could possibly kill Johnny Marshall or even hurt him. I was going to kill him and I was going to frame her if I could. The champagne bottle seemed like a good idea—but you know about that."

I went back to the dresser and drained my drink. I sat down again because I felt old and tired and beaten, and the hole in my leg ached like the devil. I couldn't stop the throbbing in my head nor find the answers for my questions; I didn't even know where to begin.

"You really did give Johnny a Mickey that night on the train, didn't you?" I said.

"And for that you should really thank me, shouldn't you, Alan?"

She was right about that but it didn't register then. I said, "You couldn't have Johnny and so no one else was going to have him."

She nodded and the story came out and I wondered why I had

not known before. Of all the motives which drive women to murder, hers was easily number one. A woman loves a man and he cheats or throws her out and she kills him. It happens all the time and I only had to read the papers to know. With Linda it was the same motive many times magnified.

When first she went to work for Johnny she expected to marry him. Instead he married someone else and she stayed on because she loved him and they had been intimate for a little while and he had promised her things. And the years went by and he married others, and hate and resentment began to warp the love she felt. Always there was the waiting, the hoping. She was, she said, never anything but a stand-in and finally, when Johnny announced he was going to marry Carol, something snapped and Linda made up her mind to kill. It was all there. She'd even told me these things herself if only I could have been able to understand.

"You're a good actress, Linda," I said. "You're pretty wonderful. You cried because Johnny'd given you a twenty-five thousand dollar bonus. You took advantage of every break and I guess I gave you one when I suggested Carol sleep in here with you. You used the chloral hydrate—or whatever it was you gave Johnny—the night you killed Garlin too, didn't you? How?"

"In some warm milk we had sent up."

"And then you swore to Dunbar that Carol could not possibly have left the room without you knowing it. You gave Carol an alibi so you could have one yourself, knowing that Carol could not wake up to trap you. I suppose you'd already made the date with Garlin. It was like we discussed it when Carol was here. He was killed just as we figured and for the same reason—only not by Penzance. Garlin didn't see Penzance the night Johnny was killed; he saw you."

"Garlin was a fool," she said. "I would have been all right except for Garlin—and this leg. If I could have gotten away before too long and had this tended to I would have been all right—except for Garlin. And you."

She went on in a low, bitter monotone. "Garlin was good at his job. He went outside that first night after he heard Johnny say he was going to the wine cellar. He went out because Penzance had been here and quarreled with Johnny, and Garlin was watching out for Johnny. I didn't know what would happen at the wine cellar but I remembered the exploding bottle and I thought if I went down there—and was lucky—maybe I could work it. So when I went upstairs before Carol and Johnny left, I continued down the backstairs and out on the road. Garlin saw me hurrying towards the winery.

"It didn't mean anything, but since he couldn't figure it out he moved along behind me. Then Johnny and Carol came. I heard them quarreling inside and what happened then was better than I had hoped for. Carol started to run and Johnny caught her and then he slipped or something and fell and hit his head. When she ran out and got into the car, I went in and the scarf was there and Johnny was still unconscious." She sighed heavily. "He never knew what happened."

"You knew whose scarf it was. You left it deliberately."

"Yes," she said.

"And then Garlin walked in on you. That must have been bad," I said. "What did you do, act some more?"

"It *was* bad." Linda's lids were almost touching. "But Garlin was a fool where money was concerned. If it had been Penzance like I tried to make you believe . . ."

"I did believe it then," I said, but she didn't seem to hear.

". . . it would have been the same. I talked fast and I knew what to say. Johnny was gone. Garlin was out of a job and he could see that I paid for it by getting me convicted of murder, or he could get paid in cash. I already knew about the check—as though Johnny could pay me for what he'd done to me," she said disdainfully, "and twenty-five thousand was a lot of money to Garlin. Also there was the report Johnny had about Penzance.

"Johnny had given Penzance a copy—just to prove he really had what he needed to break the lease—and I thought the other copy was in the study desk. I said I'd give it to Garlin. Penzance had money. It looked like a good shakedown to Garlin. Anyway, he decided to play along. Here was a chance for more money than he had ever seen and it was just too much for him."

She laughed abruptly and a mouse ran up my spine. "The only thing was, the report wasn't in the study desk. The briefcase was gone."

I said I thought Spence Haughton had taken it. "I think he hid it in the boathouse that first night and went back the next when he had more time. That's when he locked us in. I think he threw it in the lake."

She looked at me and then at the glass in her hand. "I don't know," she said. "But I knew I'd have to kill Garlin. I had my check for twenty-five thousand dollars, but it would never be enough. I'd always pay to a chiseler like Garlin . . . I took care of him."

"Using the gun you brought for Johnny," I said.

"It was easy. I said I'd get out of the house and meet him up at the gorge. And I did. The night you came back from Elmira. He was a little tight and I said we had to be sure we weren't seen. Oh, I convinced him all right, and chiefly, I think, because he was one of those big, strong, he-men who just never could conceive of a woman getting the best of him."

"I heard the shots," I said. "I nearly caught you."

"You nearly got shot. I'm pretty good with a pistol. I could have hit you. I guess I should have."

"I guess you could," I said. "Yeah. Garlin was a fool."

"That's what I told you . . ."

I took a breath before I went on. The room seemed hot and stuffy now and I realized I was a lot more weary than I had supposed. Linda's face seemed a little hazy and I blinked until it cleared. I tried to concentrate so I could find out the rest of it.

"That's almost everything," I said, "except about tonight. Penzance didn't hypnotize you. He had never hypnotized you. You lied when I asked you about that the other day."

"A little. The day early this summer when we went to see Penzance Johnny was sure the Doc could do it. He couldn't. And I could see Johnny getting mad and—I don't know, a woman does a lot of funny things to humor a man she likes—so I pretended I was hypnotized."

"So well," I said, "that Penzance believed it." I shook my head to clear it. "Well, you did a beautiful job tonight. You didn't have any idea about Penzance like you told Carol. *He* had the idea about you. He phoned you and you knew what you had to do. You had Carol get me because you knew she and I would be excellent witnesses."

I tried to put remembered things together. "He suspected you and he must have known that if you had killed Garlin you'd know where the gun was. He was going to make you find it, and you let him go. You led him to the gun, knowing I'd be watching you. He even said the right words to make us believe he was ordering you to commit suicide. 'You will get that gun,' he said. 'You will do as I told you.' "

"He meant I was to hand it over," Linda said.

"And you put it to your head, knowing I'd yell—and Dunbar and Corrigan being there made it even better—and then the shock would bring you out of the trance and you'd act instinctively and shoot your tormentor and no one could ever question your actions. Very good," I said. "We believed it too."

I leaned forward in my chair and nearly fell on my face. I'd been thinking maybe I could jump up and knock the glass out of her hand and now I wasn't sure I could even stand, I was so tired.

It scared me when I realized how I felt. We'd been talking about hypnotism and I wondered if Linda had some such power. My body seemed to weigh a ton and my head was a balloon and I blinked hard and peered at Linda.

Then I saw her, clearly. For just a second or two, just long enough to see the bright hot gleam in her narrowed eyes, the half-crazed look of satisfaction on her tight, ashen face. Then I knew. I wasn't sure I could move but I could think, and never will I know such fear again, nor feel such utter helplessness.

"You put it in my drink." I tried to yell at her but I could hardly hear myself. "*The same thing you gave Johnny on the train. The Mickey!* There was some left after you gave it to Carol the other night. You put it in my glass when you put the poison in the others."

And I pushed out of the chair towards the bedside table, and stumbled to one knee, and before I could get up Linda had a glass of poisoned whisky in each hand. She swung her feet to the other side of the bed, still holding the glasses, and stood up.

"Yes," she said, "damn you!"

The bed was between us now. I didn't try to lunge across it because I was afraid if I went down I couldn't get up. I backed up and clung to the bedpost and started around the foot, steadying myself with my hands. And Linda was talking. I could hardly see her but I could hear and my mind still worked.

"If you hadn't sent her for the doctor she might already be

dead. But no, you had to spare her feelings. You didn't want her around while you looked for the hole in my leg. All right, so I had to fix something for you too."

I pulled myself a little farther along and she kept talking.

"I didn't think I had poison enough for three of us but I had enough for two, and I had this other. It was good enough for you. I knew you wouldn't wait for your drink. You needed one and you took it when I gave it to you. And I had to be sure, you understand?"

I took another step and saw her put the two glasses on a high-boy along the wall.

"I couldn't take a chance," she said, her voice shrill. "I didn't know you'd spot the perfume bottle and find out that way, but you're pretty smart sometimes and I was afraid something might happen to make you suspect me. Maybe I'd do something wrong, or maybe you'd smell the bitter almonds. I had to be sure you'd be out of the way before Carol got back."

She was facing me now and suddenly she started to meet me, to keep me away from that highboy. I grabbed for her and she hit me in the face. I went to one knee again and came up and she put her fists on my chest and pushed.

I guess I knew then that I could never reach those two glasses. Linda was small but she was wiry and I had no strength. I staggered when she pushed and while I was off balance she pushed again and I half turned and went to both knees.

I don't know why my mind continued to work but it did. It kept me from lying down and closing my eyes. It made everything clear. It told me that with the piece of glass in her leg Linda was as good as in the electric chair. She was going to die and she knew it, but first she must make Carol die too—because she hated her so.

And it would be so easy now. Linda would be downstairs

waiting when Carol and the doctor came. She would have a cold drink for Carol. She would say I was out in the kitchen getting more ice or something and maybe while the doctor took off his coat Linda and Carol would drink. It would be so simple. Carol couldn't refuse when Linda told how she had waited before taking her own drink. . . .

Linda was laughing. She was behind me and I could hear the tight, high sounds. I don't know where the idea came from. I don't know if the laugh had anything to do with it or not. I only knew then that Carol could not die that way. I could not reach the glasses nor stay awake, but there was a way and I got one foot under me and pushed towards the door.

Linda was a little late. I got there first, reached up and yanked the key from the lock. I turned towards the window, six feet away. Then I was crawling and Linda was on my back.

She got an arm under my throat and tried to haul me back. I put my head down and crawled. She got in front of me and I wrapped one arm around her knees and pulled. She came down on top of me, clawing, crying in strangled, muffled tones.

I was sobbing too; sobbing for breath, for strength. I had four feet to go, three. I couldn't make it. Complete collapse was over-due and in another second it would come. I got one knee forward and dragged the other after it and Linda was tearing at my closed fist—and the key.

I pulled her with me and got a handful of robe. I butted with my head and yanked and the robe ripped off and Linda was on her knees beside me. She was beating her fists against my head and I put it down and crawled again and felt the wall.

I pushed at her once more with what little strength I had left and hit the window with my elbow. The glass collapsed and I held my fist out blindly into the night air and opened it and the key fell out.

The floor came up to meet me and I was flat, my cheek against the rug. I was vaguely aware that for another moment Linda's rage and frustration kept her pummeling me; then the room was still. As from a great distance I heard someone's tortured breathing and I thought:

"Linda can't get out. Linda can't get out and Carol can't get in. Linda can drink her drink, but now she'll have to drink alone."

The air along the floor was cool and fresh and everything was comfortable and relaxed. Maybe I dreamed it but it seemed to me that I was thinking about myself. It sounds silly now but I was thinking, *Brother if you can take what you've taken in the past hour without cracking there's nothing wrong with your head. You're not sick. You haven't been sick in a long time. When your knee's right you can get back in the Marine Corps.*

24

THEY tell me I had quite a sleep. Dunbar came in right after Carol and the doctor; there wasn't any extra key for Linda's room so they had to break the door down. They found her on the floor beside me and the doctor knew right off what had happened, only at first they thought I'd had some of the same dose.

I don't remember anything until about nine the next morning. The doctor was there and gave me some stuff and though I felt rocky it wasn't long before I was hungry too. So while I ate, Dunbar got the rest of the story from me, and Carol, Helen Bradford and Spencer Haughton sat around and listened.

At first Dunbar was sore. He threatened me with complicity and being accessory to Linda's suicide and a lot of other things, but when I'd given my statement to a stenographer he'd brought along he calmed down and seemed pretty well satisfied. But there were still some things Carol wanted to know.

"I still don't understand," she said, "why Doctor Penzance was suspicious of Linda and why he sent for her."

"Oh, that?" Dunbar said.

"Yes," Helen Bradford said. She was sitting next to Spence Haughton, and rather close, and the way things looked, she liked being there. "Why, Lieutenant?"

"Penzance was out that first night too," Dunbar said. "After he left here he walked along the road and went up on the hillside and sat down to brood. He saw all the comings and goings at the winery. He saw you drive back"—he glanced at Carol—"and then Linda and Garlin came back. When Marshall didn't show, Penzance decided he'd have a look and maybe do some persuading."

Dunbar shrugged. "He found him on the floor and when you came," he said to me, "he had to hide. He slugged you because he couldn't afford to be seen. He didn't know whose scarf it was you were carrying, but he saw the blood and the tear and left it as evidence pointing away from him."

"Did he suspect Linda then?" Helen asked.

"No. He figured it must be Linda or Garlin but he didn't know which and he was afraid to tell the truth to me. He was at the murder spot and he had a swell motive and it would be his word against their combined testimony, so he was afraid to do anything. Of course when he learned about Garlin he knew it had to be Linda."

Dunbar chuckled. "Also by that time I was putting the pressure on. There's a process for getting fingerprints from cloth and I'd told him I'd sent the scarf away for analysis. When he saw what was coming, he tried Linda Jordan, knowing if he could hypnotize her into showing him where the gun was he'd have a case for me. The thing was, she shot too straight—and she didn't hypnotize."

"What about the Talmains?" I said.

"Just what I told you would happen. They were picked up last night in Geneva." He paused and his gray eyes were suddenly speculative as he studied us. "Funny thing. They had over ten thousand in cash on them. Said it was theirs. And with the Doc dead we can't be sure."

He kept looking at us, first one of us and then the other. No one said anything but there was one fleeting instant when Helen caught my eye and I saw her sudden consternation; then she was fumbling with her cigarettes and Dunbar was talking.

"They're wanted in Chicago, you know. The Doc too. A four-year-old rap in some medium racket they were working. That's one of the things Mr. Marshall turned up in his report. The Doc was going to have his lease broken and also stand trial in Chicago. It wouldn't have been so good for the Brotherhood of Horus, would it?"

He cleared his throat. "Incidentally, I found the briefcase off the end of the dock." He looked at me. "You were right about hearing the splash that night someone locked you and Miss Jordan in the boathouse. It isn't important now but I'd like to know who the guy was."

I looked at Haughton and he was busy lighting Helen's cigarette.

"Okay," Dunbar said dryly. "You people have held out on me from the start, so this is nothing new. Just one thing, Mr. Wallace." He paused until I looked at him. "I know all about your idea of the piece of bottle being in Miss Jordan's leg—on account of the story she told you about the boil. But there was something else. You must have had something to make you remember that much. You must have suspected her for some definite reason before you'd dare to look at her—ah—at the boil."

"I did," I said. "I forgot to tell you. It was the scarf."

"What about it?"

"You said you found it hidden between some casks not far from where I was slugged."

Before he could answer Carol spoke up. "Oh, no," she said. She smiled and seemed embarrassed at her sudden contradiction. "I mean didn't Linda say something about it being hidden among the bottles?"

I was proud of her. I beamed at her to think that she had remembered what Linda had said when we were re-constructing the murder in her room. At that time we thought Penzance was the guy and we figured how he'd used the scarf and Linda said, "*Then he hid it among those bottles . . .*"

That had been it, though at the time it took me a minute or so to realize the significance of the remark. Now Dunbar was shaking his head.

"But it wasn't among any bottles," he said.

"That's what tipped me off," I said. "You found it in among the casks where Penzance had hidden it *after he had found it on me.* I found it among the bottles. Only one other person knew it had been there—the one who had hidden it there originally. The killer."

Dunbar stared at me with one eye and then with both. He blew out his breath. "Well, I'll be damned," he said. "A little thing like that."

"It was enough," I said. "Enough to make me think about the missing piece of bottle and the boil on her leg."

"Sure it was enough. It was plenty."

"She talked too much, that's all," I said. "We were building a case against Penzance and she forgot how much she was supposed to know."

Dunbar got up. "Okay," he said resignedly. "I guess you can be glad she didn't have another half ounce of that poison . . . Well." He stretched. "I guess that'll be all for now. I may be back this afternoon if—"

"Will you wait just a minute, Lieutenant?" Carol was on her feet and without waiting for an answer, motioned to Helen. The two of them went into the kitchen. Presently Dunbar shrugged and moved into the hall, so I leaned towards Haughton and kept my voice low.

"Who was the poison for? Were you going to use it on Johnny or yourself?"

He thought that one over awhile, his face sober and distance in his gaze. He peered at me through those horn-rimmed glasses.

"I don't know," he said. "I've asked myself the same thing a dozen times. I guess I was going to use it on myself first—I'd made up my mind I couldn't go on the way things were—and then, on the train, I got to wondering if maybe there was a way I could use it on Johnny without getting caught." He sighed and shook his head. "I don't know exactly what I was going to do, Alan. I really don't."

"Okay," I said. "And just for my own record—you were the guy in the boathouse. You swiped the briefcase and gun from the study desk the first night."

"Yes," he said. "You nearly caught me in Johnny's bedroom. I didn't find the contract there and I kept on looking. I took the briefcase—and the gun was there and I took that too, though I don't know why—and I had no time to search the case so I hid it in the boathouse. I'd found the contract the next night and was just starting out of the boathouse when you and Linda came."

Carol came back before I could add anything and I went to meet her. Helen was right behind her and we all went into the hall. When Dunbar glanced round Carol said, looking at me, "It's eleven o'clock and there's a train from Bath for New York at eleven fifty-three. Bert says we can make it if we leave here by eleven thirty."

"What?" Dunbar bristled and his eyes widened. "Now wait a minute. You're not going anywhere."

"Yes, we are," Carol said. "I am at least. I'm most certainly not going to spend another day here."

I loved her then, the proud lift of her chin, the firm sweet line of her mouth, the way she looked at Dunbar.

"You and me," I said.

"And me," Spence said.

Even Helen Bradford lost her customary austerity. There was a sparkle in her eyes. "Me, too," she said.

"You're going to stay right here," Dunbar said. "Or at least in Bath, where I can get you if I want you."

"You're going to have to arrest us if you think so," I said.

Dunbar swallowed air. He looked at the four of us and we looked back at him defiantly and he weakened just a trifle.

"No!" he said. "I may need you."

"Nuts!" I said. "You don't need a thing from us and you know it. But even if you do, you know where we live." I went up to Carol and took her arm. "The only thing," I said, "is that we'll have to take a day coach. It'll probably be crowded."

She looked up at me and smiled and everything I wanted was there in her eyes for me to see. Everything was just as I remembered it—only better because I'd missed it so.

"I know," she said. "That might be fun."

It was.